Angeon
Broken Promises

Joseph Seeker

Copyright © 2018 Joseph Seeker

All rights reserved.

ISBN-13: 979-8-3623-7073-2

Acknowledgments

I would like to give a special thank you to Kimberly Pinzon for editing this book and helping me to improve as a writer.

Contents

One
Ken - 1

Two
A New Start - 14

Three
A Fated Meeting - 22

Four
Serena's Story - 34

Five
The Farmer - 42

Six
Heart of Fire - 55

Seven
Missing Angel - 66

Eight
The Puppet King - 78

Nine
The Storm - 88

Ten
Gangsters - 103

Eleven
Confrontation - 112

Twelve
United Front - 130

Thirteen
The Hunt Begins - 148

Fourteen
Daemon Grimshear - 161

Fifteen
Going Home - 187

Sixteen
Family Reunion - 200

Seventeen
Broken Promises - 211

Eighteen
Angeon - 224

Nineteen
The Deal - 240

Twenty
Enock and Eliezer – 261

CHAPTER 1

Ken

Wow, what a beautiful day it turned out to be, Ken thought lazily while staring out the classroom window. It was impressive that he could see anything at all through his long, light brown bangs which dangled to the tip of his nose. In the back of his thoughts, he could hear his teacher lecturing on some subject that he didn't care to listen to. He placed his hand under his cheekbone to rest his head, and then used his other hand to play with his shoulder length hair.

Ken gazed at his transparent reflection in the window while looking into his own dark emerald eyes. He quickly grew bored of glaring at himself and began to nod off.

"So, as you can see class—" Mr. Fadas, Ken's math teacher, stopped his lesson when he noticed Ken falling asleep.

"Mr. Malachite, I know you don't care whether you pass or fail, but at least pretend you're interested in what I have to say," he said in a snooty manner.

Ken didn't answer. Instead, he snored loudly, causing the other students to chuckle.

Mr. Fadas was not entertained. He poked Ken with his ruler. "Wake up, Malachite!" He said while giving Ken a loathing stare from above his nose.

Ken still did not respond.

Mr. Fadas tapped the side of Ken's wrist with the ruler, then reared his arm back and swung it.

Ken swiftly reacted by catching the ruler in the palm of his hand, creating a loud smacking noise.

The entire class responded by crying out, "Oooooo!"

Ken turned his head to look at Mr. Fadas, but his face nearly met with his teacher's bulbous stomach which hung over the front of his desk.

"Are you pregnant, Mr. Fadas?" Ken asked mockingly as he snatched the ruler from his teacher's hand. He laid one end of it on the desk while clutching the other end tightly.

The students laughed at Ken's joke which made Mr. Fadas furious.

"Give me back my ruler!" Mr. Fadas demanded, showing clear signs of frustration in his voice.

Ken smiled and then pushed down on the middle of the ruler causing it to break. "Oops," he said casually with a mischievous grin.

The class once again reacted to Ken's antics.

Mr. Fadas got nose to nose with Ken; his mustache was almost touching the space between Ken's nose and mouth. "You're lucky you're a student, Mr. Malachite."

"You're lucky you're a teacher, *Mr. Fat-Ass!*"

The students in the class erupted with laughter.

Mr. Fadas glared at Ken and bellowed over the other students. "IT'S MR. FADAS! GO TO THE PRINCIPAL'S OFFICE!"

Ken stood up irritably, causing his chair to fall on the floor. "You don't have to tell me twice! If you got any closer, I'd swear you were trying to kiss me!"

The class continued to laugh as Ken walked out of the room and slammed the door.

Ken opened the door to the principal's office and saw Mrs. Lane the counselor, sitting behind her desk. Her black hair was pulled into a bun like usual. She gave Ken an accusing stare from above her glasses.

As he approached, Ken thought about how Mrs. Lane always had the, 'hot librarian look,' going for her.

"Mr. Fat-Ass wanted me to see Principal Washburn," he said in a frustrated tone.

Mrs. Lane gave Ken a stern look.

"I mean *Mr. Fadas*," Ken recanted.

Mrs. Lane pointed to the chair in front of her desk. "Why am I not surprised?" she said apathetically.

"It's not my fault, Mrs. Lane. The man hates me! I was resting my head while looking out the window when he decided he wanted to put his gut in my face and hit me with his ruler!" Ken reasoned.

"He hit you!?" Mrs. Lane asked with a concerned look.

"No, I caught the ruler and broke it, but he still tried," Ken said while glancing off to the side.

Mrs. Lane sighed and paused for a moment, "How many times have you come to the office this week?"

"This makes the fifth time in the past three days," Ken replied.

"What am I supposed to do, Ken? I am always sticking up for you. No other student has had as many chances as you! What would your mom say right now?"

Ken's head popped up at her statement, "I don't know, Mrs. Lane. Let me go ask her. Oh wait, I can't. She's dead, remember?!" Ken shouted.

Mrs. Lane gave Ken a fierce stare. "There's no need to—"

"NO! There's no reason for you to bring up my mother! What? Are you going to ask what my father would think too? Well, don't bother. In case you didn't know, he's also dead!" Ken stood abruptly from his chair.

"That's enough Ken!" Mrs. Lane exclaimed.

"Screw this!" Ken roared as he stormed to the office door.

"Ken, I'm trying to help you!" his counselor called out.

Ken opened the door to the office and glared back at Mrs. Lane.

"Maybe I don't want to be helped," he said coldly before walking out and slamming the door behind himself.

"What was all that about?" Principal Washburn asked as he walked into the office from a side door. He was wearing his cringe worthy toupee with a mustache that was thinner than his hair line.

"Ken was sent here by Mr. Fadas again," Mrs. Lane replied while placing her hand over her forehead.

"That's it! I have had it with that kid! It's time he got expelled!" Principal Washburn yelled.

"Just give me more time with him, sir. Ken's had a rough life," Mrs. Lane said.

Principal Washburn darkened Mrs. Lane's desk, "A rough life? Everyone has a rough life, Mrs. Lane!"

"His father was killed right in front of him on the street. Ken was only twelve when he witnessed that!" Mrs. Lane replied quickly. "He also witnessed his mother's death firsthand only a year and a half ago. Can you imagine holding your father as he bleeds out after some thug shot him – or watching helplessly as your mother dies in your arms after a car wreck? Don't even get me started on his stepfather!" Mrs. Lane said while rolling her eyes.

"Remember reading about Scott Billiard? He was the richest man in town until he got arrested for embezzling from his own company. Ken's mom used every penny they had to bail him out. Now that man is a drunken slob. I'd say Ken's life has been, and still is, a little worse than rough," she concluded.

Principal Washburn folded his arms and shook his head, "His tragedies are no excuse for his attitude. Not to mention all the fights he gets in. Every week he beats up a kid or two. I can't have that at my school any longer!"

Mrs. Lane stood up from her chair, and her voice began to rise. "I've talked with a lot of the students involved in those fights, sir. He only gets into a fight when he's defending other kids!"

Principal Washburn slammed his hands on Mrs. Lane's desk, "If he is protecting other kids, then why doesn't he have any friends? You'd think with him protecting all these students he'd have at least one," he said sarcastically.

"Well, they're scared of him," Mrs. Lane replied reluctantly.

"Maybe that's because he doesn't care about protecting other people. Maybe he sees an opportunity for a fight and jumps on it," Principal Washburn said while raising his eyebrows and shrugging his shoulders.

"That's not the case, Principal Washburn. He studies and helps teach martial arts. I've talked to his instructor and the other students there. They all say he's a shining example of their discipline, morals, and positive influence," Mrs. Lane said as her eyes darted to side.

Principal Washburn could tell not everything in her last statement was true. He pulled up the chair in front of the desk and sat down while sighing deeply. "I know you put a lot of time into working with him. You don't want to see it end this way. However, I can't let him stay on this path."

Principal Washburn sat there for a moment with his hand on his chin, "He gets one more chance, Mrs. Lane, and that's it. The next time he gets sent out of class, the next attitude he gets, or the next fight he's in will be his last here at my school. I expect you to let him know tomorrow morning. Is that understood?"

Mrs. Lane looked at the window in the office door and caught a glimpse of Ken's face. He glanced at her with a somber expression before walking away.

"Understood sir," she answered in a dull tone.

Whatever. Ken thought as he walked down the hallway. *So, what if I get expelled? It's not like anyone will care.*

Ken heard a loud bang down the hall to his left and glanced over to see three seniors shoving a scrawny freshman into a locker.

"Come on, Tommy. I know your mom gives you more than two dollars for lunch!" A chubby redheaded boy shouted.

"Beating up freshman for money, Terrance? That's a new low for you, especially since he's half your size," Ken said cynically. "Not to mention you have him outnumbered."

"Stay out of this, Ken. Just go home to mommy or something. Oh wait, you can't!" Terrance taunted. He and the other two seniors laughed as he picked Tommy up by the collar of his shirt.

"Now give me the rest of your mon—"

Before Terrance could finish speaking, Ken's fist landed squarely on the side of his cheek, causing him to drop Tommy.

Terrance stumbled to the ground but quickly picked himself back up. "That's it, Malachite! you're dead!" Terrance bellowed as he clutched the side of his face. "What are you waiting for? Get him!"

Both Terrance's friends hesitated while staring at Ken, who

sneered at Terrance arrogantly.

They were each smaller than Terrance and appeared to be weaker too. Ken assumed that's why they partnered with him to begin with.

"Your friends are smart. Maybe you could learn something from them. Now give me the money and go to class," Ken demanded.

Terrance glared at his friends. "Fine, I'll do it myself. Sucks for you, Ken. You don't have a mommy to fix you after I kick your ass."

Terrance ran at Ken and pulled his fist back for a heavy punch, but Ken delivered a swift kick to his face.

Terrance dropped to the ground while holding his nose.

Ken grabbed him by the collar and picked him up, then slammed him into a locker.

"That whole bit about me having no mom is getting real old Terrance!" Ken shouted as he slammed Terrance into the locker a few more times.

"How's it feel!? What's it like to be on the other end of the beating!?" Ken barked as he held Terrance up against the locker.

Terrance smiled through a bit of blood dripping from his lip. "How does it feel to go home to no family?"

Ken's grip tightened as he bared his teeth. He yelled out in rage while punching Terrance in the face. The sound of his fist hitting Terrance's cheek echoed throughout the hallway. He struck him so hard that the bully's head bounced off the locker like a rubber ball. After that, Ken went on to knee him in the stomach repeatedly.

"Ken, stop it!" one of Terrance's friends yelled as he tried to pull Ken off.

Ken whipped around and kicked the teen in the stomach and watched him fall to the floor. He turned back to Terrance and saw him rolling on the tile of the hallway, gripping his nose as blood poured from it. He looked to the third bully and held out his hand.

"Give me the money," Ken demanded.

The senior immediately reached into his pocket and pulled out two crumpled dollars. He handed the money over while shaking with fear.

Ken snatched the money and then walked over to Tommy, who

still sat with his back propped against the locker in awe of what happened.

"Take it," Ken demanded as he held it out to Tommy.

Tommy just shook his head as he stared at Ken with his mouth slightly opened.

"Take it, Tommy! I didn't just beat these guys up and down the hall so that you could stare at me like an idiot!" Ken bellowed.

"Y…you keep it," Tommy replied out of terror.

Ken threw the money in Tommy's face, "I try to do something nice for you and you can't even appreciate it! Next time they beat the snot out of you, I'm not going to stop them! Heck, I might even help!"

Ken turned to look at the bullies he just beat up. As he glanced them over, it suddenly occurred to him how badly he hurt Terrance. His expression changed from being livid to one of worry.

"Terrance, you ok man?" Ken asked, already knowing that Terrance was in too much pain to reply.

The kid he didn't attack stared at him and started to back up.

"I didn't mean to hurt him that bad. I swear!" Ken said as his heart started to race.

The student turned around and ran for the principal's office. Ken took one more look at all the blood on the floor and sprinted for the doors that led outside the school.

Oh crap, oh crap, oh crap. They're going to call the police. I'm going to jail… I just need to get home, drink some water, and calm down for a sec! He thought as he ran frantically to his home.

Ken got to his stepdad's apartment and closed the door behind himself in a rush. He then locked it as he breathed heavily.

"What are you doing home so early?" His stepfather asked from the living room where he sat in his recliner watching TV.

Ken tried to disguise how hard he was breathing as to not arouse suspicion. "They let school out early, Scott."

Ken opened the refrigerator to look for a soda but only saw beer.

"Don't take any of my beer!" Scott yelled from the other room.

"Where are my drinks?" Ken asked, still controlling his breath.

"I didn't get any. That fifty bucks you gave me paid for my beer and my Creamy Cakes!" Scott shouted back.

"You spent that money on booze and junk food?!" Ken bellowed crossly.

"Don't catch an attitude with me, or I'll slap you silly boy!" Scott replied from the other room.

Ken shook his head and grabbed a beer from the refrigerator. He then opened the top cabinet and took a Creamy Cake.

"Don't take any of my Creamy Cakes either boy!" Scott ordered.

"I won't," Ken replied as he ran upstairs to his room. He closed the door behind himself, ripped opened the transparent bag around the Creamy Cake, and took a bite. He sat on his bed and twisted the top off the beer and gulped a swig.

Ok, maybe it's not so bad. Maybe I didn't hurt Terrance as much as I think. He's a big boy. He can take a hit. Ken pondered as he put the beer on the mantle next to his bed.

He laid his head on the pillow and stared at the ceiling. He could feel his heart pumping while taking deep breaths and trying to calm himself.

I don't get it. Every time I try to help someone I get in trouble, Ken thought.

He looked at a picture he had on the mantel just behind the beer. He picked it up and held it above his head while studying it. It was a photograph of him when he was twelve, standing between his parents.

"We took this picture three days before you died dad," Ken said before he laid it on his chest.

He closed his eyes and sighed, reminiscing about a special memory he had of his father.

It was after practicing martial arts one afternoon. Both Ken and his father were winded and sitting on the floor catching their breath.

"Ken, your martial prowess is amazing!" His father said. "I can't believe how good your Kung Fu has gotten. To think, I started training you in Long Fist when you were eight! Now, only four years later you're keeping up with me in sparing!"

"It helps to have you as a teacher, dad." Ken replied, beaming proudly from his father's praise.

"Ken, you're awesome when it comes to martial arts. You're naturally talented. I'm proud of you for always trying so hard and never giving up," his father expressed.

"Thanks, dad." Ken said happily.

"Although, there is something I need to talk to you about," his father added. His tone changed from one of cheer to a more stern nature.

Ken gave a curious mien, "What is it?"

"Bullying, son. I heard you pushed a kid down yesterday," his dad said firmly.

Ken looked at the ground with a guilty expression, "Oh, that. Well, Greg called me a jerk because I took his seat at lunch, and I didn't get up when he asked. I told him not to say it again, but he did, so I pushed him. He deserved it, right dad?"

By his countenance, Ken's father could tell his son already knew the answer.

"No, son. He didn't," he replied austerely.

"I don't understand. Wasn't he trying to bully me by telling me to get out of my seat?" Ken asked.

His dad paused. "Didn't you say you took his seat?"

Ken hesitated to answer. "Yeah, but he got up, so it was mine."

His father smiled, "What if you were sitting there, got up, and then came back only to see someone took your seat?"

Ken turned his face in thought. "I guess I'd ask him to move," he replied half-heartedly.

"What if he didn't move?" His dad asked.

"Well, I guess I'd get upset," Ken answered.

"What if that kid pushed you down after all that? Would you feel like YOU were bullying him?"

"No, sir," Ken replied with his head down.

"So, who do you think did the bullying?"

"Me," Ken replied sullenly. "But he called me a jerk dad!"

"And that was wrong of him, Son. That's true. However, that's no reason to push or hit someone. Sometimes you have to be the bigger man in those situations. I think you would have been better off just letting him have the seat. If you did, you wouldn't have got into trouble, and you might have even made a friend," his father stated.

"Then why do you teach me how to fight if you don't want me to use it?" Ken asked, appearing more confused.

"I'm not teaching you to fight, son. I'm teaching you to defend yourself. Getting into a fight is a last resort measure you go to when there is no other choice," his dad replied.

"So, I can fight, but only if I'm defending myself?"

Ken's dad smiled, "That's the basic idea, son. That and defending other people."

"You mean like if someone were trying to beat up a girl on the playground it would be ok to beat that person up?" Ken asked.

"Well, I'd want you to stop him from hurting her, and if it meant having to get into a fight then so be it," his father answered.

Ken's demeanor showed that he still didn't quite understand.

"Let me sum it up for you, son. If you can stop someone from hurting you or hurting other people, then I believe you have a responsibility to do so. To protect yourself as well as those who can't protect themselves," his father summarized.

"Kind of like a superhero?" Ken asked with an excited grin.

"Yes, like a superhero," his dad replied.

Ken's father couldn't help but laugh at his son's optimistic view of the idea.

"Just remember, there is a fine line between protecting people and becoming the very thing you're protecting people from."

Ken nodded his head, "I'll remember dad."

"Good," Ken's father said as he stood. "Because the next art I want us to learn is Tae-kwon-do."

"You don't know Tae-kwon-do yet?" Ken asked.

"Nope, never got the chance to learn it. Although I figure you and I can study it together someday," his father said.

Ken shined a grin at his dad, "I'd like that a lot," he said excitedly.

Ken opened his eyes as a tear rolled down the side of his face. He sat up on the bed and looked at the picture again. "Dad…did I become what I'm trying to protect people from?" He whispered. He sat there for a moment, staring at the picture until he heard a loud knock at the door downstairs. His eyes widened as his stomach did somersaults. He remained still, hoping it was nothing until he heard the knock again, this time it was louder.

"Ken, get the dang door boy!" Scott yelled from the living room.

Ken opened the door to his room and walked down the steps, terrified of what he was going to find. As he approached, he heard another set of loud knocks. He looked through the peephole and saw a female police officer standing at the door. Ken's stomach jumped, and he felt his heart pound relentlessly. His fears were confirmed.

"Who's at the door, boy?" his stepfather shouted.

Ken started to sweat nervously as his mind became jumbled. "It's another tax collector," he shouted back while trying to steady his voice.

"What in blazes do they want now?" Scott lashed as he got up from his chair.

Ken raced upstairs to his room, "I'll just let you handle this, Scott," he said as he closed the bedroom door.

"There's not much time," Ken muttered as he grabbed his skateboard and opened the window to his room.

He climbed out of it and ran for the sidewalk. Then he started skateboarding as fast as he could.

I need to see Master Alvin. He'll be able to help me, Ken thought as he sped down the pavement.

"HE WHAT!"

Ken heard Scott yell from the apartment behind him.

Ken got to the martial arts studio where he took and taught Taekwon-do with Master Alvin.

"Please be here!" he said as he banged on the door. "Come on, come on."

He saw a figure approach the entrance and felt slightly relieved as Master Alvin opened it.

"Ken? What are you doing here? Class doesn't start for another three hours, and what are you doing out of school so early?" Master Alvin asked.

Ken let himself in, making sure he closed the door behind himself. "Master Alvin, I need your help," he said as he walked out of view of the window.

Master Alvin's expression changed from one of surprise to one of worry. "What's wrong, what happened?"

"I got into a fight at school again, but this time I think I seriously hurt the kid. The police showed up at my door after I ran home. So, I snuck out my window to come see you," Ken uttered nervously.

Master Alvin shook he head with a disappointed grimace.

"Master Alvin, I didn't know who else to turn to. I'm just really scared," Ken pleaded as his throat choked up. He was trying his best not to burst into tears.

Master Alvin sighed deeply and hesitated to say anything.

"Please, Master Alvin, what can I do?" Ken begged.

"Leave, and don't come back. You're not an assistant here anymore," Master Alvin said sternly while pointing to the door.

"Please, Master Alvin," Ken implored.

"I can't help you anymore, Ken. You have to learn responsibility for your actions," Master Alvin replied.

Ken stood, preparing to contest Master Alvin's decision, but he was interrupted before uttering a word.

"You are by far my best student. No one here can compete with you in a fight, Ken. I respect your determination and your desire to become stronger. I have always had a special place in my heart for you as a student. However, I cannot have you teaching here anymore. I have parents concerned about you training my students. You've developed a bad reputation, and now I have students being pulled out of my class because their parents don't want a delinquent teaching them!" Master Alvin stated.

Ken was shocked by his teacher's reaction. He never thought

Master Alvin would call him a delinquent.

"I defended you when people said you were a bad kid – but when word gets out that the police are after you – I'll have a lot more students pulled from my class. I'll lose a lot of business thanks to you, Ken!" Master Alvin snarled.

Ken shook his head in disbelief, "I'm sorry, I'm sorry, but I just need you," he stuttered while fighting back tears.

"You have five seconds to get out of my dojo before I call the police and let them know you're here," Master Alvin said coldly as he pointed to the door.

"Just please hear me out, Master Alvin!" Ken cried.

"One," Master Alvin said as he walked over to the desk where the phone was.

"Just listen to me!" Ken shouted.

"Two!" his teacher yelled back.

Ken ran for the door and glared back at his teacher while gripping the handle.

"I trusted you!" he whispered darkly.

"Three!" Master Alvin bellowed while picking up the phone.

Ken pulled the door open hastily and threw his skateboard down. He took off down the sidewalk as fast as he could while wiping tears from his eyes.

CHAPTER 2

A New Start

Ken raced back to the apartment as fast as he could. *Maybe the police are gone. Maybe I can get some stuff from my room and skip town*, he thought.

He made it to the back of the apartment complex and peered around the corner. There were no signs of the cop from before. He ran to the window of his room and carefully slid it up. He crawled in and grabbed his book bag then quietly opened it to take the books out.

"Leaving so soon, Ken?" his stepfather said as he walked out from the closet.

Ken jumped at the sound of his voice. He sluggishly turned to look at his stepdad, feeling his heart leap in his chest. "Scott, please don't call the police. I'm sorry about leaving, but I just had to go," Ken said in a frightened tone.

Scott approached Ken and grabbed his shoulder. The few black greasy hairs he had were plastered to the side of his pasty white forehead. His white tank top had multiple stains and holes and smelled like he hadn't washed it in days. Of course, that smell could be from Scott not showering for days too. "Now why would I do that? I wouldn't get to talk to ya for a sec if I called the police," Scott said coolly, fixing his bloodshot black eyes on Ken.

Ken smelled alcohol on his breath and knew he was drunk.

"Come down the stairs with me so we can talk about this," Scott slurred as he forcibly pulled Ken to the door. "Walk, boy!" he demanded.

Ken went down the stairs as his mind wrestled with questions. *Why is he so calm? Why isn't he calling the police? Worst of all, what is he planning to do?*

When they got to the kitchen, Ken stood on the opposite end of the room. He anticipated that his inebriated stepdad would do something stupid soon.

Scott grabbed a beer from the countertop next to him and laughed after taking a swig. "The police came to the door today. Although you know about that already, right?" he said while scratching the top of his mostly bald head.

"Scott, I can explain everything!" Ken said, desperately trying to get through to his stepdad.

"SHUTUP! I'm talking now," Scott bellowed. He put his beer down and propped his elbow on the countertop. "So, I heard you beat the crap out of some kid today, not that it's a big deal to me or anything. In fact, I find it hilarious," Scott chuckled. "Then I found out that kid had to go to the hospital. Apparently, you broke his nose and one of his ribs."

Ken's chest sank at the reality of what he had done to Terrance. "No, no I couldn't have hurt him that bad," he said while trembling.

"I said I'm talking!" Scott yelled again. His face went red as a vein protruded from his neck. "They want me to pay for his hospital bill, and they're about to try to sue me," Scott said as he laughed with a creepy smile on his face. "Not only that, but the cop and I went up to your room to get you, and you weren't there!" he added as he picked up his beer and started toward Ken.

"Scott, I'll make things right ok? I'm sorry just, please don't come any closer," Ken pleaded as he tried to back away from his step farther. He found it eerie that Scott went from screaming to laughing. It made him uncomfortable and suspicious of what was going on in Scott's head.

Scott ignored him and continued to approach. "You know the thing that really sets me off is that while we were in your room, I found this half drank cold beer and this freshly opened creamy cake wrapper. Didn't I say you couldn't have these things?" Scott stated with his bloated beer belly pushing against Ken.

Ken didn't answer. All he could think about was how Scott was going to hurt him if kept acting like this.

"I asked you a question, boy!" Scott yelled in his ear.

Ken looked down attempting to avoid eye contact.

"Boy, if you don't answer me, I'm gonna bust your head open!" Scott said threateningly.

Ken bared his teeth and pushed Scott off him as hard as he could. His stepdad fell to the floor and rolled over quickly while Ken made a run for the door. He pulled at it trying anxiously to open it but realized the door was nailed shut. He turned and looked at Scott who was now up off the floor.

"I know you didn't just push me, boy! I'll kill you!" Scott barked. He slammed his beer bottle against the wall causing it to shatter as the beer foamed on the countertop. He held the nose of the bottle like a knife and hobbled over to Ken with the jagged shards pointed at him.

"SCOTT, STOP!" Ken yelled as his stepfather got closer.

Scott pulled the broken bottle to his side then thrust the sharp pointed end at Ken.

Instantly, Ken reacted with a crescent kick and knocked the bottle out of Scott's grasp. He then kicked Scott in the chest and pushed him back to the floor. Ken wasted no time trying to run past his stepdad to get to the stairs leading to his room. However, Scott stood back up in front of him and blocked his path.

Scott opened a drawer and grinned menacingly, "Your ugly mother left you as a problem for me to fix, and I fix my problems," he said in a drunken stupor. He reached in the drawer and pulled out a large kitchen knife and held it up to Ken. "How do you like that, boy?" he said with a sneer.

"PLEASE SCOTT, STOP IT!" Ken yelled as Scott brandished the knife.

"You ain't costing me no more money boy!" Scott hollered as he drove the knife at Ken.

Ken retorted by throwing a fast front kick at Scott's face while stepping to the side of his jab. His kick hit so hard that it made Scott's head jerk back. Ken followed up by driving another kick into

Scott's overbearing stomach which forced Scott to his knees.

Scott looked up at Ken with blood pouring from his nose, "I'M GONNA KILL YOU, BOY!" He bellowed while raising the knife one more time.

"THAT'S ENOUGH!" Ken screamed as he spun around, delivering a kick under Scott's chin which cracked loudly.

Ken gasped while holding his hand over his mouth. He stared at his stepfather who now laid on the floor with his mouth hung open. Ken feared the worst. He backed into a wall behind him. He could not take his eyes off his stepfather who did not move.

"What have I done?" Ken repeated over and over to himself. He fell to his knees as tears filled his eyes, "I didn't mean to do that," he said as he shook his head. "This is a dream, a bad dream, a nightmare. I'm going to wake up any second now," he told himself continuously while looking at his stepfather.

Suddenly, he heard a loud grunt like noise come from Scott's mouth. Ken saw his stepdad's chest rise a little as he took a deep breath which sounded like a snore.

Relief flooded throughout Ken. He thought he had he killed his stepfather. He knew he at least broke his nose and his jaw. It was still far better than being a murderer.

Unexpectedly, there was a loud bang at the door, "Open up! This is the police!" a man called out.

Ken heard the voice of his neighbors yelling at the cops outside, "I heard screaming. It sounded like there was a fight!"

Ken's chest filled with panic once again. He ran toward the steps and flew up to his room. He racked his mind trying to come up with a plan, but fear clouded his judgment. All he could think about was what would happen to him now if he got caught. *I could go to jail for this, or maybe even prison.* It was at that moment Ken decided that he was going to do everything in his power to escape.

He grabbed his book bag and looked around his room for things to bring with him, but soon abandoned the idea altogether as he heard more banging on the door. He snatched the picture of his parents and thrust into his bookbag before going to the window. He opened it up and jumped outside without hesitation.

"Hey! Stop right there!" a police officer yelled from the right corner of the building.

Ken took off running in the opposite direction. He looked behind himself and saw the cop aiming his taser. Ken swiftly rolled forward on the ground as he heard the pop of the taser firing. Both probes missed him, and he got up and ran again.

As he rounded the corner of the apartment complex, he saw another officer just a few feet in front of him.

"STOP!" The officer yelled as he reached for Ken.

Ken reacted by stepping in close to the officer and grabbing his arm. He hugged the cop's body and tossed him over his hip. He performed the technique so fast that the officer laid there for a moment in a daze.

Once the officer got himself together, he stood with his taser gun ready. Ken ran in a zigzag pattern trying to avoid any taser probes that would be shot at him. To his surprise, the cop put his taser back in the holster and chased after him.

Ken ran to the train tracks just across the road from his apartment. He followed them while glancing back to see two cops on his tail. *I'll lose them in the woods up ahead,* he thought.

He jumped off the tracks and ran into the trees. Being younger, faster, and skinnier than the two officers following him, it was easy for Ken to escape in the woods. However, his paranoia kept him running as fast as he could.

As he raced through the trees, limbs slapped his face. He powered through puddles of mud which splashed all over his clothes. He glanced behind himself once more to see if the cops were still on his tail. Suddenly, he felt himself fall and began rolling down a large ditch. He finally hit the bottom and laid there for a few minutes in shock.

Ken sat up on his knees and looked over his body, checking for cuts or anything that he had not felt yet. Other than a small scratch on his arm and another on his face, he seemed okay.

He walked over to a tree, exhausted from all the running and sat with his back propped against it. He struggled to catch his breath as he pulled the picture of his parents out and looked it over. He started to weep as he thought about how ashamed his parents would be of him right now.

Ken fell asleep for roughly three hours without even realizing it. He awoke to the sound of barking dogs in the distance. He used the tree to help him stand and was so groggy that it hadn't registered with him what the barking was yet.

"Uh! Oh crap!" he shouted, realizing twilight was spilling through the trees as the dog's barking became louder. He started to run again but kept tripping since it was getting darker and harder to see.

"I can't believe I fell asleep!" he said as he sprinted. With each step, the sounds of baying dogs and shouting voices grew. He concluded that the woods no longer provided the cover he needed to get through the night, so he decided to head out of the trees and find another way of hiding.

Ken broke out of the woods and into an open area where he saw the train tracks again. He ran up to them and stumbled on one of the rails. He caught himself with the palm of his hands and then sat on his knees between the tracks. He was tired and cold from all the mud and sweat that covered his clothes. He breathed heavily and pulled out the picture of his parents again.

"No more! I'm done running. If they want me, they can have me," he said as tears filled his eyes. The tears dropped from his face to the photograph.

As Ken waited to be captured, he saw a light coming from the other end of the tracks and realized that it must be a train coming. He looked back at the picture and smiled, "There is nothing left for me here."

He looked back up at the light which was closer to him but soundless. Then he closed his eyes and dropped the picture.

"Ken, stand up," a voice said from behind the light.

Ken opened his eyes, and the light faded away to reveal a man standing before him draped in a long brown cloak with a hood that covered his face. He stared at the hooded man in astonishment and then rose to his feet. "Who are you?" he asked.

"A friend with a way out of this mess you're in," the hooded man replied softly.

Ken continued to stare at the man incredulously, "Am I dead?"

The man smiled slightly under his hood, "No, you're still alive."

Ken rubbed his eyes and gazed back at the man dumbstruck.

"You are mentally and physically exhausted. Let me fix that for you." The hooded man said as he put his hand on Ken's forehead. A circle of light appeared on the back of the man's hand and grew brighter and brighter until it consumed Ken. The light faded away, and Ken's body was completely healed. He felt like he just awoke from a full night of sleep.

Ken stood there speechless gazing at his own hands while making weird noises with his mouth as if trying to say something.

"Still think you're dead?" the man asked.

Ken shook his head with a look of uncertainty.

The man reached his hand out to the side of Ken's face. Ken stared at it in awe waiting for something else incredible to happen, but instead of more magic, the hooded man flicked him on the cheek.

"Ouch!" Ken cried while rubbing his face.

"See you're still alive," the man said, smirking under his hood.

"Fine, I'm still alive," Ken replied in an annoyed tone. "Who are you? And how do you know my name?"

"There's not much time left till the police get here," the hooded man said, completely ignoring the question.

Ken started to grind his teeth nervously, "What can I do?"

"You were right when you said there is nothing left for you here. If you stay, your life will consist of prison cells, fear, and utter disappointment," the hooded man said, now seeming quite serious. "However, I have a task for you in a new world called Etheria. There you will have a fresh start as if all the mistakes you made here never happened," he added.

Ken looked at the man skeptically, "Another world?" he questioned.

The hooded man turned away from him and walked forward two steps, "I know you've had an incredibly rough day. This is a lot to take in, but unfortunately, our time is short."

The man held up his hands, both of which had circles with designs in them that began to shine. Suddenly, a large yellow circle of light appeared in front of him and showed an image of a sunny clearing in the woods somewhere.

Ken stared at it with his mouth hung open, "What is that?" he whispered.

"Your second chance," the man replied. "Ten seconds after I walk through this portal it will close, and the police will find you. You have until then to decide," the man said as he walked forward into the portal which rippled like water as he stepped through it.

"Wait!" Ken yelled, but it was too late. The man made it through the portal and looked back at him from the other side, waiting for Ken to make his decision.

Ken gazed at the portal knowing that time was running out. His mind raced with questions. *Can I trust him? How does he know my name? Is this actually happening?*

The portal began to shrink, and Ken could hear the dogs barking in the background. "Well, there's only one way to find out!" Ken yelled as he jumped forward into the portal as if diving into a pool.

CHAPTER 3

A Fated Meeting

Ken stepped out the other side of the portal which shrunk down to nothing behind him.

"Welcome to Etheria," the hooded man said as he reached into his cloak. "You'll need to change into these," he added, pulling out a pile of neatly folded clothes. He tossed them on the ground in front of Ken along with a pair of brown boots. He also grabbed a brown leather bag from his cloak and threw it next to the clothes.

Ken ignored the things he put in front of him, "Are you going to answer my questions now? Starting with how you know my name?"

A light shined brightly from under the man's hood. He placed his hand over his forehead as if in pain. When the light faded away, he said, "I don't have much time!"

"Oh no you don't. You still have some questions to answer," Ken insisted.

The hooded man ignored Ken's argument and approached him, "Give me your hand," he said impatiently.

Ken gazed at him indecisively.

"Just give it to me! I don't have time!" The man demanded.

Reluctantly, Ken held out his left hand. The hooded man grabbed it and put one hand under Ken's palm, and the other on the back. The symbols on his hands began to glow a bright yellow as they seared Ken's skin.

"It burns!" Ken yelled, dropping to his knees.

"I know, just hold on for a little bit longer!" The hooded man said, clutching Ken's hand tightly.

To Ken, the burning felt like someone placing a hot iron on the back of his hand. "Please, stop it!" he cried out.

The hooded man removed his hand from the back of Ken's and glanced it over as steam danced from it. He could feel Ken shaking in agony. "Almost done," he said while putting his hand back on Ken's.

"Please, no more," Ken begged with his face in the dirt.

The marks on the man's hand glowed again, but this time Ken felt the pain go away. A soothing warmth overtook the burning sensation which made him smile with relief.

"There, all done," the hooded man said. He let go of Ken's hand and stepped back from him, "I've done that for children who cried less than you," he sneered.

Ken got up from the ground and looked at the back of his hand. He had a symbol like the ones engraved on the hooded man. The design was of eight swords penetrating a circle from all sides with the tips converging in the middle. Around the center was another smaller circle with a diamond shape that encased the ends of the swords. The image was scarred into his hand.

"So, what's this for?" Ken asked while rubbing it. His hand didn't hurt anymore, but it did tingle.

"It's called a Gate. Now do as I do," the hooded man replied hastily, showing he was still in a rush.

The hooded man held his hand over his chest and clenched it into a fist. Ken repeated the moment.

"Now remember to flick your wrist and extend your fingers like this as you fully stretch your arm," he said while making the motion.

Ken looked at the man with one eyebrow up and the other down but repeated the move as instructed.

Instantly, the circle lit up and projected itself into the air three inches from his fingertips.

"Whoa!" Ken exclaimed while staring at the little circle of yellow light floating to his left.

"Now reach inside!" the man ordered.

Ken moved his hand closer to the circle which immediately grew three times in size. He quickly jumped back and pulled his hand away, "What's it doing!?" he asked with a flabbergasted expression.

"It grew. Now reach inside!" the man stated, becoming more

impatient.

"Ok, ok," Ken replied. He approached the circle once more and put the tips of his fingers inside. Then he slowly pushed the rest of his hand in. To him, it felt like reaching into a tub of warm water. He pushed his arm in until his wrist was gone. He felt an object hit the tips of his fingers which drew his curiosity. He tried to look in the portal but only saw the same design as on the back of his hand.

"Grab it, Ken," the hooded man said petulantly with his arms crossed.

As Ken reached deeper into the light, the object bounced around his fingertips like it was floating in space. He finally got a grip on it and attempted to pull it out of the circle. It had some resistance to it as if being pulled back from the other side. Soon it was halfway through, and he could identify it as a large sword. He heaved the rest of it out and held it in front of him as the light faded away.

The sword looked unique compared to any he had seen before. Its entirety was black except for the edge of the blade which was silver. The hilt felt like it was made of metal and was wrapped in a dark grey tattered cloth. There was no guard on the top of the handle. Instead, the blade was big at the bottom, being ten inches wide. The width of the sword shrunk as Ken's eyes moved up the middle to five inches, which then grew an extra inch toward the top again. He guessed from bottom to top the sword was about four feet tall. Lastly, just above the hilt, there were two holes about two inches in diameter and three inches apart from each other.

"Impressive sword. I knew you'd make an interesting weapon," the hooded man said.

"What is this? How did I pull a sword from that circle?" Ken asked while admiring the blade.

"The Gate I put on the back of your hand opens a portal into your soul. When you reach inside and pull out a weapon, you are essentially pulling out a piece of yourself. In essence, that sword is part of you. This power is called, Soul wielding," the hooded man replied.

Ken looked at the man in astonishment, "This is incredible," he uttered.

"Not all people can Soul wield, even with a Gate, and every person's weapon is different in some way. Its appearance represents who you are. As you go through life the shape, size, color, and even the weapon itself can change completely depending on who you become," the hooded man said.

Ken smiled as he continued to check out the sword, "This is by far the coolest thing I've ever seen."

The hooded man turned around and held his hands up, creating another portal.

"Wait, didn't you want me to do something for you?" Ken called out.

"I have a friend who will show you the way. Now hurry up and get changed," the hooded man stated. He turned back to look at Ken and then gasped, "What hand did I put your Gate on?" he questioned.

"My left hand, why?" Ken asked.

The hooded man smacked his palm to his forehead, "That's what I get for doing this in a hurry," he said as he turned away and walked into the portal.

"Hey, what's the big deal about it being on my left hand? Can you at least tell me your name!" Ken shouted, but it was too late. The hooded man was gone. He let out a sigh and then looked at his pants which were covered in dried mud. *I guess I should change,* he thought.

Ken stripped down and put on the pants from the pile of folded clothes. They were like blue jeans and were even the same color, but they felt like the pants he practiced martial arts in. They were loose, comfortable, and best of all practical. He picked up one of the brown boots and looked at the bottom of it which was lined with metal plates that crossed the sole horizontally. He put them both on, and they fit like a glove. He then put on a plain white shirt from the pile that felt like it was made from a thicker material than the ones on Earth. Lastly, he picked up a brown vest made of hardened leather and put it on.

He opened the bag and saw two containers of water, some apples, and a large bag of jerky, "Wow, that guy came prepared," Ken said as he put his old clothes into the bag. He struggled to tie it since it was stuffed, but after shaking it around, he managed to close it. He heard the clink of coins as he put the bag down and opened the side pocket to find a sack with some change in it, "This must be currency from this world," he said as he closed it back up.

"Now what am I supposed to do with this?" Ken questioned while holding up the sword. "Wish I could just put it on my back," he mumbled while pretending to do so. Suddenly, the sword snapped to his back like a magnet. "Whoa!" He cried as he pulled it off and then placed on his back again. "It does just stick to my back! I guess the guy did say it was part me," he concluded while trying to make sense of it. He shrugged his shoulders and put the leather bag over the sword on his back.

A bright light drew Ken's attention as it shined in the shape of a circle in midair. "Back already?" he shouted at the portal. However, a small furry creature dropped out the bottom of the light and landed on the ground. As the circle faded away, the animal stared at Ken with its black beady eyes.

"Is that a fox?" Ken wondered.

The creature was red with a white chest and a white tip on its tail. It had a circle on its back that had a similar design as the one on Ken's hand, but without the swords sticking into it. It approached Ken and sat down in front of him.

"You're smaller than the foxes on Earth," Ken said, wondering if it would talk to him or do something else incredible.

The fox tilted its head twice to the right as if telling him to walk that direction.

"You want me to go that way?" Ken asked it.

Without warning, the fox took off toward the woods and jumped on the side of a tree. It hopped from one branch to another until it was at the top. Then it leaped off a twig and spread its paws apart revealing a blanket of skin between his legs that it used to glide through the air.

Ken was amazed as he watched it circle around him in the sky,

"It's just like a flying squirrel," he uttered.

The fox shot into the woods. Ken simply stared in its direction and came to the realization that he should follow it.

He took off as fast as he could while trying to catch up with the fox. He found it jumping from limb to limb and occasionally gliding the distances it could not leap. Ken continued to run to keep up with it on all the turns and curves until he lost sight of it. "Where did it go?" he pondered out loud as he roamed the woods.

Finally, he found the fox again. It was sitting on the ground waiting for him in front of some bushes.

"You're a fast one," Ken said as he approached it. Instantly, the marking on the fox's back began to glow and a portal projected into the air above it. Then it jumped into the circle of light which faded away afterward.

Ken stood in place for a moment waiting for something else to happen but presumed that the fox was gone. As he wondered what he was supposed to be doing, he heard the faint sound of crying in the trees to the right of him. He walked into the bushes to get a better look and saw a young girl sitting on a stump all alone in the woods sobbing heavily into her palms.

"I just want my mom and dad. I just want to go home," she bellowed.

Ken crouched lower in the branches, "Poor girl must be lost out here," he whispered.

As he moved to get a better look, he accidentally snapped a twig beneath his foot.

Her head popped up and she stared in his direction, "Please just leave me alone!" she yelled as she got up and started to back away.

Ken stood and pushed the limbs away as he approached the girl, who let out a loud scream. "Hey, it's ok! I'm not going to hurt you!" Ken called out to her.

She stopped screaming and gawked at him with a frightened look in her eyes.

"I just want to help you," Ken said while crouching down with his hand out.

The young girl looked at him skeptically. It was clear that something traumatized her.

From the corner of his eye, Ken noticed a hand coming out from behind the tree next to the girl, "Look out!" he shouted.

"Got you!" a man exclaimed as he grabbed the girl by the arm and held her up.

The young girl screamed once more, "Let me go, let me go!"

"I was looking everywhere for you," the man said as he stepped out from behind the tree wearing what seemed like some medieval white armor with silver trimming around the edges.

"Drop her!" Ken demanded.

The soldier glared at him, "You dare interfere with a Monarchy soldier?" he questioned pompously.

At that moment, the girl bit the man on the part of his arm that was exposed from the armor.

He yelled and dropped her while rubbing his wrist. The girl ran over to Ken and hid behind him.

Ken took off his bag and laid it next to the girl, then drew his sword from his back. "I don't know what the Monarchy is, but you're not taking this little girl anywhere," he said determinedly.

As the soldier rubbed his wrist, he scowled at Ken. "Everyone knows who the Monarchy is but, allow me to remind you since you seem to have forgotten."

The soldier put his right fist over his chest and then extended his arm causing a Gate to open at his fingertips. His Gate's design revealed one circle in the center with four other circles on the top, bottom, left and right. All of this was encased by another larger circle. The soldier then reached inside and pulled out a sword. Its appearance was that of a military saber with the finger guard and single-handed hilt.

"The monarchy is the law and protection of this land. My platoon and I were taking this child to safety when we were ambushed. She ran away out of fear, so I came to get her back. She is perfectly safe with me," the soldier said in a haughty tone.

Ken looked at the girl to see what she had to say.

"He's lying! They took me from my family. They kidnapped me!" she yelled out.

Ken glared back at the man, "You're not getting her, so go away!" he yelled harshly.

The soldier looked at Ken fiercely and then noticed the Gate on the back of his left hand. "Well, what do you know? We have an Amony amongst us," he said with an arrogant smile.

"A what?" Ken replied, still holding his sword ready.

"Don't play dumb, fool. I can see the Gate on your left hand. Everyone knows Soul wielders of the Monarchy have Gates on the right hand and the Amony purposely keep theirs on the left," the soldier stated.

Ken let out a grunt from frustration, "I'm not with this "Amony," and I'm not giving up the girl! So, leave!" he barked.

The soldier laughed obnoxiously, "Just wait till I bring the girl and the body of a dead Amony back to Captain Ulgenda! I'll get a promotion for sure!" he said like a giddy child about to get a new toy.

The soldier took Ken off guard by running at him with his sword pointed to his face. Ken quickly raised his blade and deflected the strike above his head.

"Run!" Ken yelled to the girl.

She dashed behind a tree, and the peered around the side of it to watch.

The soldier roared as he pulled his sword back and swung it at Ken over and over.

Ken held his sword up while trying his best to block all the strikes. He kicked the soldier's chest causing a tinging noise as the metal on the bottom of his boot met the man's armor. The soldier stumbled to the ground but then quickly came back at Ken.

Ken reacted by swinging his sword at the soldier's face. Both their blades clashed, but the soldier stepped in close to Ken and flailed his sword causing Ken's to fly out of his hands.

Taking the opportunity, the soldier charged forward, jabbing his sword toward Ken's chest.

Ken sidestepped the tip of the soldier's sword just in time, which caused it to get buried into the bottom of a tree.

The soldier frantically tried pulling his weapon from the bark to no avail.

Ken took advantage of the situation and closed the gap between them. He punched the soldier in the face repeatedly then he crouched down and threw a hard punch at his stomach.

"Ouch!" Ken yelled as he jumped back while shaking his hand, "Why did I punch him in the armor!?" he said to himself.

"Well, aren't you the smart one!" the soldier shouted as he ran to his sword with blood trickling down his cheek. He tried desperately to pull it out again.

"I'm not the genius who jabbed his sword into a tree. Face it, without your weapon you're nothing. Thankfully, I don't need anything special to beat you." Ken smiled as he cracked his knuckles and walked toward the soldier who jumped back while showing off an eager grin.

"You're dumber than you look, fool," the soldier said as he extended his right arm out again and opened his Gate. The sword in the tree burst into sparks of yellow light as it faded away. Then he reached into the Gate pulled his sword back out again.

"Wait, you can do that?" Ken inquired with a baffled look.

The soldier charged at Ken again, swinging the sword at Ken's neck.

Ken threw his leg in the air, and the edge of the blade hit the metal lining on the bottom of his boot. He kicked it back and followed up with several punches to the soldier's face again and then front kicked him to the ground.

The soldier wasted no time getting back on his feet. He swung his sword fiercely at Ken while gritting his teeth irritably.

Ken backed away while jumping side to side, trying to dodge every slash. He tripped on a root while avoiding the attacks and fell on his back.

The soldier flipped his sword around in the air and then held it with point aimed at Ken's face, "Die, Amony!" he screamed as he drove it down on Ken.

"No!" Ken yelled as he held his left hand over his head for protection. Immediately, his Gate began to glow brightly. Just as the tip of the soldier's sword got to Ken's palm, a powerful blast of wind burst from Ken's hand and blew the soldier into the air, causing him to smash into a tree.

The soldier bounced off the tree and landed on the ground face first and unconscious. His sword plunged into the dirt beside him and dissipated in yellow sparks.

Ken stared at his palm for a moment, "How did I do that?" he whispered.

Ken glanced from the corner of his eye and saw the little girl staring at him from behind the tree. He stood to retrieve his sword and then placed it on his back. Afterward, he turned to the girl and dropped to one knee while holding out his hand.

"It's ok, I'm not going to hurt you," Ken said tenderly.

The girl slowly walked out from behind the tree.

"That's it, come here. I'll help you get home," Ken added.

The young girl ran to him and wrapped her arms around his neck as she cried.

Ken almost fell back from the force of her plowing into him. He was slightly taken off guard by her reaction since he never had anyone other than his mom or dad hug him before. "We should get moving. There's no telling when he'll get up or if there are any more soldiers like him around here," Ken said.

The girl let go of him and wiped the tears from her face.

Ken picked up his leather bag and put it back on. "So why did the Monarchy or whatever they're called take you from your home?" he asked.

"I don't know!" the girl replied as she got upset again. "They just came to my home and broke in...then...then..." she tried to explain but started crying again out of frustration.

"Hey, it's ok," Ken said nervously, not knowing how to calm her down.

"Maybe I should avoid the subject for a while," he thought to himself.

"Are you thirsty?" Ken asked loudly over her crying.

The girl stopped and nodded her head. Ken pulled a water bottle from his bag and let her drink some.

"Better?" he asked.

The girl sniffled and nodded her head again.

"Ok, then let's get moving," Ken said.

They started walking into the woods which were not all that thick. The trees were spread out enough for them to walk comfortably without stepping over branches and roots.

"By the way, what's your name?" Ken asked, trying to make conversation.

"Serena," the girl replied while snuffling some more. "Serena Kenshi."

"Well, my name is Ken, it's nice to meet you," he said awkwardly. He wasn't used to dealing with kids and was unsure of what to say.

Serena didn't reply, she merely continued to walk beside him.

After a few hours of walking, the sky started to get dark.

"I'm tired," Serena said quietly.

"Me too," Ken replied as he and Serena strolled into a clearing. "Let's stop here for the night," he said as he took the leather bag and sword off and laid them against a tree.

"You mean sleep here in the woods? At night?" Serena questioned. It was clear the idea frightened her.

"Don't worry Serena. There is nothing to be afraid of out here. Besides, I'll keep you safe from anything," Ken replied.

After saying that, he reminded himself that he was on another planet and didn't know what kind of animals there were in the woods. Especially after seeing a fox that could fly.

"Can we start a fire?" Serena asked.

"No, the light from the flame could attract unwanted animals or even more of those soldiers," Ken answered. He wanted to take credit for that thought but simply repeated something he heard from a movie. It made sense to him, after all, so why not go with it.

He noticed Serena was shivering as the wind started to blow around them. He opened his bag and pulled out his shirt and jacket for her. "I don't have a blanket, but these should do," he said. The clothes had small smudges of mud on them, but she didn't seem to care.

"Thank you," Serena said, wrapping herself in the clothes.

Ken heard Serena's stomach growling. He smiled and grabbed the bag. "Let's see what we have to eat," he said.

Ken pulled out both containers of water and the bag of jerky along with some apples. "Hope you like apples and jerky," he uttered with an awkward grin. He was attempting to cheer her up with his forced smile.

They ate in silence for a while. Ken felt nervous as he contemplated what to talk about with the girl. He never really hung out with a lot of people, especially not young girls.

"You wanted to know how I got out here, right?" Serena asked somberly.

"Yeah, that's right," Ken replied.

"I think I'm feeling up to talking about it," she said while gazing at her half-eaten apple.

Ken nodded his head and listened as Serena told him what happened.

CHAPTER 4

Serena's Story

Serena stirred from a nap on the living room couch. She could hear the voices of her parents talking. They were both whispering and peering at her from the edge of the doorway.

"Our precious little angel," Serena's mother, Amelia said quietly. Her deep blue eyes were focused on Serena.

Serena's father, Jace, ran his fingers through his wife's auburn shoulder length hair. "Come in the kitchen with me, I want to talk about something," he said softly.

As they stepped away, Serena sat up on the couch. She rubbed her emerald eyes as her light red hair dangled messily around her face. She gazed down at the floor and saw the red book she'd been reading before falling asleep. She stood groggily from the couch and made her way to the doorway where her parents were. The closer she got, the more she could hear murmurs of her parent's hushed conversation. Mimicking her parent's stealth, Serena posted herself by the doorway to listen to what they were saying.

"Amelia, I know you're getting tired of reading by candlelight. If living here is bothering you, please let me know," Jace said gently, his green eyes attentive to his wife.

"Honey, how many times do I have to tell you? As long as our family is safe, I don't care about having electricity. We moved to this village for a reason, and I'm perfectly happy here," Amelia answered. She approached her husband and grabbed his hand tenderly.

"But...what if he's wrong?" Jace stammered.

"You mean what your father said about Serena? Honey, you know we can't take that risk. What if she really is..." just as Amelia was about to finish her sentence, Jace put his finger to her lips.

"She might hear you, darling," Jace whispered.

Amelia's mouth curved into a smile from under her husband's finger. She grabbed his hand so that she now held both of his, "I'm happy here honey. We're hidden away from the Monarchy, that's all that matters."

Serena turned away from the door and walked back into the living room, "They always do this," she mumbled to herself. "They always talk about me, this village, dad's dad, and the Monarchy. I wish they would tell me what's going on," she said while returning her book to the shelf.

Serena looked down the small hallway that led to the back door. She saw a figure slowly pass by the window as she approached it. She grabbed the doorknob and turned it open, then cracked the door to peer outside. Serena saw two men in the backyard wearing white armor with silver trim around the edges.

"Hey, you!" one of the men shouted when he saw Serena peeking at them from the doorway.

Serena slammed the door and ran back to where she eavesdropped on her parents, "Mom, Dad, there are people wearing armor in the backyard!?" she said urgently.

"What!?" Jace exclaimed.

"Jace! Jace!" A man's voice could be heard yelling outside the front door as he pounded it.

Jase yanked it opened to find his bald neighbor standing there with a panicked expression.

"What, what's going on!?" Jace shouted.

The man trembled with fright, "Get your family out of here quick! The Monarchy has come! They came without warning! We didn't even see them till they burst through the trees!" the man cried before turning away and running off.

Jace gazed around the village and saw there were dozens of soldiers walking into several houses already. "AMELIA!" Jace yelled.

"I got her," his wife replied while grabbing Serena.

"Mom, what's going on?" Serena asked in a frightened tone.

Her mother didn't answer. Instead, she grabbed Serena's hand and held it tight.

"We'll escape out the back and make a run for it in the woods!" Jace said to his wife as he walked toward her.

Serena gazed up at her father and saw fear in his eyes. She had never seen him so flustered before, and it made her feel uneasy.

"Where do you think you're going?" a woman's voice called out in a calm yet assertive manner from the front door.

Serena saw the woman walk in the house with two soldiers behind her. She had short white hair with the sides shaved off and the back pulled into a stubby ponytail. She wore all white armor with silver trim that traced the outer edges. Over her left chest plate was a symbol of a shield that had a crown hovering above it. Inside the shield were two swords that crossed each other with a circle that had different designs in it behind them. From each side of the shield, angelic wings spread upwards to complete the image. Beneath that was an inscription that read, 'Captain,' signifying her rank.

"What is the Monarchy doing here in this peaceful village?" Jace asked.

The women looked over to a soldier behind her, "Second Lieutenant, read the order!" she commanded her subordinate.

"Yes, captain!" the soldier shouted. He reached into his armor and grabbed a scroll, then he unraveled and began reading.

By order of King Volgia, highest rank of the Monarchy. This village has fallen under our protection due to information gathered about our sworn enemies, the Amony. The information goes as follows. "The Amony have planned an attack on the village known as Sales to gain control of it and to fortify their troops, as well as to get a closer settlement to our headquarters. It is our King's wish to immediately secure the protection of the people by taking every child under the age of sixteen to the Monarchy headquarters where they will be watched over and protected by highly trained and skilled soldiers of the military. Due to limited transportation, the women unwilling to fight for the Monarchy will be given refuge

as far away from the battlegrounds as possible. All men above the age of sixteen will be required to fight in the battle!

"That is what we're doing here," the captain said casually. "Now please hand over your daughter so we can take her to safety," she demanded as her two soldiers approached Serena.

"You can't fool me. I know what the Monarchy is really doing," Jace said as he backed up slowly.

"Please inform me then," the captain replied with a touch of sarcasm.

Jace sneered at the captain heatedly, "You're not taking my daughter!" He barked as he reached into a kitchen drawer and pulled out a large knife. He charged at the captain with the tip of it pointed at her chest.

"Captain Ulgenda!" A soldier yelled as he ran in front of her and deflected the knife with his sword. The soldier followed up with a knee to Jace's stomach, causing him to fall. Jace grabbed the knife and hobbled away from them as fast as he could on his hands and knees.

"Run for it!" Jace yelled to his wife with what little breath he had left.

Amelia grabbed Serena's hand and another kitchen knife from the same drawer. She ran through the living room and out the back door.

"Stop right there!" a soldier ordered as he tried to grab her and Serena.

Amelia swung the knife at the soldier which caused him to jump back. Another soldier then leaped in front of her. He held a broadsword up with both hands.

"Mom I'm scared," Serena said while clutching her mother's waist.

Did you grab the girl yet?" the captain said as she walked out the door to the backyard. Both of her subordinates were following close behind her like shadows. One of which had Jace captured, holding both his arms behind his back.

"RUN!" Jace yelled as loud as he could.

Amelia turned to the soldier that jammed her path and swung the knife at him. He blocked her strike with his sword, but she pushed her blade down to the guard of his sword and used it as leverage to throw his weapon to the side. Amelia then ran her knife through an empty space in his armor, piercing his shoulder before quickly pulling it back out.

The soldier yelled in pain as he fell to the ground.

Amelia and Serena ran past him toward the woods with great haste.

"If you want something done right, you have to do it yourself," the captain stated while activating the Gate on the back of her right hand.

Her Gate expanded from her and floated in midair. It revealed a circle with eight diamond shapes converging to the center. Another circle encased the tips of the diamond shapes where they met.

The captain reached inside and pulled out a steel whip which seemed to go on forever as it flowed from the center of the Gate. It glided around her like a long ribbon lashing through the air.

"Stop!" Jace barked.

The captain reared her arm back and flung the whip forward. It cracked through the air and hit Amelia in the back of her shoulder.

Amelia fell to the ground screaming in agony.

"Mom!" Serena shouted as she dropped to her knees beside her mother.

"Amelia!" Jace yelled now frantically trying to escape the soldier.

"None of this would've happened if you just gave up the girl. I'm willing to let go of what you did to my subordinate if you simply hand her over," Captain Ulgenda said in a clearly frustrated tone.

"But Captain Ulgenda!" the soldier cried while bleeding out from his shoulder. Another soldier tended to him.

"Shut up, you disgrace!" the captain yelled.

Amelia whispered into Serena's ear while the captain was distracted. "When I get up, you run into the woods as fast as you can," she uttered.

"But Mom!" Serena protested.

"No buts!" Amelia interrupted. "Now go!" she ordered as she

stood up.

Amelia reached into a large hole in a tree next to her and pulled out a loaded crossbow that Jace kept outside for hunting. She held it ready and aimed it at Ulgenda.

"Run Serena!" Amelia yelled.

Serena hesitated for a moment as she glanced back at her mother, but then did as she was told and ran for the woods.

"How many random weapons do they have?" Ulgenda shouted with an inflamed look.

Amelia pulled the trigger, and the bolt flew toward the captain.

Ulgenda smiled as a circle of light with the same pattern as her Gate appeared in front of her face. The bolt disappeared into the light, and another circle appeared in front of the previous one, releasing the bolt back toward Amelia. It pierced Amelia's upper left shoulder causing her to scream and fall.

Serena heard her mother's cry and turned to see what happened. Her eyes widened at the sight of her mother falling to the ground.

"NO!" Jace yelled now trying desperately to escape.

"Now for the girl," Ulgenda said while raising her whip back.

"RUN SERENA, RUN!" Jace yelled to his daughter.

Serena hesitated as she gazed fearfully at her injured mother and captured father. *Why is this happening? Why are they doing this?* she thought before running toward the trees again with tears in her eyes.

"No, you don't!" Ulgenda shouted with a wicked grin as she flung her whip into one of the portals once more. Another circle appeared behind Serena and the end of the whip flew out from it and wrapped around Serena's body. Then the captain pulled Serena through the portal where she instantly came out the other side and into Ulgenda's grasp.

"LET HER GO! Jace yelled fiercely at the captain in a growling like tone.

"Daddy!" Serena screamed while crying profusely. She was wrapped up in the steel whip under the captain's arm.

Jace bellowed deafeningly and slammed the back of his head into the soldier's face that held him.

The soldier released his grip and grasped his nose which bled freely as he cried out.

Jace ran for the sword on the ground that his wife previously knocked out of a soldier's hand.

"Get him!" Ulgenda yelled.

"Yes, Captain!" the soldiers said all at once as they surrounded Jace.

Serena was still crying at the top of her lungs which began to annoy Ulgenda.

"That's quite enough!" the captain barked as she grabbed the sides of Serena's neck.

Serena could see the soldiers getting closer and closer to her father as her sight grew dimmer and darker until she passed out.

Serena felt a jolting bump and awoke. Her vision was blurred, but as things became clear she could see bars around her and shackles on her ankles. She sat up and looked around the area. She saw a large caravan with children in cages in front of her and behind her. The air rang with the screams and cries of children yelling for their mothers and fathers. Troops surrounded her, marching next to the caravan.

Serena got on her knees, and like the other children, began to cry. "Where am I? Where are my mom and dad? What's going on?!" she shouted through her tears.

Suddenly, Serena heard something zipping through the air. A soldier that was right behind her cage was slammed into the ground by an incredibly large sword. It was made from yellow light but was so beautiful that it almost looked like stained glass. The man lay there dead as the sword faded away.

Serena gasped and stared up to see what appeared to be hundreds of yellow swords made of light flying from the top of a hill. They began slicing and ramming into soldiers all around the caravan. The children were all screaming in fear, and the soldiers were running around trying to avoid getting hit.

Serena noticed five swords flying in her direction. She screamed as she covered her head and closed her eyes, but the swords cut through her cage and smashed into the ground without hurting her. She noticed her cage was opened but sat there stunned with fear.

Another sword flew down in her direction. She cried out as she clenched her face, but the sword landed next to her leg, cutting off her shackles.

Serena quivered and wept with terror, not knowing what to do. Then three more swords flew down and hit the cage causing it to fall over and tossing her to the dirt. She got up and glanced around at all the soldiers who were scattering like ants.

Another sword landed in front her which made her fall. She quickly turned around and ran for the woods. She noticed a soldier running right behind her. She couldn't tell if he was trying to catch her or if he was just trying to get away.

Just before she got to the tree line a sword shot down from the sky and struck the soldier into the ground which made the dirt erupt around it. Then she ran through the woods as fast as she could.

After running for what felt like an hour, Serena tripped on a root in a small clearing and fell. She pushed herself up and walked forward while trying to catch her breath. She noticed a stump and sat down on it. While still breathing heavily she began to sob once more, "I just want my mom and dad. I just want to go home," she repeatedly heaved while bawling into her palms.

Serena's head popped up instantly at the sound of a twig snapping behind some trees to the right of her, "Please, just leave me alone!" she yelled out to whoever was there.

She heard the branches rustling and stood up to run again. As she backed away, she saw a figure part the shrubs. She screamed loudly through her tears as Ken stepped out into the light.

CHAPTER 5

The Farmer

"I just want to go home and see my mom and dad," Serena stated to finish her story.

Ken noticed a tear slip down her cheek.

"I understand how you feel Serena. I lost my dad when I was twelve and then my mom only a year and a half ago," he said.

Serena looked at him and wiped the tear away, "You did?" she asked.

"Yeah, but your parents are still alive, I know they are. I'll take you back home to them safe and sound," Ken said.

Serena looked at him with a hopeful expression, "You promise?" she asked with a smile on her face.

"I promise," Ken replied while grinning back at her.

The sorrow in her emerald eyes was replaced with hope. She laid her head on Ken's shoulder like it was a pillow. This made him feel slightly uncomfortable since he wasn't used to this form of contact.

I don't know if I should let her sleep like this, Ken thought as he questioned what to do.

"Thank you, Ken," Serena whispered while closing her eyes.

"Uh, for what?" Ken asked through a stutter.

"For saving me," Serena replied softly.

Ken stared at her as she drifted to sleep. The estranged nervous feeling he had before seemed to melt away as he felt Serena breathe while she rested. Ken experienced something strange in his chest, a special kind of happiness that he hadn't felt in a long time. He laid his head against the tree. "I did it, dad, I helped someone. I protected this little girl," Ken whispered while gazing up at the stars in the night's sky through the branches above them.

The next morning, Serena screamed out loudly, causing Ken to jump from his slumber. He immediately took a fighting stance while half awake.

"What, what is it!?" Ken shouted groggily while looking around for Serena.

"It's so cute!" she exclaimed from the center of the clearing.

Ken saw her hunched over on her knees petting the fox that lead him to her yesterday, "You almost gave me a heart attack!" Ken bellowed.

"I can't help it. Flying foxes are my favorite animals," Serena said, ignoring Ken's frustration.

Ken let out a sigh and then picked up the clothes Serena was wrapped in and stuffed them into the bag, "May as well stay up now. I'm not going back to sleep after that," he uttered.

Ken gazed around the area for a while, taking in the beauty of the morning sun which peered through the trees and made the dew glisten on the grass. He then turned his attention to the Gate on the back of his hand.

I guess it wasn't a dream after all, Ken pondered.

He thought about the blast of air he fired from his hand yesterday, "I wonder if I can do that again," he said to himself while holding out his left palm. He focused intently on his Gate which began to glow yellow and then fired another burst of air that sounded like a shotgun going off.

"Whoa, I can do it at will!" Ken shouted excitedly.

He did it two more times and noticed that the blast of air lost its force after it went more than five feet in front of him. He wondered if he could use it in different ways. He tried making it suck in air, move air all around him, and make a bigger blast of air. All was to no avail. It could only do the simple blast.

"It's like an explosion of compressed air, like a pressure blast or something," Ken mumbled to himself.

"That's pretty cool," Serena said while watching him with the fox on her shoulder.

Ken smiled at her, then picked up his sword and bag and placed them on his back. "We should get going," he said.

"Can we take it with us?" Serena asked while pointing at the fox.

"Well, it is pretty cute," Ken said while holding his hand out to pet the fox. When his hand got an inch away from its nose, the fox growled while baring its teeth.

Ken quickly snatched his hand back, "On second thought, it has to go," he said while glaring back at the fox.

"Aww you scared it. It won't do it again I promise," Serena pleaded.

The fox jumped off Serena's should and ran to a tree. It jumped up to the top and sat on a branch, waiting for them.

"It wants us to follow," Ken said while looking up at the at the fox.

They started to walk in the direction the fox went and continued to follow as it jumped from limb to limb. This time it moved at a slower pace. Ken assumed it did this so they could keep up while walking.

"So, flying foxes are your favorite animals?" Ken asked, trying to make conversation with Serena.

"Yeah, when I was younger my family lived in a different town. A flying fox would visit and play with me while I was outside," Serena answered.

Ken gave her a curious glance, "Is that so?" he asked.

"Yup, it even brought me a small present for my birthday one year."

Ken pondered to himself for a moment. *That hooded man must have been watching her for some time now. I wonder why he's so interested in her,* he thought.

"Serena, this is a strange question, but have you ever seen a tall guy with a brown hooded cloak on?" Ken asked

"No, why do you ask?" Serena answered, happily entertained while watching the fox as it jumped from limb to limb.

"Just curious," Ken replied.

The fox projected a circle of light into the air above it then jumped inside and disappeared.

"Cool!" Serena stated.

"Is that the same fox from your childhood?" Ken asked.

"I don't know," Serena replied as she climbed over a large rock.

"Do all flying foxes disappear into circles of light?" Ken queried in an optimistic tone.

Serena simply shrugged her shoulders.

Ken put his hand to his forehead, *I can't believe she doesn't know anything about this guy,* he thought.

He watched as she walked beside him and couldn't help but notice her mood had improved from the night before. He smiled thinking that the fox must have cheered her up. *At least she's feeling better today.*

As they stepped out from a tree line, they noticed a seemingly endless field of trees organized neatly in rows running down a pasture. The trees looked ordinary enough except for the color of their leaves which were teal instead of green.

"It's a tree orchard," Ken said as they walked down a line of trees.

"Not just any tree orchard," Serena added excitedly. "Those are purapple trees," she said while pointing to one of the apples.

Ken gazed up and noticed that the apples were a bluish-purple color with four yellow stripes running evenly down the sides.

"Those are some weird looking apples," he muttered.

Both their stomachs growled at the same time. Neither of them had eaten yet, and they were out of food.

"Let's grab some," Ken said as he dropped his bag and grabbed the sword from his back.

"Great, purapples are my favorite," Serena replied.

Ken threw his sword as hard as he could at a limb with three purapples on it but didn't even come close. He tried several more times but continued to miss.

"You're not very good at this are you?" Serena said. She was sitting on the grass and watched Ken run back and forth as he picked up his sword and threw it again and again.

"The sword is too heavy to throw up there. I need something lighter," Ken replied. He glanced down and saw a rock sitting on the ground next to him. He picked it up and reared his arm back, ready to throw it into the branch. Then he stopped when an idea popped into his head. *I wonder what would happen if I did this*, he pondered.

Ken placed the rock in the palm of his left hand. He aimed his arm at the limb and focused on the Gate. It made a loud blast and shot the rock through the air; embedding it into the tree and causing the purapples to fall.

"Awesome!" Ken shouted as he ran to catch his prize. He caught two of them, but the other hit him on the top of his head. He yelled out in pain as he rubbed his scalp, "Those things are tough," he muttered.

Serena giggled as she approached. She picked up the one that bopped him and grinned, "I bet that hurt," she said while wiping the purapple on her shirt.

Ken cut her a look and then opened his mouth to bite into one. As he tried to bear down his teeth, he learned the skin was too hard to penetrate. It felt like a stiff rubber that hurt as he strained to eat it.

"These things are *really* tough!" Ken said while moving his jaw around.

Serena laughed at him again, "You have to cut it and peel the skin off," she said as she rubbed the purapple against the blade of ken's sword. When it made a small cut in the skin, she used her fingernails to rip off the rest. "Now you try," she said.

Ken made a small cut in the side of the purapple and repeated the same process as Serena. As he peeled the skin back, he noticed the meat of the purapple was red like the inside of a watermelon. He took a bite and was surprised to find that it had the same texture of an apple, but the flavor was like a fusion of apples, strawberries, and even a hint of grapes all at once. It was sweet and incredibly juicy.

"This is amazing, I've never had any fruit this good before," he said before taking another bite.

Serena nodded her head and smiled while chewing a mouth full.

Suddenly, they heard a voice yelling from far off, "Hey, you kids get out of my purapple orchard!" a man shouted.

Both Serena and Ken jumped behind the tree fearing they were in trouble.

"Oh man, we got busted," Ken whispered while peering around the edge of the tree.

"What do we do?" Serena asked while hiding next to him.

"Wait a second. He's not yelling at us," Ken said, noticing a stout man in overalls and a red plaid shirt wearing a straw hat standing in front of three teenagers.

"You going to make us old man?" one of the kids said tauntingly.

"If I have to I will!" the man answered.

One of the kids walked up to the farmer and pushed him to the ground.

"I've had enough of you being stingy with your purapples old man!" the kid yelled.

"Wait here and finish my purapple for me," Ken said, handing his food to Serena. He darted over to the action. As he ran, his Gate lit up and forced his sword to disappear into sparks of yellow light.

"Ok," Serena answered while contently biting into Ken's breakfast.

"Come on guys lets teach the old man what happens when you don't share," one of the kids shouted.

All the teenagers closed in on the farmer and laughed while cracking their knuckles.

"Back off!" Ken yelled as he flew through the air and hit one the teenagers with a flying side kick.

The boy he hit rolled on the ground as he grunted.

"What the—? You get a bodyguard or something old man?" one of the teens shouted.

"Leave, or I'll do the same to you punks," Ken ordered while standing over the man.

"He doesn't look so tough, Gage," said a teenager to the right of, Gage, who stood in the middle.

Ken suspected that kid was the leader.

The same teen charged at Ken with his fist reared back, but when he got close, Ken caught his punch before he could even throw it then kicked the teen in the stomach causing him to fold over.

"You losers advertise every move you make. This is getting boring, so leave before I have to get serious," Ken demanded.

Gage grabbed his friend and helped him up. "Fine. We'll go, but we'll be back. You can count on that!" he shouted while walking with his friend back to the woods. The guy Ken kicked down earlier followed behind them with a limp.

"Well thank you for that, friend. I owe you one," the man said as he stood up and dusted himself off.

"Consider us even," Ken replied.

The man gave him a confused look.

"My…uh… sister and I stumbled upon your purapple orchard and knocked some down. We're lost and out of food, so we didn't have much choice," Ken said apprehensively.

"Where's your sister?" the man asked.

Ken pointed over to Serena who was watching from behind the tree. "It's ok Serena, you can come over here now," Ken called.

Serena walked out from behind the tree and advanced toward them.

The man gasped while looking at Serena's tattered and dirty clothes.

"The poor dear, I can't just let you two wander the woods. My wife would kill me for starters. That settles it. You're spending the night with us," the man stated.

Ken was shocked by his generous offer. "Thank you, that's awesome!" he replied.

"The name is Hank, and you are?" Hank said while holding his palm out for a handshake.

"I'm Ken," Ken said while shaking the farmer's hand.

"And I'm Serena."

"Let's go back to the house so we can talk," Hank said.

They followed the farmer to his small, rickety truck and hopped in the bed for a ride.

"I didn't know this world had vehicles," Ken stated as Hank drove through the orchard.

"This world?" Serena asked with a puzzled expression.

"I mean this area," Ken answered, trying to cover up what he said before. He worried that people would think he was crazy if he told them he was from another world, so he decided to keep it secret.

"There it is," the farmer called out to them. "There's my home sweet home."

Ken and Serena looked from the back of the truck and saw a white house with a brick chimney on the side that was two stories tall with a beautiful garden in front.

"Wow, it's pretty," Serena said as Hank parked in the front yard. They followed the farmer up the front porch and into the house.

"Peggy I'm home, and I brought guests with me," Hank shouted.

Upon entering the house, Ken and Serena could smell the aroma of a freshly cooked meal coming from a room to the right. Ken couldn't help but wipe a little saliva from his lip. Even before coming to Etheria, he couldn't remember the last home-cooked meal he had.

A hefty woman with greying hair and an apron came out of the kitchen. "Now, Hank, you didn't say anything to me about bringing guests," she said while coming through the doorway.

The woman instantly gasped upon seeing Serena. She ran to her and dropped to her knees while looking her over. "What happened to this poor darling? She's a complete mess." She said, rubbing dirt off Serena's face.

"My sister and I have been lost in the woods for a while now," Ken answered.

"Well come with me, dear, and we'll get you fixed up. I have some clothes I picked up for my granddaughter that will fit you just fine," the woman said as she grabbed Serena's hand. "Hank keep an eye on lunch for me," she ordered.

"Alright, Peggy," Hank said as his wife took Serena upstairs. "Come with me Ken, I need to talk to you," Hank added as he walked into the kitchen. Ken followed him in and sat on a chair by the table just as Hank did.

"My wife tells me I have the ability to look into people's eyes and tell if they're lying or not. Now, I can look at you and tell you're a good person. That's why I'm trusting you in my home, but I can tell you're lying about Serena being your sister," Hank said.

Ken felt his stomach drop at Hank's statement, *How can he tell?* he thought.

"You don't have to tell me the truth about that though. I just want to know one thing. Are you with the Amony?" Hank asked while pointing at the Gate on Ken's left hand.

Ken glanced at his hand then back over to Hank, "No, I'm not with the Amony or the Monarchy," he replied while looking into Hank's eyes.

Hank stared at him for a moment and then smiled, "Ok, I believe you, Ken," he replied.

Ken felt relieved upon hearing Hanks approval. He stayed seated as Hank got up to check the food in the oven. He couldn't help feeling like he needed to tell Hank something.

"Serena's not my sister," Ken said blandly.

Hank turned to look at Ken, "I told you that you didn't have to say anything," he said while sitting back in his chair.

"I know, but I need you to hear me out on this," Ken said. He explained how he found Serena and about his fight with the Monarchy soldier.

"I told you this because I need to know. Who are the Monarchy and the Amony? Why would they take Serena from her home?" Ken asked.

Hank leaned back in his seat and closed his eyes for a moment. "There are two things to know when it comes to the Monarchy. One is what the Monarchy claims to be the truth about how they operate – and the other is a well-developed rumor about the Monarchy that they aren't fond of," he said.

"Can you tell me both?" Ken asked with intrigue.

Hank nodded his head and leaned forward on the table. "Where to start?" he grumbled while putting his hand on his chin.

"Why not tell me what the Monarchy is first?" Ken asked, ready to hear what Hank had to say.

"Well, the Monarchy is a military government. They are the law and order around this entire continent. They protect the peace and the people," Hank said.

"So, they're like a dictatorship?" Ken enquired.

"Yes, very much so. See the reason they call themselves the Monarchy is because their commander in chief's *rank* is known as King." Hank stated.

Ken crossed his arms and nodded his head. "Ok, so I get that they run this continent. Why don't you tell me more about what they do," he said insistently.

"Slow it down, youngster, I'm getting there," Hank replied. His tone suggested that he was getting annoyed with Ken interrupting him. "To tell you the Monarchy's side, I have to start with the Amony," he added. "The Amony are the sworn enemies of the Monarchy. Their one and only desire is world domination which can only be achieved by defeating the Monarchy and taking over this continent," he said grimly.

"So, they want to rule the world?" Ken asked.

"Yes, and in attempt to do so, the Amony stage invasions here on villages and towns to try and take control of an area. They do that to get closer refuge to the Monarchy headquarters. However, the Monarchy has spies in the Amony that tip them off when these invasions are going to happen. So, they send soldiers over to the villages to take all the children back to a secure, protected area for safety. Unfortunately, they force all the males sixteen and up from that village to fight with the monarchy. As for the women who are unwilling to fight, they get taken to an area away from the battle in hopes that they don't get captured or killed," Hank said.

"That's horrible," Ken replied.

"Yeah, but such is the nature of war," Hank stated while folding his arms. "That's a very basic explanation of how the Monarchy operates, but there is also a rumor you should know."

Ken stared at him awaiting the information.

"The rumor is that the Monarchy and Amony are secretly in league with each other, the only people knowing about it are the highest ranking such as the King," Hank said.

"That doesn't make sense at all," Ken stated with a skeptical tone.

"Listen, and you'll see the connection," Hank replied irritably. "See the reason they do this is because of the guardians," Hank added. He stopped when he saw Ken give him a bewildered look.

"What's a guardian?" Ken asked.

Hank placed his hand on his face, "Are you serious?" he questioned with a puzzled gaze.

Ken shrugged his shoulders, "Excuse me for not understanding," he said sarcastically.

"Well, I have to tell you what a guardian is before I can tell you the rumored plan," Hank sighed.

"Some people are born into this world with special powers deep within their soul. These people are known as guardians. However, the guardians are unable to use these powers because they are trapped within the flesh of their bodies," Hank said.

"Then how do they know they have powers?" Ken asked.

"I'm getting to that!" Hank stated.

Ken picked up on Hank's annoyed tone and decided to stop interrupting.

"Now to continue, again!" Hank said. "A guardian can't use its own powers. Nor are they aware that they have any. However, when a guardian dies, its soul bonds to the person that it was closest to during its lifetime. Like a friend, brother, sister, and so on. The person they bond to becomes known as a host. And the combination of guardian and host is referred to as an Angeon. See when a guardian bonds to a host, it can pass its powers *to* the host. Does all this make sense to you so far?" Hank asked.

Ken nodded his head, "Basically, guardians have powers but can't use them until they die and bond to a host, right?" he questioned.

Hank shook his head in disagreement, "The guardian cannot use its powers at all, whether it's bonded or not. It can only give its powers to the host so *that* person can use them," Hank clarified.

"So, guardians have special powers but can never use them; and they have to die just to share them? That kind of sucks." Ken said while leaning back in his chair. "Why are they called, guardians? Do they protect the host or something?"

Hank shook his head. "You're putting too much thought into this. They're called guardians because their soul floats around the host like a guardian angel. Guardians can't actually interact with the world around them, so they can't physically protect the host. But they can pass their powers *to* the host, so that the host can protect themselves."

"Ok, I think I got it. An Angeon is what people call a host that has a guardian. The guardian's soul bonds to the host and can pass its powers *to* the host for them to use. Is that right?"

"Yes. You have the basic idea. Look, I'm not an Angeon and I've never really dealt with them before. I'm not the best person to explain what they are. I'm just a farmer after all."

Ken nodded his. "Fair enough, I think I got the gist of it."

"Now let's get back to the rumor," Hank said. "Supposedly the Monarchy and Amony are working together to collect guardians. It's said they have a way to detect where a guardian is. So, when they find one, they call each other in and tell them they need an invasion in that area. Then they take all the children to their headquarters. At the end of the battle, a lot of children are left orphaned and given a home with the Monarchy. It's there that the Monarchy makes the military look great to the orphaned children, filling their heads with how wonderful and glorious it is to work and fight for them. It makes the kids want to join when they get old enough. Inevitably a guardian joins the Monarchy and gets partnered with someone. Sometimes they even get paired with the opposite sex just to make them bond quicker. That way when they kill off the guardian, it bestows its powers onto that soldier making the military that much stronger," Hank continued.

Ken stared at Hank with a look of skepticism, "There is one thing I don't understand. If the Amony and Monarchy have secretly joined forces, why try to make a stronger military? There's no one else to oppose them, right?" he asked.

Hank shrugged his shoulders, "No one has an answer for that. Just remember that this is all a rumor, I don't know which is right or wrong. I just stay neutral to the whole mess. There are people out there who believe that rumor to be gospel. Of course, there are others who think the Monarchy is perfect and only wants to protect the people," he said as he got up to recheck the food.

"What do you think?" Ken asked.

"I don't think the Monarchy is perfect, but I don't think they have some crazy plan to kill off people for power either. I'm like you. That rumor doesn't make sense to me," Hank said while smelling the food in the oven.

"So, why tell me all that?" Ken inquired.

"Because you asked, and that's what I know about it," Hank replied frankly.

"Enough of all that. It's time for lunch. Besides, look at your little sister now," Peggy said as she walked down the steps with Serena.

Serena was outfitted in a pink dress with lace around the stomach and shoulders. She also wore white gloves that ran up her forearm. Her hair was pulled up into a bun and smelled like flowers indicating that she had a bath.

"I just love getting children all dressed up," Peggy said as she walked over to the stove and started to prepare the food. She had a satisfied glow about her, like a grandmother spending quality time with her granddaughter.

"You look good sis," Ken said with a slight chuckle. He could tell by Serena's expression that she didn't enjoy getting dressed up like a doll.

Serena gave him a deathly look, "I blame you for this," she whispered as she pulled up a chair between Ken and Hank.

Ken couldn't help but laugh as she folded her arms. He wanted to pick on her some more but decided to back off. After all, he still hadn't got to know her enough to push things like that.

CHAPTER 6

Heart of Fire

After lunch, Ken volunteered to help Hank with his chores and duties around the orchard. From picking purapples to chopping wood, he worked till it started to get dark. Finally, after a hard day of labor, he went back to the house to rest.

"How are you feeling?" Hank asked as Ken got a large glass of water and gulped it down.

"Tired, very tired," Ken replied after finishing the glass. When he sat, his wet sweaty bangs fell on his face. He could feel the cold, moist tips of his hair touch the back of his neck and began running his fingers through it to stop the chilly dripping of sweat.

"May I use your bath?" Ken asked while still playing with his hair.

"Yes, and leave your clothes outside the door, so I can wash them," Peggy answered. She was washing dishes by the sink.

"Yeah, you stink," Serena said while covering her nose.

"What did you do all day?" Ken asked her while fanning himself off with a plate.

"I helped Grandma Peggy around the house," Serena answered.

Ken gave her a puzzled look, "Grandma?" he asked.

Peggy approached Ken from behind and took the plate away, "Yes, I told her to call me Grandma Peggy. Now quite fanning yourself with my dishes and take a bath," she ordered.

Ken gave Hank a semi scared glance as he got up.

"I'd be afraid, too. You don't mess with the woman's kitchen wears," Hank said as he laughed.

Ken laid down in the bathtub as steam rose around him. He heard Peggy walk by and grab the clothes that he left outside the door. He relaxed in the water for half an hour, enjoying the heat and feeling his aching muscles relieve their tension. After his bath, Ken dried off and wrapped the towel around himself then opened the door to find some replacement clothes waiting for him. They were red plaid pajamas. They weren't his style, but he figured they would do for now. After he put them on, he went downstairs.

"Your clothes will be dry later tonight sweetie," Peggy said as she put the food on the table.

"Thank you, this looks awesome by the way," Ken replied as he admired the spread.

Peggy served mashed potatoes with green beans, corn and what looked like an oven-baked chicken. Ken was surprised to see that the food was similar to food from Earth. He was expecting purple potatoes with orange beans and blue corn with maybe a three-headed goose. Of course, the lunch she served earlier was a standard meatloaf and was also delicious. So, to him, it made it all made sense.

"I helped make it, too," Serena said as she sat down next to Ken. Ken smiled at her and waited for everyone to get seated.

After supper, Ken helped wash dishes. "That was a great dinner, Peggy," he said while cleaning a plate.

"You're welcome," Serena replied.

Ken looked at her oddly.

"I helped remember?" she said with a big grin.

"I think it's time you go to bed for the night Serena," Peggy said as she dried the dishes Ken washed.

"Ok, I guess I am feeling a little tired," Serena answered.

"I have clothes upstairs for you to change into," Peggy said.

Serena nodded and went upstairs.

Peggy noticed all through dinner Ken was brushing his hair out of his eyes. "We need to do something about this mop of yours," she said while grabbing the back of his hair.

"You want to cut my hair?" Ken questioned reluctantly.

"That sounds like a good idea. You were pushing your hair out of your face all day," Hank added.

"I don't know, maybe we should hold off on that," Ken muttered, hoping they would drop it.

"Nonsense, sit down right here," Peggy insisted while pulling up a chair. She practically forced him to sit on it, "I just love cutting hair," she added as she snapped a pair of scissors twice behind Ken's head.

"I don't think my hair is all that bad," Ken replied nervously.

"Well if you're going to take Serena home you might need to see where you're going," Hank said with a chuckle. "I'll be on the porch if y'all need me," he stated as he got up and walked outside.

"Don't be such a baby," Peggy said as she cut some hair off the back of Ken's head.

Ken grunted slightly. He didn't like haircuts. He had no reason to hate them other than wanting to grow his hair out. Plus, he enjoyed having his bangs cover his eyes at times.

There was a moment of silence between them while Peggy was cutting Ken's hair.

"Hank told me about Serena. I talked to her for a while and found out you're planning to take her back home," Peggy said in a more serious tone.

Ken was caught off guard by her statement, "I...uh.... That's right. I made her a promise that I would," he said timidly.

"I think it's noble that you want to do that for her. I also find it admirable that you fought to protect someone you didn't know, but did you ever think that the Monarchy could give Serena a good home?" She asked.

"What do you mean?" Ken inquired.

As Ken and Peggy were talking, Serena finished getting dressed in the upstairs room. She felt parched and made it halfway down the steps when she heard Ken and Peggy conversing.

"We don't know if the rumor about the Monarchy is true or not, but we do know that even if it is, the Monarchy takes care of the children they take from invasions," Peggy stated while cutting Ken's bangs.

"What are you getting at?" Ken asked.

"I'm saying that Serena is a growing young woman who needs a stable home. Traveling in the woods doesn't seem to be the best thing for her. The Monarchy can guarantee her a warm bed every night with dinner and a home. Can you provide that for her?" Peggy inquired.

Ken contemplated what Peggy had said, "No, I guess I can't," he answered softly.

"You need to think about what's best for her. The Monarchy may not seem like it's the best thing, but you have to look at what she'll be facing if she's with you," Peggy said as she moved around Ken to cut the hair over his ears.

"You're right, I'll have to really think about it," Ken replied as Peggy finished up his hair cut.

Serena gasped while covering her mouth. Slowly, she walked back upstairs and closed the door behind her, "He promised he would take me home," she said while climbing into the bed. "He promised he'd take me back to my Mom and Dad," she stammered while starting to cry. She fell forward onto her pillow, burying her face into it. "He won't go back on his word, will he?" she whispered to herself.

"There, it's all done. Why don't you have a look?" Peggy said with a look of accomplishment on her face.

Ken stood up and looked in the mirror Peggy had on the kitchen door. The back of his hair was cut tight to his head while the sides were shaven away from his ears. His bangs were left a little longer as they were just above his eyes.

"Well, what do you think?" Peggy asked. Her tone suggested she was ready to be praised.

Ken stared in the mirror for a while, reminding himself over and over about his promise to Serena. "I can't take her to the Monarchy. I promised I would take her home, so that's what I'm going to do. There is no better place for her than with her parents," he said without paying attention to the haircut.

Peggy gave him a dissatisfied look. Ken couldn't tell if it was because he didn't say anything about the haircut, or if it was about

Serena.

"You need to think hard about what's best for her," Peggy said sternly.

Ken ignored what Peggy said and completely disregarded her thoughts on the matter. "I lost my parents a long time ago. If I knew they were still alive out there, I would stop at nothing to find them. When I look at her, I see a bit of myself. Lost and scared with no one to turn to. I want to be the person who recuses her from that insecurity. I don't want her to become like me," he said in a somber tone.

Peggy opened her mouth to talk but was interrupted by the yells of her husband. "FIRE, FIRE, MY TREES ARE ON FIRE!" he shouted from outside.

Ken ran out of the kitchen and met him by the front door.

"Come on!" Hank yelled as he and Ken raced to the truck.

Ken hopped on the back, and they took off down the field of trees leaving Peggy by the front door watching as they went.

Ken smelt the smoke but couldn't see the fire even though it was getting dark out. "Where's it at?" He yelled over the wind that whipped by them as they drove.

Hank pointed to an orange glow just ahead.

"Do you have anything to put it out with?" Ken shouted.

"If it's where I think it is, then there should be a pond we can get water from with those buckets in the bed of the truck!" Hank bellowed back.

As they approached Ken saw there was only one tree ablaze, but it was engulfed by flames. Then he noticed three dark figures in the light of the fire. "It's those brats from before!" he exclaimed while clenching his fist.

Hank parked the truck and ran over to the tree while Ken went straight for the teenagers.

"Look, boys. The bodyguard is back, and he brought his jammies this time!" Gage said while he and the other teenagers laughed and pointed at the pajamas Ken was wearing.

"If you help us put out this fire your ass whopping may not hurt as bad!" Ken yelled threateningly.

Gage laughed even harder with his friend next to him, but the one behind them seemed a little more frightened. "Give me another one Jake," Gage said to the timid teenager.

"No, we took it too far this time," Jake replied.

Gage walked over to Jake and pushed him aside, "I'll do it myself then," he said as he grabbed something off the ground and then lite it with a match.

After it ignited, Ken realized what it was. Gage had a bottle with a rag soaked in kerosene sticking out the top of it.

"So that's how you started the fire," Ken stated.

Gage smiled sinisterly, "And it's how I'm going to get rid of you," he shouted. He reared back to throw the bottle, but his friend Jake grabbed his arm to stop him.

"NO! We need to stop before we hurt someone!" Jake exclaimed.

Gage elbowed Jake in the stomach and watched as he fell to his knees. "Hold him for me, Chris," he demanded the other teen.

The other teenager grabbed Jake and pulled him away.

"Now, where were we?" Gage said as he looked over at Ken.

"Don't throw it at me or you'll regret it," Ken said confidently.

"Only one way to find out," Gage yelled as threw the kerosene bottle.

Ken held his left hand up just as the bottle closed in on him. The Gate on his hand lite up and did a pressure blast. It caused the container to burst into pieces and ignite the kerosene. It was like he shot back a giant ball of fire toward Gage.

"AAAHHHH!" Gage cried as he ducked to the ground and covered his face. Luckily for him, Ken was too far away for the flames to make it to him before they dissipated.

"Gage, you alright?" the other teenager asked as he ran up.

Ken could hear Hank yelling out to him from the other side of the tree, "Ken, if we don't put this thing out the fire will spread to the other trees through its branches!" he bellowed.

Just as Ken started to run toward Hank, he heard a limb snapping.

He looked up and noticed a large branch about to fall where Gage and the other kid were standing. "Move, you have to get out of there!" he yelled at them.

"Why don't you make us!" Gage yelled back. Apparently, he thought Ken was trying to push him around some more.

Ken heard another snap and noticed the limb move a little more. He ran toward them as fast as he could.

"Coming back for more?" Gage yelled as he took a fighting stance with his fists up.

Suddenly, they heard a loud pop and saw the limb start to fall toward them. Before they could even scream; Ken jumped to them using both his feet to kick them out of the way. As he fell, he held his left hand up and released another pressure blast that pushed the limb over to his side just before it hit – causing it to land next to him.

Ken quickly got up and moved away from the burning branch as he released a sigh of relief. "I'm so glad that worked," he said while wiping sweat off his forehead.

"Let's get out of here!" Chris said as he struggled to get up with Gage

"Yeah let's run!" Gage shouted in agreement. Both of them ran into the woods.

"Ken, I need your help!" Hank yelled out.

Ken ran over to him as quick as he could.

"We can't let those flames get to the other tree's branches," Hank said as he pointed up to the limbs. They were engulfed in fire and getting closer to the branches of the tree next to it.

"I have an idea!" Ken cried as he held his left hand over his chest. He threw it to the side, causing the Gate to project off his hand. He reached inside and pulled out his sword.

"What are you going to do with that?" Hank questioned.

"Chop it down!" Ken hollered as he ran to the base of the tree. He gripped his blade with both hands and swung at the trunk with all his strength. To his surprise, it went halfway into the tree with one swing. He tried to pull it out but the heat from the flames was too much. He ran away from the tree leaving his sword stuck inside it.

"Now what?" Hank asked. His tone suggested he was getting worried.

"I'll keep doing that until the tree falls," Ken replied as he opened the Gate on his hand again. His blade disappeared into a burst of yellow sparks in the fire, and he pulled the sword back out from the gate.

Ken ran back to the tree and slammed his sword into it again. This time he slashed a few inches above the previous cut. It was at an angle so it would take a large chunk out of the tree. Then he ran away from it again due to the heat.

"Be careful Ken!" Hank called out as Ken summoned his sword again.

Ken repeated the process of slashing the tree and running away three more times until it cracked and popped as it fell to the ground. Thankfully, it fell away from the other trees.

"We need to put that fire out! Here take this, there is a pond over here we can get water from," Hank shouted as he passed Ken a bucket and pointed the way to the pond.

"What can I do?" Jake asked as he ran up to Hank.

Hank looked surprised to see one of the teenagers stayed to help. He immediately put a bucket in Jake's hand and told him to get water with Ken. "While the two of you get the water, I'll dig a fire break around the tree," he shouted.

For over an hour Ken and Jake ran back and forth pouring water on the tree while Hank dug around it. Finally, the flames were gone, and the tree laid there smoking and steaming.

All three of them sat on the back of the truck catching their breath, exhausted from the running and digging.

"Well, boys that should do it. The firebreak will keep it from spreading if it reignites. Plus, it's soaked, so I think we can sleep easy tonight," Hank said.

Jake stood up from the truck and turned to Hank, "I'm sorry for what we did sir. I don't know what I was thinking, going along with their plan like that. I'm going straight to the Monarchy officers and turning Gage in along with myself," Jake said with a guilty expression.

Hank stood up and held his hand out to Jake for a handshake, "It takes a big man to stand up to your friends when you know they're doing the wrong thing. And it takes a bigger man to take responsibility for your actions. You can come eat purapples with me anytime," Hank said.

Jake gazed down at Hank's hand and cut a slight grin as he took it for a handshake.

Ken got up and approached him as well, "You know what Jake? You've given me something I gave up on a long time ago," he said.

Jake looked at him curiously, "What's that?" he asked.

"Hope. I used to get into fights with bullies and jerks all the time back home, but I never had one come back to me and say he was sorry. I gave up on the idea that people could change, but maybe I was wrong," Ken said.

Jake smiled at him, "Gage and Chris aren't bad guys, they just need better guidance," he said.

"Well, they're lucky to have you then," Hank added.

"Thanks, I better get going. It's gonna to be a long night," Jake said as he turned and started to walk toward the woods.

"Good luck!" Hank shouted as he watched him go.

Both Ken and hank got back in the truck and started to drive back to the house.

"Did you mean what you said Ken?" Hank asked.

"Yeah, it seems like everyone I knew was greedy and only out for themselves. They were willing to bully and hurt anyone for anything. I felt like there was no one good left in the world and that I had fallen on the same path they were on," Ken said in a drab tone.

"So, you thought you were just as bad as them?" Hank asked.

"I think I'm still just as bad, but I'm learning to be better," Ken said as he looked down.

Hank shook his head, "You really think you're a bad person? Let's review, shall we? You rescued a little girl who was lost in the woods, you stopped those kids from hurting me this morning, you helped me get a lot of work done today, and you also helped me stop the fire. I don't know many people who would run to a burning tree just to chop it down and save my orchard. I believe you're already a good person!" Hank stated.

Ken gave a melancholy smile, "My past suggests otherwise," he uttered.

Hank gave him a disapproving glance, "Remembering the past so you don't make the same mistakes is an important thing; but living in it is self-destructive. Without you I'd still be fighting that fire and probably would have lost half my orchard by now. You're a good person Ken, and I don't care who says otherwise, even you," Hank stated.

Ken couldn't help but grin at the sound of someone being thankful for what he did. He felt a warmth of happiness building inside him. In his heart, he felt like he made his father proud.

When they arrived at the house, they told Peggy all about what happened with the teenagers and the fire.

"Well, it's a good thing you were here, right, Ken?" Peggy said while winking at him. Ken just smiled and looked away as his face went flush.

"I think we've had enough excitement for one night. We should all get some sleep," Hank said groggily.

"Oh! Don't lie in my clean beds until you both take another bath!" Peggy barked.

Ken looked in the mirror and realized he had soot and ash all over his face and clothes.

"I'll go get the clothes I cleaned for you today Ken," Peggy said. "And by the way, I know no matter what you decide to do with Serena that you'll make the right choice. Even if it's taking her back home," she added with a sincere smile.

"Thank you, Peggy," Ken replied with a nod as he went upstairs to take his bath.

As Ken laid in bed that night, he thought about all the things that had happened in only two days. He wondered who the hooded man was and what his connection to Serena could be. He also thought about how proud his mother and father would have been to see him stick up for the farmer. However, the one thing he couldn't get off his mind even more than his parents was the Monarchy. He kept trying to decide if he thought they were dangerous or just misunderstood. He made up his mind about one thing before he fell asleep. No matter what happened, he would make it a point to learn more about the Monarchy and who they really are.

CHAPTER 7

Missing Angel

The next morning Ken awoke to the smell of pancakes wafting into his room. He quickly got out of bed and dressed in the clothes the hooded man gave him. Afterwards, he raced downstairs toward the source of the scent. "That smells great," he said while entering the kitchen.

"Good morning. You know what time it is?" Peggy asked while putting a plate of pancakes on the table.

"No, not really," Ken replied.

"It's almost noon," Hank said from the table.

"Already!?" Ken questioned.

"Yeah, we let you sleep in because of how late we were up last night," Hank replied.

Ken noticed Serena sitting at the table with her eyes focused on her plate. She didn't say anything or even look Ken's way when he came in. "Thanks, I was worn out," he said to Hank. "Hey Serena, you want to hear about what happened last night?"

Serena didn't answer him. Instead, she continued to stare grimly at her plate.

"You ok Serena?"

"I already regaled her with the story of how you bravely ran to the burning tree and chopped it down," Hank said with a jolly laugh.

Ken gazed at Serena's dismal countenance, wondering what was bothering her.

After breakfast Ken, Hank, and, Peggy talked for a while around the table. "So, what's your plan for today?" Hank asked.

"Well, I guess the first thing we need to do is get a map. That way we can be on the right track," Ken answered.

"You're gonna have to go to town for that. It's not that far though. By the way, do you have any money?" Hank questioned.

"Yeah, I think so?" Ken replied.

"You think so? Show me," Hank ordered with a curious look.

Ken walked over to his bag in the corner of the room and pulled a small sack out the side pocket. He poured the coins on the table for Hank to look at.

"You got about a hundred fol here," Hank said while inspecting the coins.

"Is that good?" Ken asked.

Hank gave him a puzzled glance once more, "It's ok," he replied. "You're gonna need some more though. Peggy, can you grab my jar?" Hank said to his wife.

Peggy got up from the table and walked out of the kitchen.

"You don't have to do that," Ken said modestly.

"But I want to," Hank answered while still looking at the coins.

"I hate to take some money that you might need," Ken replied. He understood the struggle of not having enough to get by on all too well. He also hated getting money from others like a charity. It was always one of his pet peeves.

Hank put down the coins and gave Ken a stern look, "Purapples are a scarce fruit. They only grow in this region of the content and they also grow all year round. I make more money than you think I do. Just don't repeat that to anyone," he added with a wink.

Peggy walked back into the kitchen with a large jar full of coins.

"Now I'm going to give you four hundred. So, you'll have five hundred in total. Make sure you take good care of Serena with it. Get her clothes and food but stick to the essentials. Don't forget to take care of yourself too. You can't care for her if you can't take care of yourself," Hank said while counting out money and putting it into the sack.

Ken looked at the coins for a moment and noticed the numbers on them. Some had twenty and others had fifty. They seemed like what he'd see on Earth. It brought him some relief to know that the increments were the same.

"You got that?" Hank said while handing Ken the sack.

Ken was reluctant to take it at first. However, he knew he needed it for Serena's sake. "Yes, thank you for this. I really don't know what to say," he answered humbly.

Hank looked at him and replied with a smile, "Consider us even," he said. "Well, you guys have a long way to go so let's move this outside," Hank added.

They all stood up from the table and walked to the front porch.

"Are you sure we can't get you to stay longer?" Peggy asked.

"No, we have to get going," Ken replied.

Hank approached Ken while holding his bag, "Here, you almost forgot this. By the way, Peggy packed it last night. Then I repacked it because it was too heavy for me to pick up," he said while glaring at Peggy.

"I just wanted to make sure they had enough food and water," she said defensively.

Ken and Hank both laughed but Serena didn't react at all. Ken gave her a concerned glance again. He wanted to ask what was wrong, but Hank got between them while pointing to an opening in the trees.

"See that trail? Follow it for about ten minutes. It'll connect to a road that you can follow to the next town. It should only take an hour if you walk. I would drive you, but I have too much work to do right now," Hank said.

Ken put the bag on then shrugged his shoulders, "It's fine, we'll have to get used to walking anyway, right Serena?" he said while grinning at her, but she turned her head away.

"Yeah, I guess," Serena muttered under her breath.

Peggy got on her knees to get face to face with Serena and gave her a hug goodbye. Then she gave Ken one as well. Hank hugged Serena and shook Ken's hand.

"You stay safe now," Hank said as they started to walk away. "Oh! One more thing!" he called out.

Ken turned and felt something hit his chest. He picked it up to find it was a pair of work gloves.

"Don't let people see the Gate on your left hand. They'll think you're with the Amony," Hank shouted.

Ken nodded and put the gloves on. "Thank you," he yelled back. "Let's go," he said while patting Serena on the head.

Serena crossed her arms and started to walk with a scowl on her face.

"It turned out to be a nice day right, Serena?" Ken asked as they walked down the trail. The sun beamed brilliantly in the sky, but the temperature was warm and comfortable.

Serena didn't reply though. She merely continued to walk.

"What's wrong with you today?" Ken asked, now starting to get upset.

Serena still didn't respond.

Ken glared at her, "Well whatever your problem is, you need to get over it! I don't want to deal with this all day," he stated impatiently.

Serena grunted and maintained her pace.

Ken sighed and started to think of a plan for the day. "Hank told me that we can buy a map in town and get a hotel room for the night. He also said we can do a little shopping, maybe we can get you some new clothes," Ken said, hoping to pique her interest.

Serena still refused to talk.

"Alright fine, if this is how you want it till we get there, then so be it," Ken stated.

The rest of the way down the trail was awkward and silent. When they reached the road, Ken tried to make conversation again, but Serena still wanted nothing to do with him and continued her quiet walk to town.

"I think we're here," Ken said as they walked past a few old looking brick buildings. He looked around and saw several stands with people selling various items like fruit and trinkets. "So, is this the town?" he questioned while gazing around.

"This town is called Drez," a strange man wearing a black

overcoat said. He was standing next to a large bulletin board with wanted posters all over it.

Ken approached the man with Serena next to him, "Where can I find the hotel?" he asked.

"Just follow the rows of merchants then turn right at the end of the road. you can't miss it," the man said while looking over the posters.

Ken looked at some of the pictures and the rewards for finding them. Most of the prizes were for one thousand fol, but Ken noticed a bald skinny man valued at ten thousand. "Why is he worth so much?" he asked curiously.

The man turned and looked at Ken. He had a scar that ran up from his chin through his lip and to his hairline. "He's the puppet king. He kidnaps anyone of any age and then guts and stuffs them. Then he turns them into puppets. He calls these fleshy toys his friends," the man said with an eerie smile.

Ken started to get a bad vibe from the man and grabbed Serena's hand, "Let's go," he said.

The cloaked man got on his knees and looked at Serena, "Be careful. Some people say strangers don't do well around here," he said while maintaining his creepy grin.

Ken put himself between the man and Serena, "Yeah well, they don't get much stranger than you, buddy." He said while glaring at the man.

The stranger scowled back at Ken then walked off.

Ken looked down at Serena who was staring back at him with a worried expression. It was evident that the stranger frightened her.

"It's ok, you're bound to have some weird people around towns like this. Let's look at some of these merchant stalls on our way to the hotel," Ken said in a light tone.

Serena nodded her head in agreement. Her uneasiness seemed to take over whatever was bothering her.

They walked down the rows of stalls finding one with clothes all around it.

"Come on, Serena. Let's check out this one. Maybe we can find you some new outfits," Ken said.

Serena walked over to the stand and started to look at the clothes without saying anything. She obviously still wanted him to know she wasn't happy.

I don't know what to do if she doesn't lighten up, Ken thought.

He looked over some clothes and noticed a pair of black fingerless gloves in a pile of random garments. His hands were hot and sweaty in the work gloves he currently wore.

"How much are these?" Ken asked the lady behind the stand.

"Five fol," she answered.

Ken approached her with a coin that had the number twenty on it and gave it to her. She then gave him back three coins with fives on them.

"Just like currency on Earth," Ken said to himself.

He carefully removed the work gloves, so no one could see the Gate on the back of his hand and then put the other gloves on.

"That's better," he muttered while admiring his new purchase.

Serena came around the corner wearing a new outfit. She wore blue pants with a light pink shirt that had a flower design in the middle, along with a blue short-sleeve jacket that came mid-way down her torso.

"Is that the outfit you want?" Ken asked.

Serena nodded her head while looking herself over in the mirror.

Ken noticed she was fighting back a smile while admiring the clothes.

"How much for what she's wearing?" Ken asked the merchant.

"Seventy fol," the lady replied.

"Seventy!?" Ken shouted.

The lady gave him an unsympathetic look, "She has on my most stylish jacket and pants. Those are some of my best sellers. Now pay or put it away."

Ken grabbed the money out of the sack and gave it to the merchant, "She better get over her attitude for this," he mumbled under his breath.

Ken approached Serena who was still looking over her new

clothes in the mirror. "Hand me your old clothes so I can I put them in the bag," he said.

Serena nodded and did as instructed.

"You ready to look around some more?" Ken asked, hoping she would crack a smile.

"Sure," Serena replied indifferently.

Well, at least she said something to me, Ken thought.

They spent a few hours looking around at different shops. Ken bought a pocketknife and a map of the continent at one shop while Serena picked out a red ribbon to tie her hair into a ponytail at another. The whole time she still didn't make any effort to talk with Ken.

"There's the hotel," Ken said as they approached a big building that read Seeker's inn. The building seemed like one of the nicer places in town. It wasn't fancy by any means, but it did appear to be well kept up. "Let's stay here tonight," Ken added.

They walked inside and approached the man behind the desk. He wore a formal long sleeve white shirt with a black tie. Ken couldn't help but notice a few thin black hairs combed over a bald spot-on top of his head.

"My sister and I need a room for the night," Ken said.

"Would you like a luxury room?" the clerk asked.

"No, just something small and simple," Ken replied.

The clerk gave them a key with a tag and the number five on it. "That will be fifty fol for the night," he said while holding out his hand.

Ken shook his head and reluctantly handed over the coins. *We're going to run out of money at this rate*, he supposed.

"Upstairs, third door on the left," the clerk said while putting away the currency.

As they went up the stairs, Ken turned back to the clerk, "By the way, your bald spot is showing," he called out.

The clerk was taken back by Ken's words and immediately grabbed a hand mirror under his desk and went to adjusting his combover.

Ken and Serena reached room five and opened it up with the key. It was cramped with one bed and a couch just under the window. It also had a small dining table for two. Of course, in Ken's mind, it beat sleeping outside.

"We should eat the lunch Hank and Peggy made for us," Ken said while grabbing the food from the bag.

Serena didn't answer. She just sat at the table waiting for Ken to pull out the food.

They ate quietly in an awkward and unwelcome silence. The only sound between the two of them was that of forks hitting the plastic plates and the chewing of food in their mouths. After they finished eating, Ken decided he had enough.

"Will you please tell me what's going on with you?" Ken asked in a fed-up tone.

Serena ignored him and moved from the table to the bed. She laid down and stared at the ceiling.

Ken started to get irritated. He clenched his fist and closed his eyes while breathing deeply for a moment, "Fine, stay here! I'm going out," he grumbled.

Serena instantly popped up from the bed, "Why, what are you going to do?" she asked demandingly.

"I want to learn more about the Monarchy, so I'm going out to see what I can find," Ken replied in a cross manner.

"I knew it! I knew you were going back on your promise!" Serena yelled out.

"What do you mean going back on my promise?" Ken asked.

"I heard you talking to Peggy. She said you should take me to the Monarchy so that I'd have a better home, then you said you'd think about it. I guess you made up your mind! Well, I'm not going!" Serena shouted.

"Is that what this is all about?" Ken asked. He felt slightly relieved to know what the problem was.

"You have no idea what it's like to have your family taken away from you!" Serena barked as she stood up from the bed. "I'm not going to let you take me back to the people who kidnapped me!"

Ken gave her a stern look, "You're preaching that story to the wrong person Serena!" Ken said back. "Both my parents are dead. I'd give anything to be in your shoes right now. You can go back to your family, but mine are gone forever!" he roared.

Serena looked down and didn't say anything to that.

"I'm not taking you to the Monarchy! I promised that I'd take you home, so that's what I'm going to do," Ken said in a stern voice.

He walked up to Serena then heard her say something under her breath.

"What, I couldn't hear you?" Ken said.

"I said you're lying!" Serena yelled as she pushed Ken back causing him to trip over his bag and fall to the ground. Afterward, she ran out of the room as fast as she could.

"Serena!" Ken cried out as he picked himself up.

Ken ran out the room and down the stairs after her. He caught a glimpse of her running out the door of the hotel.

Ken shot out the door as fast as he could while calling her name, "Serena stop!" he shouted while sprinting down the sidewalk.

"Hey, leave that little girl alone," a huge brawny man said as he stood in front of Ken.

"Yeah back off her," a few other towns' folks stated as they walked up to him. They were all yelling at Ken and telling him to back off.

"That's my little sister! She and I had an argument and I need to go get her, so move!" Ken demanded.

"Why don't you make me?" the beefy man said in a taunting voice.

"Finally! Someone to take this out on!" Ken yelled as he kneed the big man in his lower stomach. Then he flipped the man over and onto his back.

The townspeople's mouths dropped at the sight of Ken throwing a man twice his size.

Ken looked over at the other people in his way. "Who's next?" he bellowed at the crowd.

All of them stepped aside to let Ken pass.

"Now which way did my sister go?" Ken asked in a commanding tone.

None of the people replied.

Ken looked at all of them and noticed a man pointing to a street. He did it with his hand in front of his chest so that his friends behind him wouldn't see.

"Thank you," Ken said as he ran off.

The guy's friend elbowed him in the shoulder. "What did you tell him that for?" One person whispered.

"I wasn't about to get beat up for some little girl I don't know," the man replied.

Ken ran down the street calling Serena's name repeatedly. He occasionally stopped to ask random people if they saw her. At first the people he asked recognized the description, but as time passed her trail got colder. It was now getting dark out, and Ken still could not find any sign of Serena.

He propped his back against a wall trying desperately to catch his breath, "What do I do? Where could she be?"

Ken threw his hands over his face, racking his mind for ideas as to where he could find her. *Maybe she's back at the hotel*, he pondered while wiping sweat from his brow.

Suddenly, a red light appeared in the air above him. It formed into a circle, and the flying fox dropped out the bottom of it.

Ken stood up at the sight of the fox who sat on the sidewalk with its tail batting around.

"Listen, I don't understand how you know when I need you – but if you realized I need you, then you must know what's going on. So... help me find her!" Ken ordered.

The fox popped up and began to sniff the ground. It scurried across the sidewalk with its nose pressed to it.

Ken followed behind it waiting for some sort of sign.

The fox lifted its head and darted off. Ken ran as fast as he could to keep up with it. Soon It stopped to sniff the ground again then ran in a new direction. Finally, it stopped at the door to a grey brick building way back in the outskirts of town.

Ken tried to open the door, but it was locked. He pressed his left hand on it to blow it down with a pressure blast, but the fox hopped up and wrapped both its paws around his arm. Ken looked at it as its body dangled from his wrist.

"What do you propose I do then?" Ken asked it sarcastically.

The fox dropped down and ran over to a small window in the building that was connected to the ground.

Ken stared it over for a moment, "I can't climb through that," he said while glaring at the fox.

The fox looked at Ken and then back at the window, then back at Ken and back to window once more. It then tilted its head and lowered its eyebrows as if looking at Ken like he was stupid.

"Oh, you want to go through there," Ken asked as he realized what the fox wanted.

The fox put its paw over its eyes as if smacking its forehead.

Ken pulled the pocketknife out and slid it under the window allowing him to pop it open.

The fox slipped inside and ran over to the door. Ken heard the doorknob click as if someone unlocked it, then the door slowly swung open with the fox hanging on to the doorknob with both paws wrapped around it.

Ken walked by the fox who dropped down and strolled in beside him.

Upon entering, they gazed around and saw wooden crates all over the room which was large and spacious. "It looks like a giant storage building for a business," Ken whispered. "Are you sure Serena's here?" he asked while scanning over the room.

The fox sniffed the ground and ran over to a door across from them. It then started to scratch at it frantically.

"Is this it? Is this where she's at?" Ken asked impatiently.

The fox nodded its head in response.

"Alright, we open this one my way," Ken said as he placed his left hand over the door. There was a loud bang from his pressure blast, and the door blew down.

Ken and the fox ran into the room and saw Serena with her ankles chained up and her hands tied behind her back.

Serena looked over at them and began to scream as loud as she could through a cloth that was tied over her mouth. Her eyes were filled to the brim with fear and panic.

CHAPTER 8

The Puppet King

"Serena!" Ken yelled as he ran to her. He pulled out his pocketknife and cut the cloth from her mouth, "Are you ok? Are you hurt?" he asked anxiously.

"No, but I know who grabbed me," Serena answered in a shaky voice. "It was that weird guy with the scar we saw when we got here," she added as tears rolled down her cheeks.

Ken's expression changed from one of concern to rage. He held his left hand over his chest and then extended his arm causing his Gate to open in the air. He reached inside and quickly pulled out his sword. He raised his blade high in the air above him.

Serena clenched her eyes and turned her head away. With a loud yell, Ken slammed his sword between Serena's legs and cut the shackles from her ankles.

"Come on! We're getting out of here!" Ken said as he took Serena's hand.

They ran out of the room with the fox behind them then stopped upon seeing a man standing in front of the door.

"Looks like I have two more friends who want to join us, right my darling?" the man with the scar said while smiling freakishly.

Serena jumped behind Ken and gripped the scruff of his pants with her fingers, "I'm scared," she said, trembling as she stared at her kidnapper.

The fox growled as the fur on its back stood up.

Ken raised his sword to a fighting position – his body quivered with fury as he clenched his teeth.

"You're going to pay for what you did to her," Ken said in a snarl like tone.

The man's smile grew as he raised his hand and placed the tips of his fingers on his scar. He laughed as he pushed his fingernails into the wound and slowly pulled it apart.

Ken's expression changed to one of disgust and uncertainty, "What is he doing?" he whispered to himself.

As the man pulled the scar apart, it exposed skin beneath it instead of blood. He ripped half his face off then threw it on the ground. The other half peeled off on its own as he giggled like an excited child.

"It was a mask," Ken said while gripping his sword tightly. "You're…that puppet guy from the wanted poster!" he exclaimed.

"That's correct," the Puppet King said while dropping the cloak he wore to the ground.

He sported a yellow tank top and blue pants covered in stains of blood. Ken noticed his arms had several scars and stitches, no doubt from previous victims.

"I prefer to be on a first name basis with my friends. So please, just call me Tyler," he said with wide eyes and a crooked grin that revealed his yellow teeth.

The Puppet King reached down to his cloak and pulled out a large cleaver while he looked at Ken, Serena, and the fox. "I've never had a pet before. It'll be interesting turning your body into a puppet," he said as he brandished his cleaver back and forth while staring at the fox.

Ken scowled at Tyler as Serena wrapped her arms firmly around his waist.

"Serena, you have let go," Ken said in a severe tone.

"I can't," she replied as her grip strengthened.

"Serena, he's going to attack. I can't protect you if you're on me like this. Please for both of us, let go and hide," Ken pleaded without breaking his view of Tyler.

Serena looked to the fox who nodded its head at her. Seeming to agree with what Ken said.

"Promise you'll stop him," Serena begged.

"Of course I will. I haven't lost a fight yet," Ken replied, trying to talk in a light-hearted tone.

Serena released her arms from him and snatched up the fox as she ran behind a crate. She clutched it in her arms like a stuffed animal and watched quietly.

"I'm so excited. I get to add three more friends to my collection!" Tyler said while tapping the side of the cleaver against the palm of his hand. "Try not to struggle too much. I hate having to sew the body back together, it never looks the same," he said while biting down on his bottom lip.

Ken yelled as he ran toward Tyler with his sword in front of him. The Puppet King raced at Ken as well with his cleaver at the ready. Ken swung his sword, but Tyler blocked his slash with the side of his blade. He then parried Ken's blade away and slashed at Ken several times.

Ken jumped back from the first swing and blocked the rest with the flat side of his sword. He walked backward as Tyler slashed over and over at his blade. Sparks flew as the sound of metal pounding metal filled the air.

He's too fast for me, Ken thought as he continued to struggle against the Puppet King's rapid flailing attacks. Ken dropped to the ground between slashes and kicked Tyler in his stomach, causing him to fall onto his back. Then Ken stepped back to create some distance.

Tyler stood up slowly and laughed while shaking his head, "I ask you not to struggle and you do it anyway. Guess I'm going to have to break out my sewing needle," he stated as his voice shook. He began to walk toward Ken once more while waving his cleaver ominously.

Ken jumped toward him without hesitation. He noticed Tyler rear his cleaver back to strike, but Ken raised his sword to meet The Puppet King's before he could swing. The blades collided in the air allowing Ken to prematurely stop Tyler's attack.

Ken rapidly followed up with a precise punch between Tyler's bicep and triceps, causing him to drop the cleaver as his arm went numb. Seeing his chance to strike, Ken jumped in the air while spinning and kicked the Puppet King in the face with full force.

Tyler landed on the ground with a thud and rolled over on to his hands and knees. He frantically made his way to a locked door behind him as blood dripped from his mouth.

"This ends now!" Ken yelled as he charged at the Puppet King with his sword.

Tyler pulled a key from his pocket and hastily unlocked the door. He forcefully swung it open and reached to a shelf for another cleaver. After grabbing it, he turned to face Ken once more.

Ken stopped and backed away a few steps, "Crap, I thought I had him for sure," he said while cutting his teeth.

Tyler chuckled as Ken backed away, "What's wrong? Did you realize I'm better at swordplay than you? I'll admit you got the best of me once, but I promise that won't happen again," he said while pointing his weapon at Ken.

Ken glared at him and shook his head, "Why are you doing this?" he barked.

The Puppet King gave Ken a dark smirk, "Because I like the way it feels to know I have dozens of friends who will never leave me, like them for example," he said while pointing to the room behind him with his cleaver.

Ken looked past Tyler and gaped at the sight of several bodies hanging by strings. He stepped back as his throat choked from complete loss of speech.

"As you can see I have quite the following. I have twenty-four friends so far and I can't wait to add three more to that number," Tyler exclaimed with an exuberant expression as he started to walk towards Ken.

Ken's body trembled from the reality of his situation. He had only heard of people who were crazy enough to do something like this. However, to come face to face with a murderer of this caliber caused an overwhelming fear to take hold of him.

"This guy is crazy, he...he killed all those people," Ken uttered while backing away.

"I recognize that look in your eyes. It's the look all my friends make when they learn they have no choice but to join me," the Puppet King said as he closed in on Ken.

"Get back! Please, stay away!" Ken yelled as Tyler continued his approach. "STAY AWAY FROM ME!" he bellowed while flailing his sword with all his strength.

Tyler leaned back as Ken's sword sliced through the air in front of his face. Then he rushed in on Ken and drove his cleaver to Ken's side.

Shock overtook Ken as he felt the cold, paralyzing sensation of steel pierce the left side of his waist.

"KEN NOOOOO!" Serena yelled out from behind the crate.

Tyler pulled his cleaver out from Ken's side and watched him fall on his knees.

Ken held his wound together with the fingers of his right hand while hanging his head down to the floor. *I'm going to die!* he thought as the pain intensified.

"If it weren't for that vest you're wearing I would have cleaved you in half," Tyler said while running his finger through the blood on his cleaver.

He grabbed Ken by his hair and forced his head up so that their eyes would meet – then he drew back his blade with a sinister smirk, "Good thing that vest doesn't protect your neck," he said menacingly.

Ken's eyes widened at the sight of the cleaver with his own blood on it. The terror was so overwhelming that he forgot the pain of his injury.

"Off with his head!" Tyler shouted.

Just as Tyler prepared to decapitate Ken, the fox jumped on to his face and scratched at it fiercely.

Tyler dropped the cleaver and yelled while trying to pull the fox off his face.

Ken stood on his knees shuddering with fear and pain. He knew he was going to die. He could feel himself becoming weaker as blood drained from his body.

"Ken, Ken snap out of it," Serena shouted.

Without Ken even noticing, she got next to him. He wanted to see her but could not force himself to look her way.

"Ken please, I need you. I need you!" Serena yelled out to him while burying her head against his neck.

Suddenly, everything around Ken turned black – as if the room had gone dark. He saw an image of himself holding his dad. Blood poured out from a bullet sized hole in his father's chest.

"Dad please don't leave me! I need you! I love you!" he begged while holding his palm over his father's wound. Then his mother appeared next to them. She was cover with blood and cuts from her face down to her legs. "Mom please, you're all I have left. Don't go!" Ken screamed while taking hold of her hand.

Both his parents disappeared from his sight as he sobbed deeply. Then Serena appeared in front of him. "Ken, I need you. Please stay with me," she pleaded, crying and reaching out to him.

Ken held out his hand trying his best to grab hers.

"Please Ken, you're all I have now," Serena said as her voice changed to sound like his own.

"I'm here, Serena. I won't leave you, I promise," Ken shouted as he grabbed for her fingers.

Ken immediately felt stronger. The pain and fear he felt were now replaced with concern for Serena. He snapped out of his dream and saw her crying with her arms around him. Tears filled his eyes as he gazed upon her.

"I will protect you at any cost," Ken said while removing his grip from the gash and placing his hand on her arm, leaving fingerprints of blood on her skin.

Serena looked up at him and nodded her head. Her eyes still brimming with fear and uncertainty.

The Puppet King pulled the fox off his face and held it by its neck, "I'll crush your throat!" He screeched as he squeezed it.

The circle on the fox's back suddenly shined as its nails grew several inches with a red glow. The fox stabbed its claws into Tyler's arm.

The Puppet King wailed as he frantically flailed his arm about – trying to get the fox off himself. The fox scurried up to his shoulder and the circle on its back started to glow once more as though charging with energy.

Tyler stopped his thrashing and looked at the fox who gazed into his eyes. Then it opened its mouth and blew fire into his face.

As Tyler screamed and ran around in agony, the fox leaped from his shoulder.

Tyler then ran up to the fox with his hands over his face and kicked it as hard as he could into a crate.

"NO!" Serena yelled at Ken's side.

The fox landed on the ground, struggling to get back up.

The puppet King reached down and grabbed his cleaver with one hand while still holding his burnt face with the other. He pointed his blade at the fox as he walked toward Ken and Serena, "You're next," he said in a livid tone.

"Get behind me, Serena," Ken said as he watched Tyler approach.

"Ken, I'm scared," Serena cried while following Ken's orders.

Ken smiled as he looked up at the Puppet King, "Don't be Serena," he said warmly.

Tyler stopped in front of Ken and stared him in the eyes. The right side of his face was burned and scared by the fox's fire. "Now, where were we?" he said, flaunting his cleaver.

"RIGHT HERE!" Ken exclaimed as he used his right hand to pick up his left and thrust it onto Tyler's chest. Ken moaned in anguish due to the cut muscles in his side that moved along with his arms. A light glowed under Ken's glove as he closed his eyes from the searing pain.

"NOW GO!" Ken yelled as he let loose a pressure blast directly against Tyler's torso.

The Puppet King flew backwards at an extreme speed and crashed into a crate. He sat for a moment and then glanced at Ken with a large, splintered piece of wood sticking out from his stomach. He slowly raised his hand and pointed at Ken.

"Make…me…into…a…puppet," Tyler whispered just before his arm dropped. Then his body lay strung out across the crate motionless.

"I did it. I stopped him from killing us," Ken said to himself as he stared at the Puppet King.

"Is he dead?" Serena asked while still hiding behind Ken.

"Yeah, he's gone," Ken answered.

The fox approached them with a slight limp.

"Are you ok?" Serena questioned as she ran to it. She pat it on the head as she looked it over for injuries.

"Arraahhh!" Ken suddenly yelled out as the pain in his side became more intense. He hunched his head over knees and realized he was sitting in a puddle of his own blood. "Serena, you have to get help," he said while gripping his side and twisting his face.

"Where should I go? What should I do?" Serena replied, her voice was wobbly and insecure.

"Take the fox and run out to the road. Then start screaming for help," Ken whined as he twitched with spasms of agony.

"What if I can't find my way back to you?" Serena asked while holding the fox.

"I'll put a hole in the wall so that you can't miss the building," Ken said as he put one hand on his knee to help him stand.

"Ken, be careful," Serena said as she watched him struggle to get on his feet.

As Ken hobbled to the wall, his face clenched from the piercing pain of the gash in his side. Once again, he used his other hand to hold his left palm up as he pressed it against the wall. With a loud yell, he released a pressure blast that blew a hole in the brick barrier. He immediately fell onto his legs while gripping his side again then quickly pressed his back against what was left of the wall. He started to feel cold as the room spun around him while he breathed more heavily.

"Ken!" Serena called out as she ran over to him.

"Go!" Ken muttered. "You're my last hope, Serena. I'll die if you don't hurry."

Serena teared up as she rubbed her eyes, "I can't leave you; I'm scared. I can't do it," she said as she laid her head on Ken's shoulder.

"Serena you're stronger than you think," Ken said while still clinging to his side. "I believe in you. Didn't you believe in me when

I said I'd protect you?" he mumbled while peering at her with one eye open.

"Yeah," Serena replied through a sniffle.

"Well, now I need you to protect me. You must be brave and get help. I'll be ok as long as you hurry," Ken said as he rest his head back against the wall.

Serena stared at him speechless with uncertainty. She looked down as she felt the fox bite her pants and tug on them. It looked at her and nodded its head, confirming that she needed to get up and be brave for Ken.

Serena stood up and wiped the tears from her face, "I'll be back big bro. Just wait for me!" she said with a determined look. She then ran out the hole in the wall with the fox at her heels.

"You can do it, Serena," Ken whispered while trying to steady his breathing. "I know you can," he slurred to himself.

After a few minutes of sitting against the wall, Ken started to hear voices. "Who's there?" he said in a weak tone.

"It's us son, your mother and father," the voice replied from a bright white light in front of him.

"Am I dead?" Ken asked meekly.

"No honey," his mother replied in a soothing voice.

"We just wanted to tell you how proud we are of you while we have the chance. You've become so strong and you've learned to fight for all the right reasons," said the voice of his father.

"What if I'm not strong enough to protect her, dad. What if I'm too weak?" Ken questioned.

"You're not weak, son. You draw your strength from an unbeatable power, love. Your will to protect what you love will give you the ability to keep her safe," his father's voice answered.

Ken gazed into the light with a blank stare. "My will...to protect?" Ken asked.

"Yes, son. You'll be strong enough as long as you fight to protect what matters most. We must go now, son. Our time is up," his father said.

Ken shook his head and held his arm out to the light, "No, please don't leave me again. I need you. I love you," Ken uttered as he reached as far as he could to the light.

"You don't need us any more honey. You're strong enough on your own now," his mother's voice said.

"Please don't go! I just got you back!" Ken yelled out to the light as it faded away.

"Always remember that we love you son," the voices said as they faded into the dark.

"No, come back," Ken begged as everything went black around him.

CHAPTER 9

The Storm

Ken opened his eyes and saw a bright white light in front of him, "Mom? Dad?" he inquired while gazing into it. He turned his head to scan the room and noticed blurry objects all around him. Suddenly, he felt something warm touch his arm. He glanced and saw a fuzzy figure next to him.

"You're finally awake," Serena said tenderly.

As Ken's vision came into focus, he realized he was sitting up in a bed, "Where are we?" he asked Serena in a sluggish tone.

"We're in a Monarchy hospital," she replied.

Ken laid his head back on the pillow then glanced down at his body, "I'm wearing my clothes. Why am I not in hospital clothes?"

"The doctor said that your injury was critical. I guess there was no time to change you," Serena said while leaning back in her chair.

Ken laid for a moment as his mind processed what was going on. He sprang upright in his bed as he remembered the recent events. "Serena! Are you ok?" he shouted in a loud panic.

Serena almost flipped backward from her chair, "I'm fine!" she said in a surprised tone.

"What happened after you left?" Ken asked.

"After I ran out to get help, I found some Monarchy soldiers who heard the blast from you blowing a hole in the wall. Then I ran with them back to you. One of them stayed with you and started working on your injury while the other called for help. They asked where my parents were. But I told them that you're my brother and that our parents were dead. So, they let me stay here with you," Serena answered.

"They didn't recognize that you escaped from them before?" Ken asked curiously.

"No, I guess not. I mean they're not the same soldiers that kiddnapped me. I suppose they just don't know about me," Serena replied.

"Mr. Malachite, you're a lucky man," the doctor said as he walked into the room with a clipboard in his hands. The Doctor's eyes seemed hazy and unfocused. Ken also noticed half of a glowing yellow circle under the collar of his coat.

That symbol looks like the one on the fox's back. I wonder if...

"Are you still with me Mr. Malachite?" the doctor queried.

"Oh, yeah..." Ken answered after snapping back from his thoughts. "I wouldn't say lucky," he replied sarcastically.

"Look at your side and say that again," the doctor retorted while gesturing at Ken's side with his clipboard.

Ken pulled up the side of his shirt to see a well-healed scar where he had been injured. "How did you—"

"Mystic water," the doctor stated. Abruptly interrupting Ken. "Now let me explain what treatment we used so I can clear this room. I'll be needing it soon," he claimed while looking over his clipboard. "When you came in you were in critical condition. We thought you were going to die until a soldier told me who you killed. Then I realized you had the funds to pay for a Mystic water treatment. So that's what we used.".

"Mystic water?" Ken questioned.

"Mystic water is water that has been infused with healing properties by Sages. Only the Monarchy has access to it. We poured it over your injury and injected you with some. In a matter of minutes, you were healed up good as new," the doctor said impatiently.

"Well, what about—"

"As far as the payment for your medical work goes—" the doctor said, once again interrupting Ken. "You received ten thousand fol for killing the Puppet King. So, we used that as your payment."

Ken gave the doctor a stern look.

"Don't worry. You still have some left over. After we subtracted your room, the cost of the treatment, the food to feed your sister, and this little vile of Mystic water we are giving you for the road, the grand total you have left over is three thousand fol," the doctor said as he dropped a sack full of coins on a table next to Ken's bed. Then he laid a small vile of water with a string around it next to the sack. "Anyway, that's all I have to report to you. Now you are free to go. You have five minutes to get out so I can get the next patient in. If you are not out in five, then security will make sure you leave. Have a good day," the doctor said as he walked out the door.

"Come on, Serena, lets go," Ken said as he jumped out of bed.

"Are you afraid of the security?" Serena asked.

"No, I just don't want to push our luck any further than we already have," Ken said while grabbing the sack of coins and thrusting it into his pocket.

"What do you mean," Serena questioned.

"We're at a monarchy hospital, Serena. Last time I checked they were after you," Ken said in a rushed manner. "By some stroke of luck, they haven't recognized you or realized who you are. I think it's best that we get out of here while it's still an option," Ken stated as he moved toward the door.

He couldn't help but think about the glow on the doctor's neck. *Maybe it's not luck keeping us safe,* he thought.

"Your right, I didn't think about it like that," Serena responded while following Ken out the room.

They quickly made their way out the front door of the hospital. Ken's eyes squint as they walked out the door. It was bright and sunny. He noticed a few buildings around that seemed familiar.

"Are we in the same town we were in before?" he asked.

"Yeah, this is the same place," Serena said while putting her hand above her forehead to block the sun.

"The first thing we need to do is get my bag from the hotel. It has the map, then we can figure out the best route to get you home," Ken said as they walked down the sidewalk.

"We need to get you some new clothes first, Ken," Serena replied while looking at the blood stains on his shirt.

Ken looked around and noticed people staring and whispering amongst themselves as he walked by. He grit his teeth and made a growling noise, "We really don't have time for this," he said quietly as if talking to himself.

"Look, there's the place we bought my clothes from yesterday," Serena stated while pointing at the stand.

Ken took off the shirt covered in blood and threw it in a garbage bin next to the stand. Then put his leather vest back on his bare chest.

"Why are you still wearing that? It has a big cut in the side of it," Serena asked skeptically.

"Because I would have died without it," Ken replied as he walked into the stand, looking for new pants and a shirt.

He quickly browsed through the clothes and found a pair of dark green cargo pants with deep pockets on the side of the legs. *These are nice, why didn't I get them before?* he thought while trying them on. He put on a black shirt and put the brown leather vest back over it. He paid for the clothes and made his way out the shop hastily with Serena.

"We have to hurry back to the Inn," Ken said as he walked at a fast pace while pulling Serena's arm. He was practically dragging her with him as he moved forward. His eyes and mind focused intently on getting to the room.

Serena was struggling to keep up as she was stuck awkwardly between walking fast and running to maintain pace with Ken.

They made it to the hotel and flew up the stairs to the room and grabbed Ken's bag. He opened it and rolled out the map to try and decipher where they were going.

"What was the name of your hometown again, Serena?" Ken asked while scanning over the map.

"Sales," Serena replied while looking with him. "It's right there," she stated as she pointed to a spot on the map.

"Oh, I see now," Ken said, noticing where it said Sales on the map just above her finger. "The town we're in is called Drez if I remember right. So, let's see if we can find it on here too," his eyes darted back and forth attempting to locate it. Then he found it and gave a smile, "There it is! It looks pretty close, too," he stated. "Now we just need to plan a route there."

Ken continued looking over the map trying to find roads that connected the two towns. The trail he discovered seemed to take them a little out of the way at first but then made almost a straight shot there.

"This looks like the best route. Although I never really was good with map reading in school," Ken said as he shrugged his shoulders.

Serena simply smiled back at him.

"Well, it's the best plan we have so let's go for it," she answered. Her tone was happy and excited which resonated with Ken and encouraged him.

They returned the key to the hotel owner and made their way out of town.

"That's where we're headed," Ken pointed to a trail that went up a hill just in front of them. Then he showed it to her on the map.

It displayed a trail that went around a wooded area to the left and a large river on the right. The path was on a cliff that resided atop a steep wall that went down to the river.

"This trail looks like it'll be really nice," Serena said with a grin. She was clearly excited to do some sightseeing.

"Yeah, you should be able to see pretty far out from up there," Ken responded as they walked.

After making their way up the steep hill for a few minutes, they finally made it to the top and stopped for a break. They drank some water and sat in silence for a moment. Ken glanced over at Serena and saw she had a melancholy look on her face. He could tell she was lost in thought. He opened his mouth to ask her what was on her mind, but she spoke first.

"I'm sorry," Serena said softly. "I'm sorry for running away like that, and I'm sorry for not trusting you." She began to choke up as tears raised to the surface of her eyes. "You saved me even though you don't even know me, and now you're going on this journey to take me home. I was so mean to you, and all you've done is help and I... I …"

Ken wrapped his arms around her for a big hug, "That's enough of that now," he said sympathetically. "You're right. We really don't know each other very well. We only just started this journey together after all. So, I don't blame you for doubting me. Let's be honest, I'm really just a stranger to you," Ken said.

Serena peered at Ken from under his hug, "That's not true. I feel like I know you so well. We may not have been traveling together long, but I really do feel like you are my big brother. I trust you, Ken," she said while wiping her face.

Her words caught Ken off guard. He never had any siblings or real friends before. Hearing her say that made him feel as though his heart melted. As if she were really his little sister. It further pushed his desire to keep his word and get her home.

Ken wiped his eyes as he felt them get moist, "I promise I'm going to take you home no matter what Serena. As your big brother, I'll keep you safe and get you there one way or another," he said.

Serena beamed at him. "I know you will big bro, and as your little sister I'll do everything I can to help and make it easier," she said.

They both stood in place rubbing their faces. Ken laughed and shook his head. "I must be getting soft. Enough mushy stuff. Let's get going," he said with determination.

Serena nodded her head in agreement, and they began walking once more.

"So, Serena, in the spirit of getting to know each other better – how about you tell me about your family. Like, do you have any siblings, and what are your parents like?" Ken asked.

"Well, I don't have brothers or sisters, it's just my parents and me," Serena said as they walked. "Everyone says my mom and I look alike, but she has blue eyes, and I have my dad's green eyes. My mom is a kind-hearted person. She likes to cook and bake things for people just to make them happy. She's always been thoughtful that way."

"Oh yeah? She's good at baking then? I'll have to try some of her cooking when we get you home," Ken said.

Serena gave a joyful grin, "She'll be happy to make something special for you."

Ken could tell that she enjoyed talking about her parents. Her voice sounded upbeat and content. "What about your dad?" he asked, trying to keep the conversation going.

"Well my dad isn't a big guy, but he is strong. You can always find him working around the house or helping the village people. He's super sweet and always tells me how much he loves me and my mom," Serena giggled as she spun around once. "I remember when he used to throw me up in the air and catch me. Then he'd spin me around and around till I got dizzy," she said.

"Your dad sounds like a nice guy. I'll bet you have several stories like that," Ken said as he watched Serena spin around a few more times. He hadn't seen her this way before. So happy and free-spirited. It made him feel good to see her in such a delightful mood.

"What about your family Ken? What were your parents like?" Serena asked.

In the back of his mind, Ken knew when he started this conversation that his history would come up. It didn't bother him to tell her about his parents. However, he was concerned that she would ask where he was from. Telling her, he's from a different planet didn't seem like a good idea. Even if it was the truth.

"My dad practiced a lot of fighting styles. He taught me several martial arts and ways to defend myself. I didn't really realize it at the time, but he was also trying to teach me how to be a real man too. I guess I just never picked up on it, though," Ken said while looking up at the sky, thinking about how he treated people in school.

Serena noticed Ken seemed heavyhearted toward the end of what he said. "What about your mom?" she asked, trying to change the tone of their talk.

Ken smiled faintly, "Well, just like you, everyone said my mother and I also looked similar. She had a heart of gold and loved her family dearly. She loved us…no… she loved me so much that she put up with a lot of trouble just to make sure I was taken care of."

Ken's thoughts went to his stepdad, Scott. He thought about how horrible that man was to his mother, and how she dealt with it just to take care of him.

Ken glanced over at Serena and saw the look of uneasiness on her face. He realized that his downtrodden expression was ruining her good mood. He then gave a big smile, "I was really good at martial arts though," he said, quickly trying to improve the vibe. "My dad said I was a natural. So, I practiced every day. Then when he passed away, I practiced even harder," he said while giving Serena a thumb up.

"Why did it make you practice harder?" she queried.

"Because even though my father was gone, the things he taught me were still here. Training made me feel close to him like I still had him with me somehow," Ken replied.

"That's so sweet, Ken!" Serena said while punching the air with her fist up in front of her face. "You really are a great fighter. I'm sure your dad is really proud – watching you beat up people to protect me and all."

Ken laughed while Serena threw a couple of punches. "Well, that's what we trained for. Self-defense and to protect or help anyone in need," he said.

Serena jumped and kicked in front of herself as she walked. Still pretending to fight like Ken.

"Hey, that wasn't too bad," Ken said while rubbing his chin.

"Big bro, show me some of your moves. I want to learn how to fight too," Serena said eagerly.

Ken put his hand behind his head and chuckled, "Sure, just sit over there, and I'll show you some forms we do."

Serena looked at him curiously, "What are forms?" she asked.

Ken walked out so he had some room to move and then he did some stretches to loosen up. "Forms are just a series of movements that you do to practice your style and technique," he said as Serena sat down on a stump beneath a tree. She waited patiently for him to demonstrate.

"This is the black belt form from Tae-Kwon-Do," Ken said as he performed a series of punches and kicks in different stances" Serena watched intently as if trying to learn it herself.

"Wow, that looks really cool big bro," she stated.

Ken's face went flush as he rubbed the back of his head again. "I'll show you another form. This one is from a style called Long Fist," he said.

Ken performed another series of punches and kicks, but this time he also did some running and low stances while swinging his arms around as if swimming through the air.

"That one was really long and looked more complicated than the other," Serena said with an impressed gaze.

Ken sat down next to her trying to catch his breath, "That form…really takes…it out of me," he said between gasps.

"You looked amazing out there, Ken. I can't wait for you to start teaching me," Serena shouted while trying to get in one the stances Ken did during his form.

"When we get to the next town maybe I'll be able to teach you some stuff," Ken said with a chuckle.

Serena turned to him like she was ready to say something, but before she could, they heard thunder rumble just beyond the trees behind them. Ken stood up and walked back from the stump while looking at the sky. Dark black clouds were rolling in fast as the wind started to pick up.

"Looks like a storm is coming," Serena stated while staring at the sky.

"I guess we didn't notice it building since its coming from behind that tall tree line," Ken said as he opened the map. He looked over it trying to determine how much further they needed to walk. "Man, I wish I knew how to read maps better. I can't tell how far along we are," he mumbled.

Just then a raindrop hit him on the nose, "Let's get moving Serena. Maybe we can beat the storm."

They started walking at a quickened pace while looking up occasionally. The black clouds continued to expand in the sky as the rain began to lightly sprinkle over them.

"We're not going to make it big bro. Why don't we hide in the trees until to storm passes?"

Just as Serena finished her sentence, a bolt of lightning struck in the distance on the other side of the river. It was only a few miles away from them. Immediately afterward the rain came down harder.

"We can't do that!" Ken said while grabbing her hand. "Hiding under a tree isn't safe during a lightning storm. We have to keep going till we find some shelter," he said.

They ran as the rain came down even harder than before. "I'm soaked Ken!" Serena shouted as the rain poured over them.

"Yeah so am I!" he yelled back over the sound of the water smashing the ground around them.

Suddenly, there was a bright blue flash followed by an ear-shattering crash just to their left. Lightning struck a tree right next to them.

Serena jumped back and let out a loud scream.

"Serena stop!" Ken yelled.

Before she realized it, Serena was on the edge of the cliff that dropped down to the river.

Ken immediately grabbed her so she wouldn't fall off the edge but then slipped in the mud and fell onto his rear. Before he could do anything else, they started sliding down the side of the cliff.

Serena screamed as she grabbed Ken's shirt so hard that she was clutching the skin of his waist between her fingers.

Ken kept his arms wrapped tightly around her as they slid down the muddy wall.

Finally, Ken felt his feet hit something hard. He looked down and saw a tree that was hanging over the river beneath them. He could feel his heart racing in his chest.

Serena was still gripping Ken with eyes closed and her body clenched with fear.

"Serena, are you ok?" Ken shouted as the rain continued to pound all around them.

She looked up at Ken while still shaking, "I think so," she replied. "What are we going to do!?" She added while burying her face in Ken's chest.

Ken studied the area frantically trying to find something they could grip or use to climb. He tried grabbing the wall with his fingers to no avail. The mud was too slick, and there was nothing around he could use to help them back up the wall.

He could feel Serena shaking as the wind blew across them. He couldn't tell if she was shivering from fear or the cold chill of the wet air. He suspected it was a combination of both.

Ken racked his mind trying to think of a way out of their predicament. The only thing he came up with was jumping into the river. Unfortunately, he knew Serena would not make it through the rapids. The water was moving fast as it crashed into the rocks that were scattered throughout the stream.

The tree holding them up from the water made a loud cracking sound and shook slightly. Serena screamed once more while tightening her grip on Ken.

"Crap! I have to think of something fast!" Ken said, cutting his teeth.

A bright red light appeared above them in the shape of a ring. Then the flying fox dropped out from it and flew circles in the air above them.

"Man am I happy to see you!" Ken exclaimed.

The flying fox soared over to the top of the cliff and disappeared. Ken gazed up with disappointment as he waited to see if the fox would return. After staring at the cliff for a few minutes, he became aggravated.

"SO, YOU CAN BREATHE FIRE AND MAKE PORTALS BUT YOU CAN'T GET US OUT OF THIS!?" He barked. He let out a deep sigh of tension and shook his head. "We're so screwed."

"Hey! You guys ok!?" a voice yelled from the top of the cliff.

Ken looked up and saw a person staring down at them, "No! We're trapped down here!" he called back to the voice.

"Hold on, I have a rope. Just let me secure it, and I'll throw it down!" the voice shouted.

"Serena, do you hear that? We're going to be fine now," Ken said in a relieved tone.

"Thank goodness," Serena replied while still clinging to him.

The end of the rope fell by them, and Ken instantly grabbed it. "Serena you're going to have to hold on to me really tight while I climb up here," he said while turning around and preparing to climb.

Serena nodded her head and carefully made her way around to Ken's back where she wrapped her legs around his waist and her arms around his neck.

Ken gathered his strength and attempted to pull them up with the rope, but his foot slipped on the mud beneath them. *I have nothing to grip with my feet, and I'm not strong enough to do it with arm strength alone,* Ken thought. He pondered for a moment, trying to figure out a way to gain some sort of gripping.

"I have an idea," Ken mumbled. He placed his left hand in the mud and released a pressure blast into the wall causing it to leave a small indentation in the sludge. He then used the depression as a foothold to help him climb. He could feel the mud shift as he put his foot into it. *It's not stable, but it'll have to do,* he contemplated as he began to climb.

Ken repeated the process of using his pressure blast to make holes in the wall as he scaled. He felt mud build on the bottom of his shoes, making is feet heavier with every step. The rain continued to surge over them, and thunder clapped in the distance. Lightning colored the sky in a cobalt blue flash.

They were almost at the top as Ken reached his hand out to use his power once more. He placed his palm on the wall and discharged another blast. Immediately, he felt a sharp pain shoot through his hand and grunted from its sting. He held his palm in front of his face and looked it over. There didn't appear to be any injury on it. Yet as he attempted to make a fist his hand hurt and felt as though it wouldn't close. He shook his head and looked up at the wall. He noticed that with the hole he just made, it should only take one more blast to get them to the top.

"Ken, I can't hold on much longer. My arms and legs are feeling weak!" Serena cried out.

Ken bore down and firmly gripped the rope while stepping up

into the cavity he just made. He placed his hand on the mud once more while squinting his eyes in anticipation for the pain this blast would bring. He emitted his attack again into the wall. This time the pain was exponentially greater throughout his hand. He screamed out in agony. It felt like the muscle in his palm had torn to shreds. He tried to grip the rope with his left hand but could not get his fingers to close.

"Ken are you ok!?" Serena asked from over his shoulder.

"Yeah, I'm fine," he responded, reminding himself that she depended on him.

"Come on! Come on! Just one more step. Do it for her. Do it for Serena!" He said to himself as he gripped the rope with his left hand. With the last of his strength, he pulled up to the edge of the wall with a loud grunt.

"I got her!" the guy who threw down the rope grabbed Serena and helped her up the side of the ledge. He then grabbed Ken's arm and helped him finish climbing over the wall.

Ken hobbled over to the tree line and fell onto his back in a puddle. He laid there for a moment while catching his breath and staring at the sky as rain rolled off his face.

Ken glanced over and saw the guy who helped him. He looked like a fourteen-year-old boy who was soaked in the rain like they were. He wore his hair in a ponytail that went just down to the back of his neck.

"Thank you," Ken said in an exhausted manner.

Ken looked at his hand once more. The pain was gone, but he still had trouble moving his fingers. *I'll have to remember this power has a limit,* he mulled over to himself as he lay there.

"You guys should come to my house and get out of this rain. You're covered in mud, and I'm sure you're worn out now," the boy said.

Ken sat up after regaining some strength, "You sure that's alright," he asked while standing up.

"Yeah, it's fine. Besides, I can't just leave you guys out here like this." The boy said as he gathered his rope.

"That's really nice of you," Serena said as she helped Ken up.

"Yeah, Thanks again," Ken added. "What's your name?" He asked while rubbing his left hand with his right.

"I'm Steven, Steven Rumph. What's your name?" the boy said

"I'm Ken Malachite, and this is my little sister Serena," Ken said.

Serena smiled at Steven. "Thank you for saving us," she said sincerely.

"It's no problem. You're just lucky that fox showed me where you were. I wonder where it went?" Steven inquired.

"I guess that fox helped out after all," Ken whispered to himself.

"What was that?" Steven asked.

"Nothing, just ready to get out of these wet clothes," Ken replied.

"Follow me. There is a shortcut to my place through the woods. It's just outside of town," Steven said.

Ken and Serena followed Steven into the woods for a few minutes. Then they found a well-beaten path as they stepped out of the wood line.

"This path leads to my house. We'll be there soon," Steven said as they continued to walk.

"Hey Steven, I'm not complaining or anything – but why were you in the woods with a rope anyway?" Ken asked as they continued.

"I was using it to climb trees and grab some fruit. I was going to take the fruit and sell it," Steven answered back.

"That's a neat way to make some extra money," Ken said.

"Well, money is pretty tight right now for my family. I just want to do my part to help," Steven replied glumly.

"I hate to hear that. Did you get a nice haul?" Ken inquired, noticing the change in Steven's voice.

"Actually, I just snuck out here when the fox got my attention," Steven said while shrugging his shoulders.

"Snuck out?" Serena asked.

"Yeah, well with what's been going on around here, I'm not exactly allowed to go out on my own," Steven answered sullenly.

Ken glanced over at Serena who looked back at him. They shared an expression of concern and curiosity with one another.

"Here we are. You guys wait here, and I'll go in and tell my mom what's going on. Be right back," Steven said before running over to a large cabin.

The house looked well-kept and beautiful from the outside with bushes surrounding the exterior and a shed just behind it. The rain had stopped, but it was still dark and cloudy.

"It sounds like something was really bothering him," Serena said as she wiped mud off her leg.

"You picked up on that too? Yeah, something seems wrong," Ken replied.

The front door opened wide, revealing a woman waving over at Ken and Serena, "Come in, come in!" she yelled out to them.

"Let's go," Ken said as he and Serena made their way to the house.

CHAPTER 10

Gangsters

Ken and Serena stood on the porch with water puddling up around their feet. They were covered in mud from head to toe.

"Come in, let's get you cleaned up," Steven's mother said as she motioned for them to come inside.

Ken felt reluctant to do so since he didn't want to get her home dirty. Conversely, he wanted to make sure Serena was taken care of. With that in mind, they walked inside.

They stepped into a medium-sized kitchen with a dining table towards the back of the room. To the left was a staircase that lead to the bedrooms and washroom. The house appeared quaint and modest while still looking sizeable on the inside.

Steven's mother reached for a cloth on the table. She had long brown hair with brown eyes to match. She appeared to be in her early to mid-forties according to Ken's guess.

As they admired the room, the smell of a home cooked meal waft over their noses. Serena's stomach instantly began to growl.

"You poor thing, Steven told me what happened. Are you alright?" Steven's mother asked Serena as she wiped mud off her face with the cloth.

"I'm ok," Serena replied, her stomach continued to rumble.

"Steven, take them to the bathroom and let them clean up," the mother said. "You just leave your clothes outside the door, and I'll wash them later. Steven will bring you something to wear tonight," she stated while looking at Serena. "Same goes for you," she added while glancing at Ken briefly. "Hurry along now so you can eat. Dinner will be ready shortly."

She then turned to her son, "As for you!" she expressed heatedly while pointing at Steven. "When you get done helping them, you'll have to explain why you went out on your own after your father explicitly told you not to!" She said sternly while shaking her finger at Steven.

"Yes, ma'am," Steven replied despairingly.

Steven escorted them upstairs where Serena went into the bathroom first and started her bath. Ken waited outside the door for her to finish. He noticed a picture on the wall in front of him. It was a family portrait with Steven and his mother, an older guy who appeared to be the elder sibling, a younger boy that Ken assumed to be the youngest son, and a dauntingly muscular man that had to be the father.

Steven came down the hallway with a basket that had some clothes folded inside. He took the clothes out and laid them on the floor. Then put Serena's muddy ones in the hamper.

"Put your clothes in here when you're done," he said to Ken. "Try to make your bath fast. My dad will be coming home soon, and he hasn't been in a good mood lately," he bleakly told Ken.

"We can just go after I clean up. I don't want to cause any trouble," Ken replied.

"No!" Steven answered abruptly. "Please, stay. I saw what you did to climb that wall. You have a special power," he said in a desperate tone. He grabbed the side of Ken's shirt and continued. "We need help, my little brother is—" His voice became shaky as he tried to talk. Then he let go of Ken and hurried off down the stairs.

What was that all about? Ken pondered while waiting for Serena. *Something bad must have happened.*

The door opened and Serena reached her arm out for her replacement clothes. She was wrapped in a towel, but Ken could tell she was too shy to walk into the hall to retrieve them.

After getting dressed, she stepped out of the bathroom wearing what appeared to be boy's clothes. It was a simple white shirt with brown pants. Although they seemed to fit her well.

"Those look good on you, Serena," Ken said teasingly.

"Well, they fit, and they're dry," she replied while crossing her arms.

Serena walked down the stairs while Ken took his bath. He was sure to make it quick as Steven had asked. The entire time he washed, he wondered what Steven meant by what he said earlier. *What happened to make him so upset?* he pondered, hearing Steven's voice in the back of his head saying, 'My little brother,' repeatedly.

Ken got out of the tub and dried off. "Maybe I can find out what's going on and help," he whispered while looking at the gate on the back of his hand.

Ken made his way down the stairs to find Serena sitting at the dinner table while Steven's mother was placing bowls of food on it.

"Have a seat and eat quickly," she said to Ken as he walked toward the table. "Steven, when they get done take them to the shed and give them some blankets for the night."

"Yes, ma'am," Steven answered while staring out the window. "Hey mom, dads here," he said with a concerned grimace. "Should I just get them to go out back?" he questioned.

His mother looked out the window and saw the father was almost at the door.

"No, it'll look even worse if they try to run out the back. Just go eat and we'll deal with it," she said in an uneasy tone.

Serena gave Ken a troubled expression. He looked back at her the same way. *What did we get into?"* Ken thought as he stared at the bowl of food. *Is this guy really that bad a father?*

Heavy footsteps could be heard as he walked up the porch. The room fell silent as everyone watched the door. Slowly it opened with an eerie creak. A towering man with spiky black hair and a muscular frame stepped through the doorway. He appeared just as he did in the picture Ken saw on the wall.

He scanned over his home and saw Ken sitting at his table. His expression intensified as he clenched his fist, tightening the muscles in his arm. His eyes pierced Ken as rage grew upon his face.

"Honey it's not what you think it is!" His wife said hastily.

Ken's mind started to race. He didn't want to do anything to hurt the people that just took care of him. Nonetheless, he couldn't just let this man attack him or Serena. Mentally he prepared himself for a fight. He recognized the look in that man's eyes. They were the eyes of someone ready to kill.

"Yeah, dad, he's not with that gang. I saved him and his little sister. They fell down that slope. The one on the trail to Drez. They were covered in mud and trapped above the river. I used my rope to save them," Steven pleaded.

The father looked over at his wife for assurance. "It's true Tim. They are just passing through. When I saw that sweet little girl, I just had to do something," she added.

Tim's stare fell on Ken and then shifted over to Serena. He took a deep breath and then released it as he shuttered his anger away. His body appeared to lose its tension which allowed Ken to relax as well.

"Marie, you know we can't afford to take care of everyone who gets lost out here," Tim said firmly to his wife. His voice was deep and projecting.

He looked over at Ken and Serena, "I'm happy my son could help you, but this isn't a bed and breakfast. Eat, sleep outside, and leave first thing in the morning," Tim commanded.

"Tim!" his wife called out to him in a disapproving manner.

He seemed to ignore her as he made his way to the stairs. Unexpectedly, they heard a loud noise at the door. It sounded as though someone threw something heavy at it. Marie jumped back, and Serena gasped at the racket.

Tim rushed over to the door and opened it immediately. A man flopped down onto the floor with a beaten and bloodied face. Marie fell to her knees and put her hands on him.

"Mitchell! Mitchell! My baby, my boy!" she cried as she ran her hands across his cheeks.

Tim swiftly pulled him all the way into the house and hovered over him as well. "Son! Son! What happened!?" Tim shouted.

Mitchell moaned inaudibly while pointing at the door.

Tim's breaths became deep and disgruntled as he grunted. He then ran out the door in pursuit of the people who did this to his son.

Angeon Broken Promises

"Serena stay here!" Ken said urgently as he followed behind Tim.

It was dark outside, and the rain left large puddles of water all around in its wake. Tim ran through his yard and to the edge of his property where he found three men walking away. Ken followed behind him to find out what was going on.

"Why!?" Tim shouted crossly at them. "Why did you attack my son like that!? I just gave you two thousand today!" he yelled.

The men turned and looked at Tim with sneering crooked smiles. The one in the middle chuckled as he stepped forward, "He tried to give us a mere three hundred as a payment for what you owe. That chump change is an insult to us," he said.

"Yeah, anything less than a grand will just get you hurt," the man to his left added.

"So, you hurt my boy because he didn't give you enough money!?" Tim barked back in a rage.

Ken felt his blood boil at what he was hearing. He always hated people who bullied others, but this took it to a new level.

"You better watch your tone, old man. Remember, we still have your youngest boy hostage. If you keep talking to us like that he'll have a bad night!" the man in the middle said tauntingly.

Tim yelled out as he went down to his knees and punched the ground beneath him.

Ken's thoughts instantly went to the youngest boy in the picture from the wall, "Those monsters! They kidnapped this man's youngest son!" he said while gritting his teeth.

"You still owe us three thousand fol, Timmy boy, and we expect to see it tomorrow. Otherwise, the boss may just press that button and blow up the cage your kid happens to be in," the man said as the other two laughed.

Tim gazed up at them as tears began rolling down his face. "Please! I beg you! Let my son go and put me in there instead. Please. I'll do anything!" Tim cried out, pleading desperately to the men.

They laughed even harder while pointing at him, "Never thought I'd see a grown man this big cry like a five-year-old," one of them said through their amusement.

Tim put his head to the ground and despairingly begged them once more, "PLEASE! GIVE ME…BACK...MY BOY!" he bellowed as his voice cracked.

The men merrily continued their snickering and pointing while making remarks at Tim as he sulked in the mud. Then their amusement instantly came to a halt when a bag fell before them with a loud clink.

Ken walked up and stood next to Tim after throwing his sack of money on the ground in front of them, "He owes three thousand fol, right? Well that's three thousand exactly. Go ahead and count it. Then when you're done, let his son go; you filthy bastards!" Ken shouted.

Tim lifted his face from the ground and looked over at Ken. He seemed to be in shock of what Ken just did. Then his eyes moved toward the men in suspense. The look on their faces went from delight to disbelief. One of them picked up the bag and felt it. Then opened it to peer inside.

"It's real, there really is three thousand in here Gretch," the man on the right said.

The one in the middle, apparently being Gretch, smirked at Ken, "You must be new around here. I don't remember seeing you before," he said with a snake-like expression.

"Yeah, I am. So, what?" Ken replied impatiently.

Gretch laughed while holding Ken's bag of money, "Well, I guess you didn't pay the fine for getting into town yet. That's about two thousand fol. Plus you called us bastards, that's another one thousand right there. So, I suppose we'll just say this clears your debt. You're lucky I'm such a nice guy and that's all I'm charging you," he said while pocketing the sack of coins.

"I've had enough!" Ken yelled as he charged at the men. He readied his Gate to summon his sword, but he felt something land on him from behind. It dropped him down and pinned him to the ground. He quickly realized that Tim tackled to keep him from attacking the men.

"What are you doing!?" Ken shouted from under Tim.

"You're going to get my son killed!" he yelled back while restraining Ken.

"Wise move old man," Gretch said while jangling the money in his pocket. The gang turned and started to walk away. "Remember to have the money tomorrow, or else. BOOM!"

"Oh, and to the young guy over there. If you want to make some real money, consider dropping by. We might even initiate you as one of us," Gretch called out to Ken as their figures faded into the trees.

Tim got off Ken and put his hand to his head as he stumbled around.

"We have to go after them!" Ken yelled while pointing in the direction that the gang went.

"Enough from you!" Tim bellowed back at him. "You don't understand what is going on here! If we hurt any of those guys or do something to make them angry, they will blow up our children!" Tim said darkly.

Ken gawked at Tim, still enraged by what happened, "Children?" he asked.

"Yes, they took three kids from families around here and put them in cages with bombs in them. You get it now!? They win! There is nothing we can do!" Tim snapped irritably.

Ken stood still like a statue. His expression changed from fury to shock.

"Just leave! This is our problem to handle," Tim said, starting to walk back home.

Ken continued to stand in place, processing what happened. After a few minutes, he walked back to the house to retrieve Serena. When he got there, Steven and Serena were waiting on the porch.

"Follow me," Steven said in a somber tone.

Ken and Serena followed him behind the house to the shack. He gave them blankets and the bowls of food they left on the table.

"Shouldn't we leave?" Ken asked as Steven took back the blankets and laid them down across the wooden tables.

"No," Steven replied promptly.

He sat down for a moment and rubbed his eyes, then raised his head to Ken. His expression was one of determination. He didn't appear sad as much as he was angry with everything. "My dad's not like that at all. He's a nice guy, but this whole situation is tearing him apart. We tried getting help from the Monarchy law enforcement officers, but they're all gone. They left to help in a battle not far from here," Steven said.

"What about the officers in the next town over?" Ken queried.

"Some townsman went off to check on that, but the officers are so scarce in those areas that they couldn't send anyone. It's something we have to deal with on our own," Steven answered.

"It doesn't matter how much money you give them. They will not give your little brother back," Ken stated in a concise tone.

"I know, I've been telling my dad that this whole time. My big brother agrees with me too, but my dad is too scared to do something about it!" Steven exclaimed as he stood up. "That's why I'm asking you. I know you're a Soul wielder, and I can tell you're strong. So please, help us. Help my little brother!" he cried out while grabbing Ken's shirt.

Serena gave Ken a muddled expression. She hadn't been given the details of what was happening yet.

Ken put his hand on Steven's head and answered him in a sincere tone. "Tomorrow…your little brother will be home."

Steven's eyes shot up at Ken. His countenance was one of hope as tears welled up from his eyes, "Do you mean that?" he asked with optimism in his voice.

"I wouldn't say it if I didn't mean it," Ken replied while grinning confidently. "Now go get some sleep while I make a plan tonight."

Steven beamed at Ken as he walked away. Before leaving, he looked back from the doorway, "Thank you," he said quietly before closing the door behind him.

"What is going on!?" Serena asked as she sat down on her blanket.

Ken explained what happened and what he saw when he followed Tim.

"That's horrible!" Serena expressed as she covered her mouth.

"Serena, I know I'm supposed to be taking you home. I know I promised you we would be there soon, but… they need someone to help them stand up and fight," Ken said.

"I agree!" Serena stated firmly. "We have to help them, after all – Steven saved us. We owe it to him!"

Hearing Serena say that put a smile on Ken's face, "You know, you're really mature for your age Serena. That's selfless of you to put off what you want most to help someone else," Ken said.

Serena laid back in the covers and looked up at the ceiling with a bright glint in her eyes. Ken saw that his praise made her happy. "My dad always told me to do the right thing. So, I know he'll understand if I'm a little late getting home," Serena said in a warm tone.

"I'm sure he will too," Ken replied.

"Do you have a plan to save him tomorrow?" Serena asked.

"Not yet," Ken answered. "But I will, first thing in the morning."

Chapter 11

Confrontation

Ken woke up early the next morning feeling groggy. He sat up from under the covers and stared at the wall in a daze. He couldn't help running everything that happened through his mind over and over. As he spent the night thinking about the gang, it somehow reminded him of his own past. How he used to beat up bullies at school who picked on the weaker kids. Then he reflected on how he would lash out on the kids he saved for being too weak to stand up for themselves.

He let out a sigh and rose from the blankets, "I thought I got over all that," he uttered as he looked over at Serena, who was still asleep under the covers. As he moved about the shed, Ken noticed their clothes in a basket on the floor. He assumed that Marie washed and dried them last night. He grabbed them and got ready to change clothes.

"Good morning big bro," Serena said, sitting up and rubbing her eyes.

"Don't look, I'm about to change clothes," Ken replied while laying his clothes out.

Serena turned her head as he changed, "Did you come up with a plan?" she asked through a yawn.

"Yeah, I came up with something," he responded while pulling the shirt over his head.

He laid Serena's clothes next to her and turned away. She grabbed them and started to change as Ken continued to talk to her.

"Serena, I have something to want to tell you," he said as if confessing something.

"What?" she asked curiously.

"When I was younger, I didn't have any friends. I know it's because I wasn't nice to anyone. I would try to help people by beating up bullies, but then I'd get irritated with the kids I helped because they didn't bother to fight back. I would make fun them and tell them they were cowards for not standing up for themselves," Ken paused for a moment. "I guess what I'm getting at is, this reminds me of…"

"Some bad memories?" Serena interjected.

"Yeah, I guess it does," Ken replied in a somber tone.

"Well, I don't know what you're talking about. I haven't seen you like that at all," Serena said.

She grabbed Ken's arm while he was still facing away, "This entire time I've seen you selflessly help people. You rescued me from that soldier and the maniac who kidnapped me. You helped that farmer save his trees and now you're helping this family. Also, I haven't heard you talk down to anyone that you've helped this whole time. So, you can't tell me you're a bad guy when I've seen how caring you are," Serena said tenderly. "What brought that up anyway?"

Ken stood quietly for a moment, "Well, I have a plan to motivate this family to stand up for themselves. Unfortunately, I have to rely on my old way of doing things. I think I can light a fire under them, but I need to be cruel to do it," he said with a tone of remorse. As though speaking from regret.

Serena wrapped her arms around him for a hug, "I trust you no matter what you decide to say or do big bro. I know you're only doing what you think is best," she said sincerely.

Ken smiled faintly. "You may not think that when you hear me," he said with a light chuckle.

Serena let go of him and put the clothes they borrowed in the basket, "I guess we will have to see," she said, grinning assuredly.

As they prepared to walk out, Ken placed his hand on Serena's should, "Thanks for listening, and for what you said."

Serena grabbed his hand and pulled it as she walked, "Let's go," she said happily.

They made their way to the house with the basket to return the clothes. Ken knocked on the door and heard Marie call for them to come in. Upon entering, Ken noticed Mitchell sitting at the table eating breakfast. He had a few patches on his face from the injuries he received the night before. Ken felt relieved, realizing that he wasn't seriously hurt.

Steven was sitting opposite of Mitchell at the table, and Marie was cleaning dishes at the sink. There was a drab air in the room as if someone had just passed away.

"Thank you for taking us in last night," Ken said as he and Serena walked in.

"No problem. Just leave those clothes on the floor," Marie replied hastily.

Ken could tell she wanted them gone. Neither son bothered to look up from the plates in front of them.

"Where can I find Tim and the gang's hideout?" Ken asked, thinking he may as well get to the point.

Marie stopped washing dishes and glared at him sternly. "You need to leave now," she answered irritably.

"I want to help," Ken replied while putting down the basket.

"You've done enough. My husband told me what you did last night and—" her voice cracked midsentence. She was obviously fighting back tears.

"We appreciate you giving them that money, and I'm sorry they took it, but that's just the way it is," she muttered.

Ken shook his head in disagreement. His fist clenched at her words, "I couldn't care less about the money," he replied with his head down, trying to keep himself in check.

"You saying, 'That's the way it is,' has me burning up!" he stated while raising his eyes to her. "Is that what you tell yourself every day? That your son is at the mercy of these thugs and that's just the way it is?!" Ken questioned.

Marie scowled at Ken, "You don't know anything about this family or what we are going through! How dare you say such things after we helped you!" she yelled back.

"I know plenty!" Ken replied persistently. "I know that no matter how much you give them, they will never return your son. You must have realized this by now?"

Marie threw down a wooden spoon that she was washing. Tears filled her eyes, and she grew even more upset, "Of course! Of course, I know that! Tim knows that! We all do!" she shouted while covering her face. "What are we supposed to do!? All we can do is hold out for hope!"

"You have to make your own hope!" Ken exclaimed. "You have to stand up and fight for your son to get him back! That's what I'm going to do anyway," Ken stated with an air of conviction.

"No! You'll get him killed!" Marie replied in a panic over what Ken was saying.

"He's right mom, I agree!" Mitchell added, getting up from the table. "They will not honor their word and return Timmy. We must fight back."

Ken was stunned by Mitchell's response. He thought he would have to argue the point more or even take a punch from Mitchell for upsetting his mom.

"Enough is enough, mom!" Steven said. "If we don't do something, no one else will."

Marie broke down as Steven pulled a chair around for her to sit in. "What are you going to do?" she asked Ken through her sobbing.

"I have a plan to rescue him, but I need to know where your husband is and where the gang's hideout is located," Ken replied.

"I can take you to my dad, and I also know where the hideout is," Mitchell claimed as he approached Ken.

"I'll come with you," Steven said.

"No, you need to stay here and watch over mom," Mitchell demanded.

"I'm coming whether you like it or not!" Steven answered.

"He makes a good point you know," Ken interrupted. "Someone has to protect your mom and my little sister. I know you think it's just something to keep you from following, but this honestly is something we need someone to do. I can't think of anyone better to protect Serena than you," Ken said as he winked at him.

Steven bit his lip slightly, wanting to argue the point. However, Ken put it in a perspective that he couldn't challenge. Steven let out a disapproving sigh then glanced at Ken, "You better bring my little brother back," he ordered.

"He'll be back before you know it," Ken replied with a pat to Steven's arm.

Ken looked to Serena who smiled back at him and gave a thumb up. Then Ken and Mitchell ran out the front door. "I'll take you to my dad first," Mitchell called out as they dashed.

"Just tell me where the gang hangs out as we go," Ken said as they hoofed it down a dirt pathway leading into a wooded area.

"They stay at an abandoned warehouse just out of town," Mitchell said between breaths.

"How do I get to it?" Ken inquired.

"Just walk into town and turn left at the Monarchy Enforcement Station. Then follow that trail all way to the warehouse. It's simple to find," Mitchell stated.

"Got it! Just one more question." Ken added as they rounded a corner. "How do I get to town from here?"

Mitchell gave Ken an exhausted expression then stopped running, "Can we talk… after we… get with my dad?" he asked while panting.

Ken stopped then shook his head at Mitchell, "Come on, we got to hurry!" he said impatiently.

"He's just up ahead," Mitchell said as he started to walk forward, still breathing deeply. "We cut off the trail here into the woods. He'll be this way chopping trees."

They began walking into the woods with haste. Mitchell was still winded from running, but Ken was ready and energized. He went through different scenes in his mind trying to plan how this would go. Most of them were confrontational, resulting in he and Tim fighting. Ken continued to contemplate to himself, hoping to find a solution that wouldn't start a bout, but he knew tough love was the only way to light a fire in Tim.

As they approached, Ken heard a loud grunting noise followed by a thud. It sounded like metal hitting wood. Tim came into view in a clearing where many trees were chopped down. He was splitting thick pieces of wood on a stump.

Ken watched as Tim reared back the ax and drove it down into the lumber, causing it split and fly off in two directions. He paid close attention to the way Tim moved his body and torso as he swung the ax. Ken could see that Tim had some previous martial training, just from the way he did his work. *This man knows how to fight, I better be ready,* Ken thought to himself.

"There is a rich guy who lives out of town who pays my dad to chop wood for him. He chops from morning to night to meet this guy's demands," Mitchell informed Ken as they approached.

"So that's how he makes the money," Ken whispered to himself.

Tim looked up as he prepared to swing the ax, realizing Ken and his son were coming to him. "I thought I told you to leave!" Tim growled. "And you should be home recovering," he stated to his son.

Ken crossed his arms and sneered at Tim, "I was about to leave, but then I decided that I wanted to see for myself," he claimed in a cocky tone.

"See what?!" Tim demanded.

"See what a coward does while his son rots away in a cage," Ken said in a haughty tone.

Mitchell's eyes went wide from Ken's arrogant statement, "What are you doing!?" he shouted.

Tim moved toward Ken with his ax clutched firmly in his right hand. Nonetheless, Ken didn't back down.

"So, this is it then? This is your big plan to save your son?" Ken questioned as he stood his ground confidently.

Tim stopped moving and stared Ken down, "You don't know anything! Make another comment like that, and you'll be laying on this stump next," he said threateningly.

"I just had this talk with your wife, and she came to realize I was right. I hope you will too," Ken stated, unfazed by the threat.

Tim's eyes burned at Ken intensely, but Ken didn't waver. Instead, he continued with his point. "You'll never give them enough money to free your son. I know you understand that much."

"Then what am I supposed to do?!" Tim yelled back. "My son is being held hostage by a group of thugs with a bomb! Should I run in there in a wild rage and watch as they blow him apart!? Is that what you want!? Is that what will make you happy!?" Tim barked as his eyes dampened.

"No, I don't want that at all," Ken said, turning his head away. "What's going to make me happy is seeing your family together. Just like in that picture down your hallway."

Tim stared at Ken through his tears, but Ken continued to look away. "I hate people who bully others or treat others like trash. Even though I tend to do the ladder myself. However, I hate cowards who let those bullies do as they wish even more! I can't imagine sitting back and doing nothing while someone tries to hurt me, or anyone else for that matter!" Ken shouted. His body trembled as he spoke. He felt furious just thinking about the way this gang was manipulating people.

"You want to know why I won't look at you, right?" he asked Tim, who was speechlessly gawking at Ken. "It's because of how pathetic you look right now, crying to me about what to do to save your son. That's not who you are. I can tell just by looking at you. You're a warrior, and I won't dishonor you by looking at your moment of weakness," Ken said, gazing off at the trees.

Mitchell stood in awe of what Ken was saying. He didn't know whether to agree with him or punch him in the face. "Look, you can't talk to my dad like that in front of me!" Mitchell stated meekly from behind Ken.

"So, tell me what your plan is," Tim said firmly as he wiped his face. "I'm assuming you didn't come all this way to talk crap to me for no reason," he added.

Tim's response astounded Mitchell.

"You can look at me now, cause I'm done being a coward," Tim said as he threw the ax to the side.

"I do have a plan," Ken replied as he cut a grin of approval, "There are two more children being held hostage, right?" he asked.

"Yeah, we know both the families that those kids come from," Mitchell responded.

"Then you two go to town and gather anyone who's willing to stand up and fight. Bring them to your place and wait for me," Ken ordered.

"But they have two guys that keep watch for suspicious activity. If we do something reckless, they will tell the others," Mitchell argued.

"We'll do it," Tim said without heisting.

"How are we going to do that?" his son asked skeptically.

"I'll just take them out," Tim replied in an abrupt tone.

"Don't kill them, though. They have valuable information that I want to take advantage of later," Ken added.

"What will you do?" Tim asked as Ken started to walk away.

"They invited me to join their gang. It would be rude not to at least stop by and get a look at where they operate," he said with a mischievous air about him.

"Follow the trail we were on earlier to get to town," Mitchell called out as Ken continued to walk away. Ken held up his hand with a thumb up then ran to the trail.

It didn't take long for Ken to follow the trail to town. The place was small. There were a few run-down looking buildings on each side of a dirt road that ran between them. He guessed that there were ten building in total. Including the monarchy enforcement station that split the dirt road, as it sat in the middle of town. He could tell what it was since it appeared to be the nicest building out there. He noticed two guys off to the side who seemed to be part of the gang. He wanted to give them a good kick to the ribs, but he knew he needed to continue.

Ken wasted no time getting to the trail that was just to the left of the monarchy building. Then he followed it back into the woods. As he ran, his mind went to thoughts of trap bombs being hidden in the trees. After all, if they knew how to make bombs then why wouldn't they set traps. He thought while slowing his pace.

Ken saw the silhouette of the warehouse through the trees. He stopped walking and stared at it for a moment. It looked like a big brick gymnasium from the outside. He then surveyed the area around it. Searching for anything that appeared to be trouble.

Leaves fell around him as a light wind rustled the branches above. The air was warm, and the sun peered through the shrubs, illuminating the area as Ken glanced it over.

It's so beautiful today. I suppose this is what people call the calm before the storm, he thought as he approached the double doors that entered the warehouse.

Ken heard bushes shake behind him as he got close to the door. Two thugs stepped out from them, "About time they showed themselves," he whispered to himself. He realized they were there while he was looking for traps, but he decided they would help with his plan.

"What do we have here!? Looks like someone came to pay the boss directly." one of the guys said as he walked up behind Ken.

"Hey, I recognize him! He was at that Tim guy's place yesterday when we dropped off his pathetic older son. You know, the one we beat up." A second guy stated as he came from behind Ken's right side.

Ken felt rage rise within him. He wanted nothing more but to punch that guy in the mouth. Though, he reminded himself that for his plan to work he had to remain calm. No matter what he would hear or see. He had to stay focused to get the information he was after. Besides, sweet revenge was part of his future plans.

"Gretch offered this guy to join up with us yesterday. I'll bet that's why he's here." the thug to Ken's right claimed as he grabbed Ken's arm.

"Well, let's bring him in then!" the other thug replied while taking hold of Ken's other arm. Both men wore the same crooked smile.

Ken said nothing and allowed them to take him in.

They slowly opened the doors which squeaked ominously. At a gradual pace, they revealed a large open room with a tall ceiling. As they escorted Ken inside, he gauged the room around him. Taking note of what he saw.

There were wooden crates on both the left and right side of the area by the doors. They went roughly halfway to the middle of the building. They seemed to have space between them as if randomly put down without being pushed together to conserve room.

Once they made it to the center, Ken noticed that the back of the building had two sets of stairs that led to a platform where a man in a regal black suit sat with slick back dark hair that formed a widow's peak on his forehead. His skin was pale, and the smile on his face was just as crooked as the people working for him.

Ken swiftly noticed three cages on the ground just to the right of the platform. Each cage housed a different child. The first two cages held boys, and the last one was a girl. They all watched as he was brought in. None of them said a word. The guise of their faces was sorrowful and depressed. It appeared they were too scared to even call out to him.

Ken saw a set of wires that ran down the platform. They were strung together all the way to the floor where they split off one to each cage. *Those must be the wires to the bombs,* Ken thought as he continued to observe.

He spotted a set of large windows on both sides of the room. Two of which were just above the cages and on the same side that the wires hung down from. He noticed that the cages had roofs covering them. Ken looked back at the children. A part of him wanted to tell them that help was on the way. That they would be saved soon, but he knew for their sake he had to remain quiet.

"Hey, Giovanni. Look what we found!" one of the guys called out to the man in the suit.

"He was sneaking around outside, and we thought you might like to see him!" the other one yelled from directly behind Ken's ear.

Ken didn't react even though it caused his hearing to ring. He couldn't take his eyes off the cages that the kids were in. There were blankets on the floor and a bucket sitting in the corner of each pen. Ken assumed that was for using the bathroom. It appeared they had a few toys or things to keep themselves occupied with. He could feel rage pulse through his veins at the sight of those children being held captive. Contained like wild animals. He bit down on the inside of his lip to help stay focused.

Not yet, not yet. If you do something now, then they may get killed because of you, he thought. *Just focus on what you came here for, they'll be safe soon enough,* Ken reassured himself as they finished approaching.

The boss stood up from his chair and looked down at them, "If you came to pay what you were told you owe, then show me the money now!" the boss proclaimed from atop his platform.

"I actually came to join this group," Ken replied, shuttering from the disgust of his own lie.

"You what now!?" Giovanni retorted.

"I told him to, boss!" a voice came from behind a crate. The man stepped out from the shadow to explain himself. "He's the one I was telling you about, the one that gave up three thousand fol for Tim's kid, then called us all bastards!"

Ken recognized the guy as Gretch. One of the thugs that he saw the previous night.

"Oh, so this is the guy?" Giovanni questioned. "You want to join my gang? After calling us bastards?" he yelled out scornfully. He snapped his fingers and one the guys next to Ken balled up his fist and swung at Ken's stomach.

Out of habit, Ken's leg twitched as though to raise his knee and block the attack, but he stopped himself and took the punch. Then he fell to his knees. It didn't hurt him much since he was used to taking hits, yet he knew he needed to put on a good show.

"Why are you attacking me? That Gretch guy said my money covered what I called you," Ken asked, pretending to be upset and in pain.

"Gretch isn't the boss here, I am! I can tell them to beat the snot out of you as much as I want!" Giovanni bragged with a satisfied smirk on his face.

So far, I've only seen the two guys holding me, Gretch, and the boss. That's not including the guys watching in town. Does that mean they only have six members? Ken wondered as he scanned the room some more. *No, they have more than that. I need to lure them out for a better count. This is going to hurt though,"* he thought.

Ken stood up quickly and kicked the man to the right in the back of his knee, causing him to let go of Ken's arm. Then with his liberated fist, he punched the other guy in the face.

"GET HIM!" Giovanni bellowed. Six men ran out from behind the wooden crates.

Ken saw how many there were and felt his stomach drop, "Crap! I figured two or three more, not six! This is really going to suck," he whispered as they closed in.

Ken kicked the first guy that approached him square in the face, landing him on his back with a bloody nose. Then the second man tackled Ken and held him down while the rest started to beat him.

"Alright! That's enough!" the boss ordered with his arm raised high. They all got off Ken, and two of them raised him up by both arms. Ken was roughed up from the attack with a swelling eye and some blood dripping from his mouth.

"We don't want to kill him! After all, he brought three thousand fol in for us. He may have more money, or he may be able to make us some more money," Giovanni said, giving a twisted smile as he gazed upon Ken.

"Here's the deal. Since you like Tim's family so much, I'll put you under the same demands as him. Bring me five thousand fol in the next three days, or I'll blow up his kid." Giovanni held up a small device with a wire that ran from the bottom of it to the rest of the wires that led to the cages. It appeared to have three small buttons on it.

"That's the last thing I needed to see," Ken said to himself as if completing his mission.

"Now take him outside so he can make me some money!" Giovanni barked to his underlings. As they grabbed him, Ken saw the boy from the picture in Tim's house watching. He winked at the kid and gave a slight grin. To which the boy smiled back with a glimmer of hope in his eyes.

They dragged Ken by his arms to the door, then pulled him down the trail a few feet. They let him go and watched him fall onto the dirt. Laughing as they walked away.

Ken slowly stood up and started knocking the dirt off himself. He could feel a few spots on his arms, legs, and sides where they got a few good hits in, but he was able to block and protect the more sensitive areas.

"If that's all they got, then this will be easy with the right number of people," Ken said as he made his way back. He was still in some pain, but it was nothing that he couldn't walk off. He wasted no time going back to Tim's place. He walked through town quickly and then followed the trail back to their home.

As Ken approached, he saw two men standing outside of Tim's house, "Oh no! Am I too late?" he gasped as he continued to close in.

One of them walked inside the house briefly. Then came back out with Tim, who gave the other two a thumb up before walking back inside the house. Ken smiled and felt as though the world was lifted from his shoulders. *They were successful then,* Ken thought as he walked up the stairs.

"You ok, buddy?" one of them asked as Ken approached the door.

"Yeah, I'm fine. I got some important info for everyone so let's go," Ken said as he entered the house. To his surprise, he saw several people gathered in the kitchen. They were wall to wall, filling the room to capacity. Getting a rough count, he figured there were twenty people in all.

Tim was standing at the dinner table talking with everyone. Then he looked up at Ken, and all the voices fell silent. All the eyes in the room were focused intently on him. Waiting to hear what he had to say.

"I told everyone here that you're the mastermind behind this," Tim said, breaking the silence.

"How's my little girl? Is she okay?" a man to Tim's left asked with a worried expression.

Ken felt nervous as the attention of the entire room was on him. It was something that he was definitely not used to. However, he knew these people wanted answers and that they needed someone to stand up and deliver. He wasn't going to let a little stage fright get the best of him.

"All the children looked safe and unharmed," Ken answered.

There was an air of relief in the room as many of them let out a breath to release their anxiety.

"Thank goodness," the man said quietly as he placed his hand on his forehead.

"But the conditions they're living in are terrible, and they look distressed," Ken added as everyone went silent again. "I don't mean to burst anyone's bubble here, but you need to know the truth."

"Hey, are you hurt? You look like they beat you pretty bad," one of the men asked as Ken made his way through the room.

"I'm fine. What's important is that we go over the plan," Ken grumbled. "I was able to get a good look in the warehouse and get a count of how many people they have."

Ken explained to everyone about the crates and the layout of the room, as well as the platform and the wires that connected to the cages. "The thing that got my attention was the windows," he said while continuing to explain. "There are four big windows, two of which are above the cages and directly to the right of the platform. That's what we will use to save the children," Ken stated confidently.

"How, how will we use them?" a man asked from the crowd.

"We'll get two men to sneak to up to each window as I distract the gang. Then when I give the sign, our guys will bust through the window and shoot an arrow at the wires to cut them," Ken explained.

"Why don't we just shoot the boss? He can't press the button if he's dead," a guy called out. Many of the others murmured amongst each other in agreement.

"Because he's a moving target, if you miss the shot then he'll be able to blow up a cage. Besides, even if you do hit him the buttons will still work. Someone else could run up there in the confusion and use it," Ken shouted over them.

The people continued to talk amongst each other. Ken even heard someone say that he raised a good point.

"What if the bombs are set to go off when the wires are cut?" someone asked.

"Oh man, I didn't even think about that," another person stated. Their squawking grew louder as panic built between them.

"This is hopeless, no matter what we do they got us cornered."

"That's enough!" Tim yelled.

Everyone hushed once more.

"You people think I would put my son's life in this guy's hands for no reason!?" Tim shouted. "I want my son back, and I'm tired of living in fear!"

"I trust him, too! We're getting my daughter back today! With or without the rest of you!" the man next to him exclaimed.

"And I'm willing to do anything to get my boy back as well!" Another man said from the crowd. Ken assumed that was the third child's father.

"Listen to what he says before you start to doubt," Tim ordered everyone in the room.

They all went quiet once more, and all eyes fell on Ken. He was surprised to hear that so many people were putting faith in him.

He quickly solidified his resolve and continued with the plan. "Did you guys catch the thugs in town?" Ken asked as he searched among the people.

"They're over here," Tim answered while pointing to the corner of the room. They were tied up and appeared to be used as punching bags.

"Perfect!" Ken said as he approached the thugs. "Answer this for me. Will the bombs go off if we cut the wire?" he asked one of the men who were bound.

"Don't tell them nothing, Jasper!" the other thug said hastily.

Ken punched the one who spoke in the side of his head, causing him to pass out. "Your name is Jasper, then?" Ken asked as he looked the thug over with a sinister smile.

Jasper trembled. He turned his head and braced for a hit.

"Look at me, Jasper," Ken ordered as he grabbed the man's hair and forced his head around. "When this is over, these people are going to do whatever they want to you. You may not even live through whatever it is they have planned," Ken said ominously.

Jasper's eyes grew with terror as he quaked, "Please, they forced me to join them. I just want out of this, please let me go. I'll tell you anything," he replied in a panic.

"Then tell me if the bombs will go off when we cut the wires," Ken demanded.

"They won't. The boss even told us that they won't. I promise!" Jasper spat.

"That's good to know, but I got to tell you something. We're going to leave you tied up till this is done. So, if we cut those wires and the bombs go off, I will personally come back here and break every bone in your body before turning you over to these people," Ken stated, nose to nose with Jasper.

The people looked at Jasper with fury in their eyes. Jasper seemed to feel the malice in the room grow towards him as they glared. "I swear it's the truth. They will not go off!" he cried.

Ken stood up and looked back at the townspeople, "Do we have any good archers here?"

"Keith is a great archer! He bow hunts all the time," someone called out.

"Yeah, I could do it." a skinny man said from the crowd. "I got my bow and some arrows outside. It's just a lot of pressure since everyone is relying solely on that shot," he said.

"We need at least two archers!" Ken added as he looked around the room. "Is there no one else who can shoot a bow?"

"No, but I'm good with a knife," a short guy said as he stepped forward. "The name's Jack," he added

"That's not going to help at a distance," Ken replied skeptically.

"I'm also really fast. Keith will shoot the arrow from one window while I jump down from the other and slice the wires," Jack said optimistically.

"We really need someone who can hit it quickly at a distance," Ken said.

"Well, no one else here can do it. Come on, we're putting our trust in you. So, put some in us too. Besides, it's just a backup plan. Keith will hit the target, but I'll be halfway to it by the time we see if it cuts or not. Plus, I'll be there with you when things get hairy," Jack said confidently.

"Alright, I guess we don't have much choice. Besides, we need to get moving soon. They'll notice two of their guys missing any minute," Ken said.

"So, what's the final plan here?" Tim inquired.

"I'll go through the front door and pretend like I have money to give. That will distract them long enough for everyone to hide in the trees and bushes around the warehouse. Then the guys who are going to the windows can take position. After that, just wait for my signal. When you see it, everyone rush in and fight with everything you have," Ken stated as he looked over all the people in the room.

"What's the sign?" one of the men asked from the back.

Ken had a plan, but it involved his pressure blast. He worried that if he told them about his power, they would question how he got it. He also feared that they would forego the plan out of mistrust.

"You'll recognize it when you see it," Ken replied, hoping that would be enough.

"We need to know what we're looking for here," Keith said in an irritated tone.

Now what do I do? Ken thought. He gazed around anxiously hoping the answer would hit him.

"Look, we don't have time to keep going back and forth," Tim shouted crossly. "Ken said we will know the sign. That's good enough for me. Everyone gather your stuff and get ready to go to the woods. When Ken heads out, we'll begin," he commanded.

Many of the people cheered in agreement, and they all started to go outside to prepare. Ken breathed a sigh of relief as they left.

"Don't worry about your little sister," Tim said as he walked by Ken. "Steven and my wife are with her upstairs. They're all safe."

"Thank you, I was wondering where she was," Ken replied.

Tim's eyes fell to the glove that covered Ken's left hand. Then went back to his face. "I'm trusting you," he said as he walked out.

That look he gave me — does he know? Ken pondered as he watched Tim walk out. He shook his head to regain focus. "It doesn't matter. What's important now is saving those kids," he stated as he walked out of the door.

Chapter 12

United Front

Ken walked outside and saw the townspeople gathering their weapons. Some of them had simple tools such as shovels, hoes, or pitchforks. Others had swords, knives, or in Keith's case, a bow, and arrows. As they got their things together, Ken thought that he better prepare himself as well. He began to stretch his legs, arms, and back in various ways.

"You're not bringing a weapon?" one of the townsmen asked as he watched.

"I'm the distraction. If I have a weapon, they may just kill me before I can get inside," Ken replied.

"What will you do when the fighting starts? You'll be unarmed," the man questioned.

Ken rubbed the back of his head and chuckled nonchalantly. "I suppose I'll just have to fight well," he answered.

The man laughed and shook his head as he walked away.

Of course, if things get bad, I can always summon my weapon, Ken thought as he peered down at his left hand.

"We need to get going," Tim said as he approached Ken. He had a saber that was sheathed in a white scabbard with silver trim around it.

Ken eyed it up and down, thinking about how it looked like the armor of the monarchy soldier he fought when he first found Serena.

"You nervous there, Ken?" Tim asked.

Ken smirked back at him. "I'm just excited to get some payback," he replied, brimming with tenacity.

After their talk, Ken made his way to the trail, "Here we go everyone. You ready!?" he hollered to the townspeople.

They cheered as Ken gazed over at them. "Let's go!" He yelled as he ran down the trail.

The town's men went into the woods toward the warehouse, purposely taking a covered route so they could hide in the trees until Ken gave the sign.

Ken ran down the trail with butterflies in his stomach. Questions ran through his mind as he pondered. *What if they figured out what we're doing? What if they don't cut the wires in time? What if... someone dies?*

Ken stopped running, then stood in the middle of the trail. He glanced up and felt the warm air on his skin. The sun shined on him through the tree branches, and everything that surrounded was quiet. "If someone dies, it'll be my fault. If someone gets hurt, it will be because of me," he said in a hushed voice.

Ken took off the glove covering the Gate on his left hand. *Can I use this power to protect them? Is it enough?* He wondered as doubt clouded his judgment.

Then an image of Serena went through his mind. He could see her as if she were standing in front of him, smiling in the face of all that opposed them.

"If I can't help these people, then how do I expect to get her home. How can I protect her from an entire military if I get second thoughts about a small gang?" Ken said to himself.

He put the glove back over his hand and clenched his fist. "No! No second thoughts! I promised Serena I would take her home, and I promised Steven I would bring his little brother back. So that's what I'm going to do! No matter what," Ken stated as he stared down the path in front of him with newfound determination. "There are too many people counting on me now. It's all or nothing!" he claimed as he darted down the trail.

As Ken sprint through town, he noticed how empty it was. It was as if it were abandoned. He turned left at the Monarchy Enforcement Station and continued down the path. He soon saw the warehouse as he approached. The men that caught him before didn't bother to hide in the bushes this time. One of them had a bandage on his face from when Ken kicked him. Ken felt slightly prideful when he noticed the dressing.

"You didn't waste any time coming back for another beating," the thug with the bandage said begrudgingly.

"Actually, I came back to pay what I owe," Ken replied as held up a bag with coins in it. The thug reached for it, but Ken snatched it back.

"Give it to me, I'll take it to the boss," the thug stated in an impatient tone.

"I don't trust you to take it to him. How do I know you won't pocket it and walk away?" Ken replied smugly.

"I'd never take money from Boss Giovanni," the thug said with a warped grin.

"Yeah, now give it up!" the other gang member demanded.

For my plan to work, I need to go inside, Ken contemplated as he stared them down. *I have no choice.*

"Alright guys, you win. Here you go," Ken said as he threw the money up in the air.

Both thieves raised their arms to catch the bag.

Ken spun around rapidly and delivered a side kick to the bandaged thug's face. He immediately followed up with a punch to the side of the other one's head. They both fell to the ground unconscious as Ken held out his right hand and caught the bag. Afterward, he scanned the woods, trying to see if he could spot any of the townspeople. After searching for a moment, he saw a hand wave at him from behind a tree.

Ken gave a self-assured grin, "Yes, they're here. Time to get the show started," he whispered.

As Ken walked to the doors, he noticed Keith and a few others make their approach from the right side. They were preparing to scale the wall of the warehouse where the windows were.

Ken opened the double doors and stepped passed the threshold. He saw two thugs talking off to the side. Giovanni was in his usual seat on the platform, and the children were still in the cages.

"Who let you in here? Where are the guards from outside?!" Giovanni yelled as he stood from his chair.

Ken knew he needed to buy everyone some more time to get in place. What's more, he knew that what he said next would define how the entire situation would play out.

The other thugs began to surround Ken as he continued his approach. He counted eight, then realized all the remaining members were here. He held up the bag of coins and shook it, "I came to bring you the money I owe!" he called out as the coins rattled and clanged. The gang members encircled Ken, stopping him from making his approach.

"Just give the money to them," Giovanni demanded. "And where are my guards that were outside?"

The gangsters started to pull out knives and steel pipes. Readying to attack at any moment.

"They tried to stop me from warning you, so I knocked them out," Ken replied with a roguish smirk.

"Warn me about what?" Giovanni asked skeptically.

"To warn you about an attack the townspeople have planned," Ken answered with a hint of nerve in his voice.

The thugs looked around at each other with concerned expressions. "Let him through," Giovanni ordered.

Ken made his way to the boss slowly. He looked over at the kids in the cages. Seeing the fear in their eyes. He smiled at them and then winked as he did before. They merely continued to stare at him as he approached the boss. Their expressions were bleak and portrayed hopelessness.

"What do you mean they are planning to attack me?" Giovanni queried.

Ken glanced up at the windows and saw a figure in each of them. *Good, they're ready,* he thought while turning his attention back to the boss. *Time to get started.*

"Before I tell you, let me give up the money I owe," Ken held the bag up in his left hand and extended his arm toward the boss. He stood still as he moved his arm around slightly as if taking aim.

"Well hurry up and give it to me!" Giovanni bellowed.

Ken grinned impishly from behind his hand. "If you say so."

Suddenly, there was a loud bang that erupted from Ken's palm. The bag he held tore to shreds as it flew, releasing dozens of coins that soared at the boss like a volley from a shotgun. The coins pinged and slammed into the platform.

Giovanni cried out as he tried to duck down. The ringing of coins reverberated through the warehouse as they smashed into the metal rails and fell to the ground.

As the thugs dashed toward Ken, the two windows above the cages shattered. Keith wasted no time taking aim while Jack jumped down to cut the wires.

Giovanni stood back up quickly holding the side of his face. Blood was dripping down from where a coin hit him in the cheek. "I warned you! I said I'd blow up a kid!" he screamed while holding the button in his right hand.

Ken felt panic rise within him as he looked to Keith. "Take the shot!" he shrieked.

Keith released his arrow and watched as it flew toward the group of wires. It was as though time stood still while the arrow soared its path.

It's going to hit! Ken thought as it closed in.

The arrow caught the wires with a glancing strike but didn't cut them all the way through. Both Keith and Ken's eyes widened in disbelief as they watched their hope fly into a wall.

"Now die!" the boss yelled as he pressed the first button on the control pad.

"NO!" Ken screamed as he looked over at the children in the cages.

Everyone fell silent as they stared at the pens, but nothing happened.

"Looks like I made it just in time!" Jack said as he approached Ken with his knife held high.

Ken stared beyond Jack and saw where the wires hung after being slashed through. "You... you did it!" Ken cried out in awe.

"We got more important things to worry about," Jack said, watching as the gang members came at them.

With a loud burst, the doors opened, and the townspeople all rushed in, yelling as they charged.

"Ken look!" Keith called from the window. Giovanni ran to the back of the building and opened the door to escape. Keith shot an arrow but missed as the boss took off.

"Damnit! Go after him, Ken. We can handle this!" Jack yelled as he passed.

Ken nodded his head and ran for the door that Giovanni went out of. He looked back just before opening the door and saw the townspeople taking down the thugs. It was twenty against eight. He knew at this point that the gang didn't stand a chance. So, without further hesitation, he made his way out the door and up a small hill behind the warehouse.

Ken searched frantically for the boss as he rushed. When he topped the hill, he saw Giovanni standing before him. Then he noticed a small device clutched in his hand. It had a wire that went directly from the device and into the ground.

"What is that?" Ken asked.

Giovanni smiled malevolently and laughed as though he had gone mad, "You ruined everything! I was making a killing! These people would have kept bringing me money until I was tired of them, but then you just had to show up and screw it all to hell!"

"It's over! Just drop it and move on," Ken demanded as he stared the boss down.

Giovanni snickered at him even more, "You're not the one calling the shots here, buddy!" He shouted. "You want to know what this does?"

Ken didn't reply. Instead, he looked on quietly as he stood his ground, contemplating what to do. Giovanni didn't seem to like his silence.

"Well since you're not interested, I'll just demonstrate!"

"No!" Ken yelled in a panic. "Tell me, what does it do?"

Giovanni gave a sinister grin, "It's a button to several bombs that are set up all throughout that building we were just in."

Ken glared at him while baring his teeth, *exactly what I was afraid it was! Damnit!* he thought while racking his brain for a plan. He considered summoning his sword, but the distance was too great. He would never cut the cord before Giovanni pressed the button. He also had nothing to shoot with his pressure blast.

"Ken it's over! We did it!" Tim yelled as he ran up the hill. "We just need to get the keys from the boss!"

Tim stopped as Giovanni came into view.

"No one else comes out, or I'll blow them all up!" Giovanni commanded.

A few other men came out the door and started to make their way up. Tim turned to them and yelled for them to stop.

"I said no one else comes out!" the boss barked.

"They're going back in right now," Ken replied calmly. "Listen, if you just hand over the key and drop the button, then I'm sure we can work something out," Ken added, trying to ease Giovanni's nerves with a soothed tone.

"You think I'm stupid? If I give up my bargaining chip now, then I'll lose. Of course, if I press the button, it'll make a great distraction for my escape," Giovanni said threateningly.

"Please, my boy is still in there. Walk away, and I'll let you leave. Just drop the button, and I swear I'll personally stop anyone who goes after you!" Tim cried desperately.

"No, I like my other plan better. I told you people not to cross me, and here we are!" Giovanni shouted.

Ken and Tim stared in suspense. "You can't do this!" Ken yelled.

Giovanni chuckled once more as they pleaded with him, "you say I can't do it? Watch me then."

Giovanni dropped his thumb down to press the button. Just as sheer horror overtook Ken, he heard something whiz by his ear as the boss pushed down. There was a loud click from the press of the button, yet once more nothing happened.

Giovanni gazed down and saw where the wire was cut. Just behind him was an arrow that still shook from its impact on the ground.

Ken turned back and saw Keith standing on top of the warehouse, still holding the position with his hand next to his face, and his bow held high.

"That should make up for my mistake earlier!" Keith yelled out.

Giovanni dropped the device and ran for the woods, but Ken wasted no time running him down. He jumped through the air and kicked the boss in the back. Causing him to fall on his face. Then Tim placed his knee between Giovanni's shoulders and pressed his weight down. Giovanni cried out in pain as they tied him up.

"Where are the keys!?" Tim bellowed as he picked Giovanni up and slammed him into a tree.

"In my right pocket! Please take them, but don't hurt me!" the boss begged fearfully.

Tim grabbed the keys then dropped the boss in the dirt. "Watch him while I free my son," he ordered Ken.

"Wait!" Ken replied. "What if he booby-trapped the cages to go off with a certain key?" he inquired.

Tim stopped in his tracks. "That's a good point, bring him!" he commanded as he made his way down the hill.

Ken and another townsman carried Giovanni back to the warehouse. Then they sat him next to the cage that Tim's son was in.

"Will this key blow up the cage when I open it?" Tim questioned the boss sternly.

"No, I swear it!" Giovanni squalled.

Everyone gathered around, looking on as Tim prepared to open the cage, "If you're lying to me, then you're going to die with us," Tim stated while pulling Giovanni over to the door of the cage. He slammed him against the bars and held him close as he put the key in. Then he glared back at the boss expectantly.

"I told you that it's over. The cages won't go off," Giovanni groaned once more.

Tim turned the key and swung the door open. "Daddy!" his son Timmy howled as he jumped to his father.

Tim wrapped his arms around his son and held him tightly. "My boy!" he cried as he dropped to his knees.

The other families retrieved the key and let the rest of the children out as well. There were three groups of families huddled to together, crying and holding their loved ones tight. Mitchell approached his father and little brother and joined in the display.

"This is all thanks to you," Jack said, slapping his hand on Ken's shoulder. "If you didn't talk some sense into us, these kids would still be suffering right now."

Ken smiled as he watched the families reunite, "I didn't do much. I just gave them a small push. If they hadn't agreed to stand up and fight, then this never would've happened," he said humbly.

Jack shook his head and chuckled, "Stop trying to be so modest," he uttered before going over to the other townsmen.

While Jack was talking, Ken continued to watch everyone as they came together. The tears of joy on their faces made him feel proud of what they accomplished. Yet, he could feel a slight pain in his chest. He thought about his mother and father and how he would never get to have this kind of moment with them. Then he thought about Serena and the promise he made to her. How her reunion with her parents would be just like this. He smiled at the notion, and the pain went away.

Her parents are probably crying for her right now. Worried and afraid of what happened to their daughter. I'll bring her home soon, Ken thought as he wiped a tear from his eye.

"Hey, you guys listen up!" Keith announced to everyone. He was standing next to Jack and few of the other townsmen. All of which had the gang members tied up and surrounded. "Those who just got your family back should go home. I know the rest of your loved ones are ready to see these children safe and sound. We'll take care of these guys!" he shouted.

Tim stood up holding his son's hand. "Are you sure?"

Jack and Keith nodded at him assuredly.

"We'll trust them to you then," Tim said as the families made their way out the warehouse.

"You should go with them," Keith said to Ken who was watching them leave.

"You don't want any help with these dirtbags?" Ken asked.

"No, we have enough people here to deal with this. Go, see what you've accomplished," Keith replied.

"Besides, there is something Tim needs to talk to you about," Jack added.

Keith elbowed him in the side with a peeved expression. Jack shrugged his shoulders and walked off.

Ken was curious as to what they meant, but he did have a feeling that he needed to see Serena anyway. Part of him was compelled to leave just for her sake.

As Tim's house came into view, they could see Maire, Steven, and Serena standing on the front porch waiting for them. Marie gasped and covered her mouth as they rounded the corner of the trail, revealing her son sitting atop his father's shoulders. Tears welled up in her eyes as she ran down the steps towards them. Tim put his son down and watched as he dashed toward his mother.

"Mama!" Timmy cried out as he shot to her with arms spread open.

"My baby!" Marie yelled back as she cradled him. She wept profusely as she squeezed her son tight.

"I missed you, mama!" Timmy said through his tears.

Marie tried to reply but was unable due to being so choked up. Steven approached them and hugged his little brother as well. Then Tim and Mitchell gathered around with them.

Serena wrapped her arms around Ken as they watched, "I knew you would do it big brother. I just knew you would save them," she gazed up at Ken and saw tears fall from his eyes. "Big bro? Are you alright?" she asked.

Ken wiped his face and gave a warm smile back at her, "You're next Serena. No matter what's in front of us. I'm taking you back home!" he said with determination in his voice.

"I believe you, especially after this. I know I'll be home soon," she replied.

Tim and the rest of his family made their way to the house. He looked back at Ken and Serena then called out to them, "What are you waiting for!? Come on!" he said while waving them over.

Ken and Serena followed them into the house where everyone talked about each person's role in the attack. They explained how Mitchell and Tim knocked out a guy together and tied him up, and how Keith shot the last wire with his arrow.

Timmy explained what his incarceration was like. Tim got upset hearing how his son was treated but was able to look past it now that everything was over. Soon the other townspeople showed up to get the other two thugs Tim was holding. When they picked them up, they explained what they were doing with the gang.

The townspeople broke into the Monarchy Enforcement Station so they could use the jail cells to lock up the criminals. Ken asked if they would get in trouble for breaking into the building. They just laughed and said they would have to prove the criminals didn't do it themselves.

After they left, Ken and the rest of the family enjoyed a great meal prepared by Marie. Once the feast was over, Ken stepped outside to get some fresh air. The sun was still bright in the sky. He could hear a light breeze blow through the trees as he peered out among them. While taking in the view, he felt a sense of accomplishment about himself.

The door opened behind him, and Tim walked out and took a seat just to Ken's left.

"It feels like it should be later than this, doesn't it?" Tim asked as he gazed at trees with Ken.

"Yeah, I guess it's because of all the excitement," Ken replied. They sat in silence for a moment. Staring out at the woods and listening to the air blow around them until Tim spoke once more.

"I owe you an apology for the way I treated you. I was in a dark place at the time, and that's just not the kind of man I am," he said. Even though he was apologizing his voice still sounded rugged and commanding.

Ken shook his head, "Don't worry about it. I'm surprised you were as nice as you were. Given the circumstances."

Tim gave him a stern look, "Don't tell me not to worry about it. I was a jerk, and that's that. As a man, you either accept my apology, or you don't."

Ken was taken back by Tim's response. He simply shrugged his shoulders, "I accept?" he replied reluctantly.

Tim chuckled and leaned back in his chair, "Good, because I also wanted to thank you for telling me what a piece of crap I was. After all, what kind of father lets his son live in a cage?"

Ken once again didn't know how to respond to Tim's comment. He couldn't tell if he was serious or being sarcastic.

"Honestly, if you hadn't lit a fire under me – my son would still be there. He would be at the mercy of those thugs, and that's a scary thought," Tim said in a somber tone. "You forced me to man up Ken, and I owe you my life for that."

Ken went flush from the compliment. He stayed quiet while taking a seat.

"Shy now, are you?" Tim said jokingly.

"I didn't mean what I said when I was insulting you," Ken replied while rubbing the back of his head.

"Don't take it back now. You spoke the truth. Stand by your words and your actions Ken. It's what makes you a man," Tim stated.

Ken let out a sigh, *I don't know how to take this guy,* he thought as the conversation continued.

"I have something important I need to talk to you about," Tim said as his tone went serious again. "Look at this for me." He pulled a folded piece of paper out of his pocket and gave it to Ken.

Ken opened it and saw a picture of Serena on the front. His body went tense with shock.

"It's a missing person poster," Tim said as Ken looked it over. "It says the Amony attacked a caravan that was transporting her to safety. It goes on to give a description of the suspected person who kidnapped her. It matches you almost perfectly, except the hair. You have shorter hair then the description," he added.

Ken trembled as his eyes scanned over the picture. *Is he going to turn me in?* He pondered as panic took hold of his mind.

"Just calm down for a minute, Ken," Tim said, noticing how pale Ken became. "Look, I don't know if you knew this or not, but I used to be a soldier in the Monarchy."

Ken's fears only worsened from Tim's proclamation. *That explains the saber that matches the armor the Monarchy wears,* he worried while clutching the paper with both hands.

"I'm not turning you in or anything, so you can relax," Tim added calmly. "Just hear me out, okay?"

Ken didn't know what to do. He knew he couldn't run since Serena was still in the house. He gazed at Tim's face and saw peace in his eyes. *I just need to calm down, if he wanted to turn us in, he wouldn't have come out and said all this,* Ken considered as he folded the paper. He let out a deep breath and tried to relax.

"Good, now listen, I didn't make it all that high in the ranks. I wasn't even a Soul wielder. In fact, I was just a normal soldier. I didn't agree with the way the Monarchy did a lot of things. So, I retired early and decided to live a simple life," Tim stated. "That being said, I recognize a Gate power when I see one. Or in this case, hear about one. My son told me about your power, and then Keith and Jack confirmed it for me. What's more, they told me it was on your left hand," Tim said while staring at Ken with a stoic expression.

"What are you getting at?" Ken asked.

"I'm not going to ask if you're with the Amony, or even what you're trying to do. You saved our whole town when you could've just left. I know you're a good guy. I know you didn't kidnap that girl either. I don't think she would be that found of you if you did. The only thing I want to know is, what are you going to do with her?" After asking, Tim relaxed in his chair waiting for Ken's response.

Ken didn't want to tell him where they were going in case Tim sold them out. Yet, against every part of his mind that screamed for him not to say anything. He decided he would inform Tim of his plan.

"I promised I would take her home to her family. So, that's what I'm doing," Ken answered. His tone was decisive and stern.

Tim smacked his own forehead. "I knew you were going to say that. I have some bad news for you Ken," Tim said grimly. "The battle in Sales didn't go well."

Ken was surprised by Tim's statement. "How do you know where she's from?" he asked.

"I still have a lot of connections in the Monarchy," Tim answered. "Plus, that paper says where she is from if you look it over closely," he added. "Now to get on with my point. After the children were taken to safety, the Amony launched a surprise attack. They didn't have time to remove the women and seniors from the area. There were massive casualties. They say only a handful of the villagers survived."

"What are you saying?" Ken queried. "Are you telling me that—"

"Her parents may have died, Ken," Tim said darkly.

In the back of his mind, Ken knew this was a possibility. He knew since it was a battle, that her parents may not have made it out alive. He just didn't want to believe it.

"What will you do now? There is a chance that they are alive, but I doubt it," Tim said, his voice was dismal and didn't inspire optimism.

Ken sat in silence with his head down for a moment before responding, "I'm going to keep my promise to her," he replied quietly.

"What if her parents really are gone? What will you do then?" Tim questioned.

"I'll keep protecting her. That's what big brothers do," he replied. "Besides, there is no proof that her parents are dead. It's just a possibility. So, if there is even a slight chance that they are waiting for her, then I have to take her home."

Tim shook his head at Ken. "You know that's probably the first place they'll look right?"

"I don't care, I promised I would do this, so that's what I'm going to do," Ken answered firmly.

Tim let out a disapproving sigh, "Which route are you taking to get there?"

Ken opened the map and showed him the road he and Serena discussed before.

"It's just as I thought," Tim said. "If you go too far up this road, you'll run into a route the Monarchy uses regularly. You'll have to go another way."

Tim looked over the map and showed him another spot, "Go down the trail you were originally going to take until you get here," he said while pointing on the map. "It's a small rest area where you guys can sleep and eat for the night. Then, instead of continuing down that road, take this northern route in its place. It'll carry you to an abandoned town called Vorit. There you'll find a bar run by a guy named James. Tell him I sent you, and he'll help you get where you're going."

"That's a little out of our way," Ken said skeptically.

"Well, it's either that or get caught," Tim replied.

Why would he run a bar in an abandoned town? Ken wondered.

"It's up to you to take me up on the help I've offered," Tim said impatiently.

Ken rolled the map back up and put it away, "I appreciate the help, thank you," he replied.

"There is one more thing," Tim added. "I hate to do this but, I need you to leave as soon as you can. It's not that I don't appreciate what you did, but if the Monarchy finds out that we've had you here—"

"Say no more." Ken interrupted as he got on his feet. "You just got your family back. If we stay, it could cause you more trouble. We'll leave immediately," he replied. "Besides, the sooner we leave, the sooner I can get Serena home."

Tim stood up and held out his hand to Ken. Ken grabbed it firmly and shook it. "Thank you, Ken," Tim said as he opened the door.

When Ken walked inside, he was surprised to see Serena sitting at the table with her hair dyed black and cut just above her shoulders.

"What do you think, big bro? Marie gave me a little makeover."

Tim put his hand on Ken's shoulder and winked at him. He assumed that meant they helped disguise her.

Ken nodded back at Tim then smiled at Serena, "It looks great, I like that look on you."

Serena grinned back at him as she admired it from a hand mirror once more.

"I think it's about time we left, Serena," Ken said as he grabbed his bag.

Serena got up from her chair and stood beside him, "Okay, I'm ready when you are," she replied happily.

"You guys are leaving already?" Steven asked in a disappointed manner.

"Our parents are waiting for us at home. We can't let them worry," Ken replied with a blatant lie.

Steven rushed to Ken and gave him a hug. Ken rubbed his head, purposefully messing up his hair. "Hey!" Steven cried out through a chuckle. Then Mitchell shook Ken's hand and thanked him.

Afterward, Marie approached him with Timmy at her side and gave him a hug.

"Thank you for bringing my baby back," she said earnestly.

Ken's face flushed as he moved toward the door, "We better get going," he said as Serena followed.

"One more thing Ken," Tim said as he shoved three bags into Ken's hands. "Take these with you. Two of those bags have metal ball bearings that my son uses with his slingshot. The other is five thousand fol, to replace what the thugs took from you."

"Five thousand!?" Ken questioned. "But I only gave them three thousand."

Tim grinned at Ken as he followed them out the door, "Consider it a thank you. When they picked up the guys we had tied up here, they gave back all the money they took from me, and then some. Oh, and I'm sure you know what to use those metal balls for." Tim added

"I don't know what to say," Ken replied, looking back at them from the porch.

"Just say you'll come to visit us again one day," Steven replied.

Ken gave him a thumb up as he and Serena made their way off the porch. Everyone yelled bye to each other as they walked off. Soon they were too far away to hear them calling out anymore.

"I'm surprised you were willing to leave so soon, Serena," Ken said as they made their way down the trail.

"I knew you were ready to go. Plus, the sooner we left, the better. It means we're closer to getting home," Serena replied cheerfully.

Ken felt a wave of guilt hit him from her statement, *That's right, she doesn't know how the battle went. She doesn't know that her parents could be…* Ken thought as they walked.

He pondered whether he should tell her about her parents. About how there was a good chance that they didn't make it. Then he saw how happy she was as they walked.

I don't want to ruin her mood, but she also deserves to know. Ken suddenly had an interesting thought after that. *What if she already knows. What she's just holding out hope.* He stared at her, trying desperately to decide whether he should tell her that her parents may be dead.

"You okay big bro?" Serena asked.

"Yeah, I'm fine," Ken replied half-heartedly.

I'll at least wait till we get settled in for the night, he thought as they walked. *She does deserve to know about our change in plans at least.*

"Hey Serena, we need to take a different road than we originally planned," Ken said.

"Okay," she replied, shrugging her shoulders.

"That's it? You're not going to ask why?"

"I trust you no matter what, big bro. If we must go another way, then that's fine. I wouldn't mind knowing why, though," Serena answered.

Her response surprised Ken, "You really trust me that much?" He asked.

"Of course, after everything we've been through. I know you'll get me home," Serena replied, her eyes beaming up ay Ken.

Ken felt a tenderness in his chest from what she said. He was happy to know how much she thought of him and how confident she was in him. *I'm not going to let her down. I'll do whatever it takes to get her home safely,* Ken thought.

Chapter 13

The Hunt Begins

As they made their way to the rest area, Ken explained the new plans to Serena. He told her about the new route they needed to take, and how a guy named James was supposed to help them. Then he showed her the missing person picture that Tim gave him.

"This picture… they took it from my house!" Serena bellowed.

Ken figured that's how they got it, but he still knew it would be a shock for her.

"It shouldn't surprise me, though. Since they attacked my parents and took me away," Serena said grimly.

This may be a good time to talk with her about her parents, Ken assumed as Serena folded the poster. He opened his mouth to speak but noticed she was deep in thought with a bleak glaze over her face. She was probably rehashing everything that happened to her. Ken knew just how painful it was to remember tragic scenes constantly.

"Well, it won't be long until you're home," Ken chirped, attempting to lighten her mood.

Serena appeared to break from her trance and gave a melancholy smile, "You're right, we just have to keep pushing a little further," she said, passing the paper back to him.

Ken felt relieved to see her smile, sad as it may have been, it was still an improvement.

"You said Tim used to be a soldier for the Monarchy, right?" Serena asked.

"Yeah, that's right?" Ken replied, curious about her question.

"What if he's setting us up?" she queried.

"I thought the same thing at first, but I don't believe he would do that. Especially after I helped save his son," Ken answered, wondering what made her ask that. She never seemed to be the pessimistic type before.

"If Tim was with the Monarchy before, this James guy may still be with them," Serena said.

Her words took Ken by surprise. He didn't think about James being part of the Monarchy too. "That's a good point, Serena, but to be honest, I still think we can trust them. So, what gives? You were fine with the change in plans earlier. You didn't even care that it would take longer to get you home. Now you sound like you're afraid that we're walking into a trap?" Ken said, wanting to uncover the motive behind her skepticism.

"I don't know, I guess seeing that wanted poster got me a little stirred up," Serena replied dully.

That makes sense. It's one thing to know someone is looking for you, but it's quite another to feel like the world is out to get you, Ken thought as he put his hand on her head.

"It's not a wanted poster. It's a missing persons picture. If anyone is wanted, then it's me," Ken said lightly. "I should've thought about how seeing that would make you feel. Sometimes I forget how young you are. After all, you're so mature for your age," he added while messing up her hair.

"Hey! You really like doing that, don't you?" Serena said while running ahead of him with a chuckle. She fixed her hair and stayed an arm's length away from Ken so he wouldn't mess it up again. To her, it was like a game.

"How much longer till we get there?" She asked.

"We should be there any minute."

A dark brown wooden building came into view as they rounded a corner. Then they saw another building that looked similar just in front of it. The second one was smaller, so it was safe to assume the first one was the inn and the other was a place to eat.

"Looks like we're here," Ken said as they approached the inn. He scanned around and noticed those were the only two building in the rest area. The space around them was cleared out, but trees decorated the scenery of the outside landscape. He looked for the trail Tim told him about but didn't see it.

"Come on big bro, I'm hungry," Serena said as Ken continued to gaze around.

"Alright let's get a room," he replied.

Once they paid for the room, they didn't waste any time going to check it out. After sleeping outside, in a shed, and in a hospital, they were excited to finally have another room of their own for the night.

"It looks nice," Serena said as she walked in.

The room was small and had a wood floor. You could hear every footstep as she made her way to one of the two beds.

"Is there not a bathroom in here?" Serena asked as she looked around.

"No, remember? The innkeeper said we had to go downstairs," Ken responded.

"I wasn't paying attention," Serena said as she pouted.

"You need to go?" Ken asked.

"Yeah, but I also wanted to change my shirt. This one feels itchy for some reason."

"Has it always been that way?" Ken inquired as he reached into the bag for another shirt.

"No, I think I walked into something. I don't know, but I need to change," Serena said hastily while scratching at her sides.

Ken threw the shirt to her and turned away so she could put it on with privacy. He could hear the wooden floor creak beneath her feet as she got dressed.

Without warning, Serena screeched and threw the shirt down.

"What's wrong!?" Ken asked urgently as he turned around.

Serena was standing in front of the bed shirtless with her back to him. Ken immediately noticed a black design drawn on the center of her back. It had two circles encompassing a diamond in the center. From each point of the diamond a line stretched out and connected the diamond, middle circle, and outer circle. The symbol was the same as the Gate on Ken's hand but without the swords piercing it.

"What the...?" he whispered while gawking.

Serena glanced back at him from the corner of her eyes. "Stop looking at me like that!" she shouted.

Ken's face went red as he turned away. "I wasn't trying to... I mean... I heard you scream...and then—" he continued to stumble on his words as tried to explain himself.

"You can look now," Serena said in an irritated tone.

Ken gazed back at her and saw her holding the other shirt which had some small moving black dots on it.

"I had Itch ants on me. I don't like bugs, so I screamed," Serena said as she threw the shirt at him.

"Itch ants?" Ken asked, unaware of what that actually was.

"You know, Itch ants. They don't bite, but when they walk on you, they feel itchy," Serena replied as if it were common knowledge.

"Oh yeah, of course, Itch ants," Ken said, still not understanding what they were.

"Look I wasn't peeping I just—" Ken hesitated to finish. He didn't know if he should even mention that he saw the mark on her back. Then he realized it could have some connection to the hooded man that put the gate on his hand.

"You just what?" Serena asked impatiently.

"I saw the mark on your back. It caught me off guard." Ken continued as he rubbed the back of his head.

Serena's expression changed from anger to dumbfounded. As if she had forgotten it was there and Ken just reminded her of it, "You haven't seen it before?" she asked.

"Well, I don't normally watch as you change," Ken replied sarcastically.

"Good answer. Did you...see anything else?" Serena asked bashfully.

"No! Of course not! Just the mark on your back I swear!" Ken said defensively.

Geez, she's only ten. It's not like she has anything to hide, Ken thought as he put the shirt down and began to pick off the ants.

"You don't really think I'm like that do you, Serena?" Ken asked.

"No, I was wondering why you kept looking. Now it makes sense that you were staring at the mark," Serena answered.

"What is that anyway?" Ken asked as he checked the shirt for more ants.

"I don't know. I've had it for as long as I can remember," Serena replied.

"You never asked your parents about it?" Ken questioned.

"They always said they would tell me when I'm older," Serena said.

Ken let out a sigh as he finished looking over the shirt, *so much for getting some answers*, he thought. He put the shirt back into the bag and put it on his back. "You ready to eat?" he asked.

"Yeah, why don't you leave the bag here?" Serena queried.

"I would, but I think we should keep anything valuable on us from now on. We are on the run after all. Never know when we might have to take off again," Ken replied, thinking about how they had to retrieve the bag from the hotel in Drez when they left.

"I didn't think about it like that. It's a good idea," Serena responded.

They left the inn and went to the restaurant to eat. When they walked in, they saw five round tables scattered throughout the room with chairs all around them. The tables had candles housed in glass on them. Their footsteps became audible from walking across the wooden floor, same as the hotel room.

Ken looked around and saw a man standing behind the counter with a menu written in chalk on a board.

"Hey big bro, I really have to go to the restroom now," Serena insisted.

"Go ahead, I'll read over the menu while I wait," Ken replied.

Serena darted toward the lady's room. "I may be a while!" she called out as she went in.

Ken chuckled while sitting down, "At least she isn't shy about it," he said as he placed his elbow on the table and propped his cheek on his palm.

He watched as the man behind the counter cleaned off some plates, then his eyes moved up to the board. As he studied it, he heard the door behind him open, *Someone else is here? The place was barren a minute ago,* he thought as looked back.

Ken's eyes widen as he stared at the person walking in. It was a woman wearing white armor with silver trimming. Her hair was white and cut short with the sides shaved down by the ears.

Ken quickly turned back as he felt his heart race. *Don't panic, just act natural,* he thought as he stared back at the menu. He could hear her boots hit the wooden floor as she strolled into the room. Each step grew louder as she approached.

Is she walking up to me? he pondered as his fingers twitched on his face while holding the position he was in before. The sound of her footsteps seemed like she was right next to him as he closed his eyes.

Crap! Was all he could think to say to himself.

The soldier then walked past him and made her way to the counter. Ken opened his eyes again and saw her approach the man behind the booth. He let out a deep breath as his chest tingled from suspense. "I have to cool it. She has no reason to think I've done anything wrong," he said to himself as he let out a few more breaths to calm his nerves.

Serena is in the bathroom, as long as she stays in there, we should be fine. After all, this chick might just be getting some food and taking off, he contemplated as he watched the soldier.

"How are you doing today, Captain Ulgenda? I haven't seen you around here in a long time," the man running the restaurant said as he continued to clean.

"She's a captain!?" Ken said quietly as he sat back in his chair. *I wonder what the rank of that other soldier was. The one I beat up when I found Serena,* he wondered while putting his arm over the back of the chair, attempting to look relaxed.

"I'm here because of this, Derek," the captain said as she handed the clerk a paper.

"A missing girl, eh?" Derek said as he looked over the paper.

Ken's heart sank as he heard the conversation. *We're so screwed!* He tapped his foot as his mind raced nervously.

"I can't say that I've seen her," Derek said as he gave the captain back the paper. "You want to get some food?" he asked.

"No, just trying to find this poor little girl," the captain replied.

She turned around and saw Ken sitting at the table with his arm back as he leaned into the chair, "Well, you look like you're comfy," she said sarcastically as she approached him.

Ken's stomach felt heavy as her footsteps beat down on the floor once more. *I can handle this. It's just like that time I got caught selling Scott's creamy cakes at school. If I just act casual, she'll ask what she wants and then leave,* Ken planned as she approached.

"Care if I join you?" the captain asked as she pulled up a seat.

"Knock yourself out," Ken replied while trying to seem nonchalant.

The captain sat down in a chair next to Ken and then laid the paper out in his view, "You haven't seen this girl around, have you?" she asked, wearing a wicked smile.

Her voice sounded like she was used to being in charge and giving orders. "No, I've never seen her before," he replied calmly.

She let out a sigh as she leaned back in her chair, "It seems my trail went cold then," she said in a disappointed tone.

Ken thought that if he was too distant that she would be suspicious. He argued to himself that he could make conversation with her to get information. At the same time, he didn't know how much longer Serena would be in the bathroom.

"So where are you from?" The captain asked as she grabbed the paper.

Her question stunned Ken. He didn't expect to be asked something like that. "I'm...a traveler," he replied reluctantly. "I've been wandering around since I was a kid," he added.

"That's sad to hear. No family or friends?" The captain asked as her eyes moved to Ken's hands.

He quickly placed them behind his head as if lying back on them. He remembered how Tim looked at the gloves and was worried she would want to see what was under them.

"No, my parents are long gone, and it's hard to keep friends when you're always running around," Ken replied. "I hate to hear that your trail went cold. She looks so innocent in that picture. I can't imagine a little a girl being out on her own like that," Ken said, trying to change the subject.

"Yeah, it caught me by surprise," the captain said as she peered over to Derek. "Bring me two waters please," she called out to him.

"I had a good lead for a while," she said as she turned back to Ken. "By the way, my name is Captain Ulgenda. Commander of the Retrievement Team," she stated as she held her hand out.

Ken hesitated to grab it but knew he had to play along. He shook it and put his hands back behind his head and waited for her to continue.

"I had good information on the girl when my team found one of our soldiers knocked out in the woods. He said he couldn't remember much. Yet he did recall that he saw her with a man that was described in the poster," Ulgenda said.

Ken assumed that was the guy he fought when he ran into Serena for the first time.

"Several people in Drez saw the little girl accompanied by this man. Only his hair seemed to be cut at this point," Ulgenda added as Derek gave her the waters. She passed one over to Ken.

"Thank you," he said lightly.

"After that, we came across a few people in this small town we that said they saw her and that guy," Ulgenda continued.

Ken felt his stomach churn anxiously as she spoke, *Tim didn't sell us out, did he?* he wondered while trying to maintain his composure.

"Someone said they were staying with a family in the woods, so I just had to pay them a visit," Ulgenda said as she started to smile.

Her grin made Ken feel uneasy.

"Of course, these people acted like they never saw them before, but I knew they were lying," she said as her eyes narrowed. "I think when I catch the guy who kidnapped that sweet little girl, I'll get him to confess. Then I'll arrest all the adults in that family," she sneered as she took a sip from the cup.

Ken didn't like hearing her say that, but he knew he had to keep focused. Doing something stupid now would cause a lot of trouble.

"I've rather enjoyed our chat. What's your name?" Ulgenda asked while crossing her legs to get more comfortable.

"I'm Ken," he replied. Instantly regretting what he just said. *Damnit, why didn't I make up a name!* he screamed at himself internally.

"You know you don't have to be so nervous around me Ken," Ulgenda said seductively.

Ken felt his guts quiver from her statement. *She thinks I look nervous?*

"I mean I understand why you would be nervous," the captain stated as she leaned in toward Ken, hovering inches away from his ear as he sat completely still. "I am a gorgeous, strong, intimidating woman after all," she added in a heated tone.

Ken stayed seated as his eyes darted back and forth, unsure of how to react to that. Then Ulgenda laughed as she leaned back once more, "I'm only messing with you, lighten up a little!" she thundered while smacking Ken on the back.

Suddenly, they heard a light creak from a door just to their left. Serena stepped out the bathroom and called out to Ken, "Sorry I took so long. What are we…?"

Serena's mouth fell open midsentence when she saw Ulgenda.

Ken saw the terror in her eyes as she stared at the captain. He quickly got up and moved over to her. Attempting to get between their views of each other. Ken's heart fluttered once more with anxiety, but he tried to calm himself down as he remembered that Serena's hair was cut and dyed. *Maybe the Captain won't recognize Serena,* Ken hoped as he took Serena's hand.

"Who might this be!?" Ulgenda called out as he walked away with Serena in tow.

"Don't look at her and leave the talking to me," Ken whispered as Serena gazed up at him. She was pale and absolutely traumatized.

"She's my little sister. I was waiting for her to use the bathroom since our room doesn't have one. Unfortunately, it's past her bedtime so we need to get going," Ken said as he rushed to the door.

Ulgenda stood up from her chair with eyes pressed on Serena, "I thought you didn't have any family?" she asked curiously.

"I said my parents were gone, I never said anything about having siblings," Ken retorted, hoping she would drop it.

"I see, my mistake," Ulgenda said as she cut a smile.

Ken turned away and pulled Serena's arm to start walking again. He could feel her hand tremoring as they moved. Then Ken heard a familiar sound coming from behind them. He glanced down at one of the glass encasements around a candle and saw a light shining from the captain's hand as she threw her arm out.

Ken instantly reacted by pulling Serena behind him. He turned and activated the Gate on his left hand. Hastily, he reached inside the circle of light it created and pulled out his sword. Just as he got it, Ulgenda flailed her steel whip at Ken as it flowed out of her Gate like a snake thrashing about.

Ken used the flat width of his sword to block the whip at the last second. The sound of metal smashing metal rang throughout the room as Ulgenda rushed at Ken while pulling her whip back.

"You were obvious from the start!" she yelled viciously as she jumped at him with a wild and dangerous grin.

Ken quickly dropped to one knee and held out his left palm. Then he released a pressure blast as she closed the gap. With a loud bang, he fired his attack off at her abdomen, sending her flying back over the counter where Derek hid for cover.

Damn, I fired too early. If she got just a little bit closer that would've really messed her up, Ken thought as he stared over where she fell.

"Let's go, Ken! Serena yelled as she pulled his arm.

They ran out of the restaurant to find it was dark outside. The moon was shining brightly as they scampered, giving them some light to go by.

"Stop right there!" Two Monarchy soldiers yelled as they approached them. One held a medieval English looking broadsword, while the other wielded a military-like saber.

Ken reached in his pocket and grabbed one of the bags with metal ball bearings in it. He held it up in the palm of his left hand and then fired another pressure blast, sending the metal balls rocketing at them. As the balls hit their armor, a loud ping echoed out from the attack on the soldiers. Both of which fell on the ground grasping their face and sides while yelling out in pain.

Ken and Serena ran north into woods. As they raced, Ken scanned the area for more troops but saw none. He powered through the branches and twigs as they smacked and slapped him.

Ulgenda hastily limped out of the restaurant while grabbing her stomach. She hobbled over to her men who were laying on the ground, still gripping their faces.

"Where did they go!" she barked, hovering over them while still holding her mid torso.

"I don't know!" One of them cried out.

"He blasted our faces! We couldn't see a thing!' The other one bellowed.

Ulgenda gritted her teeth as she yelled out in anger, causing her to fall to her knees from the pain in her stomach.

"You useless scumbags call yourselves soldiers!?" she bellowed as she took slow deep breaths.

"We didn't know he had a Gate power, Captain," one of them replied. "Should we send word for reinforcements?" he asked.

"Are you a complete idiot!?" Ulgenda shouted as she struggled to stand. "It's one guy and a ten-year-old girl. You want me to tell my superiors that a Captain and two Lieutenants lost to one man!?" she screeched furiously. "We will handle this ourselves. I won't be the laughingstock of the entire Monarchy!"

"How are we supposed to find them if we don't even know which way they went?" one of the soldiers asked as he looked at the palm of his hand for blood.

Ulgenda reared her leg back as if she were going to kick him but then put it back down. "We found them after looking this long. It won't take much to find them again." She gargled and spit a glob of blood down in front of her subordinate. "I will not be outdone by my brother any longer," she said crossly

Ken and Serena continued to run blindly through the woods until Serena tripped and fell.
"Serena! Are you okay?" Ken asked as he helped her up.
Serena panted violently as she sat up and propped herself against a tree. "I'm too tired," she said between breaths.
Ken sat down next to her, breathing heavily as well. "I don't think they followed us," he said.
They sat for a moment as they recovered.
"That woman, she's the one who attacked my family and took me from my home," Serena said as she teared up.
Ken moved over and leaned his back against the tree with her. Then he put his arm around her shoulders to comfort her.
Serena moved in closer and placed her head on Ken's chest as she cried.
"If I knew that, I would've hit her twice as hard," Ken said lightly, trying to cheer her up.
"She attacked my mom and dad. She hurt them so bad Ken! To be honest I…I…I don't even know if they're still alive!" Serena bellowed as she cried harder into his chest.
Ken was shocked to hear her say that after she talked so much about seeing them again. He wondered if that had crossed her mind before, but never wanted to ask her outright. He wrapped both his arms around her tightly as she continued to cry. He could feel her pop up between breaths as she gripped his shirt and buried her face into his torso.
Ken's eyes started to well up also, just from haring her despair. It broke his heart to hear her talk about her parents possibly being dead. As if she was giving up on everything they were working towards. He wanted to tell her what Tim said but hearing her this

upset made him decide that he couldn't. Besides, she already realized that it could've happened. That was the only point there was in telling her in the first place. To help her prepare for it, just in case. Of course, as he knew better than anyone. There was no real way to be prepared for that kind of news.

Ken held her tight as she continued to cry, "I can't say I know if they are okay or not Serena, but I can promise you that I'll take you home no matter what. I can promise that we will we find them together and that I will be with you every step of the way. Just like a big brother should," he said as he wiped a tear from his own eye.

Serena switched from gripping his shirt to hugging him back, "Thank you, big bro," she said as she sniffled.

Ken continued to hold her as the night went on. Soon she stopped crying and fell asleep on him. He felt sad for her, and for everything she was going through. Then he thought about the marking on her back and the hooded man who put the Gate on his hand. *Why doesn't he help her? Why did he want me to watch over her instead of just protecting her himself? If he can create portals and make these Gates, then he should be powerful enough to keep her safe,* Ken wondered as he looked up into the starry night's sky through the branches. *One thing is for sure, he's got a lot of explaining to do when I find him.*

Chapter 14

Daemon Grimshear

Ken awoke the next morning with Serena's head laying on his lap. She was sound asleep and seemed comfortable using him as a pillow. The sound of chirping and fluttering wings filled the air as birds flew from tree to tree around them. The sun peered through the branches above and Ken felt the warmth of its light on his skin.

Ken let out a long yawn as he stretched his arms while trying not to wake Serena. He stayed up most the night, listening to the sounds of owls and other random creatures howling and hooting. He was prepared to escape with Serena in case Captain Ulgenda picked up their trail during the evening. He guessed that he got two hours of sleep altogether.

Serena stirred and rolled her head around on Ken's thighs. Then she sat up while rubbing her eyes.

Ken stood up from the tree and felt a slight pain run down his back. The tree's unforgiving bark did not make for a comfortable bed. Ken didn't move from his place the entire night though since Serena was sleeping so securely.

Ken reached down and touched his toes causing his back pop and crackle. He continued to do a series of different stretches to loosen his stiff muscles.

Serena sat silently and watched as Ken was doing his morning exercise. After he finished, he looked back at her and saw she had a few scratches on her face and arms from the branches smacking her as they ran. Then he searched himself and found far more scraps and cuts on his body. It was inevitable since he ran in front of her while pulling her arm.

"Are you okay?" Ken asked in a light tone.

Serena only nodded for her reply. Her expression was despondent and listless.

"I'm sorry you got scratched up," Ken said while continuing to stretch.

"It's alright. Why didn't you use your sword to cut the branches down," Serena asked while pointing at Ken's Soul Wielding weapon. It was laying on the ground next to the tree where they slept.

Ken forgot that he even laid it there, "It would've taken longer to cut through the branches. Not to mention it would have made a trail for them to follow us," he said as he threw a few light kicks into the air.

Serena glanced off to side, "I didn't think about it like that," she said dully.

Ken wanted to take credit for that stroke of genius, but he got the idea from watching investigator shows when he was on Earth.

Serena's stomach growled as Ken continued to stretch and practice.

"I guess we didn't get anything to eat last night, did we?" Ken said while rubbing his own stomach.

Serena let out a sigh with a worried grimace, "Are we going to be okay?"

Ken stopped practicing and walked over to the bag which laid by his sword. He pulled out the map and laid it on the ground, "Yeah, we'll be fine. We just need to go see that James guy. He can help us find a route to your home," he said while scanning over the map.

"You're still taking me home? After all that?" Serena asked.

"Of course, I am! I made you a promise, didn't I?" Ken answered while focusing on the map.

"But what about the Monarchy soldiers that are after us?" Serena inquired while approaching him.

"We always knew they were after us. The only difference now is that they've found us," Ken replied. "I still believe James can help us though, so, I'm not going to worry until I hear what he has to say."

Serena was staggered from what Ken said. This run-in with the Monarchy made her feel hopeless. Yet Ken made her feel optimistic again with his positive outlook.

"Thank you, big bro," she said as she hugged him from behind.

Ken smiled and patted her arm. Then he rolled up the map and put it back in the bag.

"We couldn't find the trail that Tim told me about. However, we still managed to run north toward Vorit, like he said. I'll bet if we keep going this way, we'll find it," Ken said while making his Gate glow. Suddenly, his sword dissipated into yellow sparks of light.

"Why did you get rid of your sword?" Serena asked curiously.

"Having a sword on my back may look suspicious to some people. I'll just summon it again if we need to," Ken answered.

Serena's stomach growled once more.

Ken chuckled as he started to walk with her at his side. "Hopefully this James guy will have some food at his place," he said.

"Yeah, I'm starving. Do you think they're out here looking for us?" Serena asked, referring to the soldiers they bumped into the night prior.

"Yeah, I'm sure they are," Ken replied.

"What if they called for more soldiers?" Serena said in a concerned tone.

"Don't worry about it, everything will be alright once we talk to James. Until then you just need to relax. Upsetting yourself over the details won't do you any good," Ken replied.

Inside, Ken was also worried about the same things. However, he knew it was pointless to run through those scenarios over and over in his head. He also didn't want Serena to get distressed any more than she already was.

"Besides, one of those soldiers I beat up was a Captain! It didn't take much for me to handle her," Ken said with a confident flair. "I doubt they have anyone who can handle me," he added while winking at Serena.

Serena merely rolled her eyes with a smile.

As Ken pushed a branch back, a small town came into view. They both grinned excitedly as they gazed around. The area looked like a ghost town. Many on the houses and building were collapsed or missing parts of the walls or windows. The land around them was overgrown with grass and weeds in some spots, while it was barren and dusty in others.

"I don't think anyone lives here," Serena said as they stepped out of the woods.

As Ken scanned the area, he saw one building that was intact. It was made of dark wood and shaped like a barn. Ken thought it resembled a bar from an old western movie or T.V. show. It was the only place that wasn't falling apart. "That must be it," Ken said.

They walked to the door cautiously while checking the area around them. They noticed there was no sign of life anywhere in the town. Not even so much as a stray animal.

They opened the bar and walked in slowly. There were a few tables scattered around the expanse with chairs at them. A counter stood at the back of the room with bar stools lining the front of it. It appeared dim and dank inside. The only lighting was that which came in through the windows that surrounded the bar. Dust sat on top of many of the chairs and tables.

They made their way to the counter, which was suspiciously clean, along with the bar stools. Meaning someone must have been there to wipe them down.

Suddenly, a door to the left behind the counter opened. An older looking bald man walked up to the counter with a scowl on his face. He wore a light blue apron and was holding a cup. He noticed Ken and Serena, and he became flabbergasted.

"I'll be damned, they're customers in my bar," he said in a raspy tone as he approached them from the behind the counter. He gazed over at Serena and let out a long-drawn-out breath, "No children allowed in here buddy," he said in an irritable way.

"Can I get my sister some food and water? She hasn't eaten in a while," Ken replied, ignoring the comment.

The man glared at them for a moment and then sucked his teeth. "Fine!" he answered. He turned around and began preparing two sandwiches.

"Is your name James?" Ken asked as the man worked.

"Who's asking?" the man replied gruffly.

"A friend of yours sent us here. Tim Rumph," Ken said as the barkeep placed a sandwich in front of him and Serena.

Ken pulled out a few coins and gave them to the man. The bartender raised his eyebrows as he pocketed the money. "I wasn't going to charge you that much for two sandwiches and water," he said as he leaned back against the counter behind him. Then he crossed his arms and watched as they ate. "So, Tim sent you here, eh?" How's he doing?"

Ken explained what happened with the gang and how they saved the children.

"Sounds like quite the tale," the barkeep replied in an unenthusiastic tone.

"Well anyway, Tim sent us here and said James would be able to help me get my sister home," Ken said while finishing the sandwich.

"Where you headed to?" the man asked.

"I'm taking her back to Sales," Ken answered reluctantly. He had a feeling even mentioning Serena's hometown would stir trouble.

The man shook his head while grabbing the dirty dishes from them, "Yeah, my name is James," he said as he cleaned them off. "Let me guess, that little girl's name is Serena isn't it?"

Ken and Serena both gaped at his statement.

"You know me?" Serena asked.

"No, I don't," he said as he pointed to the wall on his right.

Ken and Serena both gazed over and saw the missing person paper with Serena's face on it. Serena put her hands to her mouth as she gasped while Ken blew through his teeth out loud.

"Don't worry, I'm not turning you in or anything," James said as he finished cleaning the plates. "However, I am telling you to get the hell out of my bar," he said, frankly.

Ken stood from his stool and slammed his fist down on the counter. Serena jumped from his sudden outburst. "Look, I'm trying to take my little sister home, and you're the only one who can tell me the best route to get there without crossing Monarchy territory!" Ken shouted.

"Who do you think I am! A magic genie? You think I can give you all the answers just like that!?" James yelled. "Listen here, buddy; you're wasting your time trying to take her home. There is nothing left there! The place was destroyed in the battle!"

"That's not true!" Serena bellowed.

The room fell silent as everyone gazed around at each other. James let out a sigh and rubbed his eyes with his index finger and his thumb. "It's like I said, the place is destroyed. Besides, if you go there, you'll almost certainly be caught. That's the first place they'll think to look for her," he said as the tension in the room lightened.

"I don't care," Ken replied. "If there's even a slight chance I can reunite her with her family, then I'm going to try!"

James raised his eyes skeptically, "Why? Why are you trying so hard to help this girl? I know she's not really your sister. So why are you helping her? Why make yourself an enemy of the Monarchy by fighting them just to take her home?" he asked while tugging at his chin.

Serena looked up at Ken anxiously. She too had wondered why Ken just decided he would help her as much as he had.

Ken didn't want to tell them that the hooded man sent him on this journey. Mainly because that wasn't his reason. Originally, he did it solely for that purpose. Yet, when he found Serena, he gained a new motivation. One stronger than just doing what he was told.

"I do it because she's just like me," Ken said in a somber tone. "She was lost and alone when I found her. Her whole world crashed down around her, and she had no one to turn to. That's a feeling I'll never forget. It's a feeling someone as young and innocent as she is, doesn't deserve to experience," he said as his voice cracked.

Serena put her hand on his to help him calm down.

James stared at Ken for a moment with a serious expression. Then closed his eyes and turned his head away.

"It's a sweet story buddy, but I've heard many of them in this place, so my answer is the same. Go away! I can't have the Monarchy knocking on my door."

"What stories have you heard!? There is no one here! Who comes out to an abandoned town to drink at a bar run by a grumpy old man!? Ken yelled furiously at James.

James's face changed back to its scowl. He opened his mouth to yell back at Ken, but the door leading outside opened behind them. As James stared at the person walking in, his expression went from being irritated to utter shock.

Ken noticed the change in James's appearance and felt his stomach do a flip as he heard footsteps against the hardwood floor approach them. It was déjà vu for him, like when Captain Ulgenda walked into the restaurant the night before.

Ken slowly turned his head back to see who was approaching them. It was a daunting man, standing over six feet tall. His body was covered in what appeared to be black tights from head to toe. He had black metal bracings around his forearms and the outsides of his biceps like an armor. His chest and legs also had chunks of black steel covering specific areas of them, like his thighs, shins, and upper torso. The most peculiar thing about him was that he wore a thin black metal mask that had cut outs for the eyes and small vertical slits over the mouth. Written over each piece of metal was a red circular symbol that was the same as the one on Serena's back. There was even a red symbol on the forehead of his mask.

The man sat down on the stool to Ken's right without even looking his way.

"I never thought I would see the great General Daemon Grimshear walk into my bar again," James said as he placed a cup in front of the stranger.

Ken jumped back and pulled Serena behind him, "He's a General!?"

"Give me the usual," the man said. His voice was so deep that it reverberated in Ken's chest. "Don't call me that again either. I renounced that name a long time ago," Daemon added as James poured a dark brown liquid into his cup. Daemon reached for his mask and popped a latch that was under his chin. He turned his head away from Ken and lifted the mouthpiece and drank.

James averted his eyes from Daemon as he finished his cup. Then

Daemon closed the mouthpiece and held his finger up for another drink.

Ken couldn't help but gawk at him in silence.

Daemon turned his attention to him and stared back as James refilled his cup. He glared into Ken's green eyes with his, which were a deep brown. As they exchanged looks, Ken could see a fire in Daemon's eyes. As though determined to accomplish something. Yet, they also appeared cold and piercing, like he was looking through Ken and not at him. They said nothing to each other as they stared.

Once James finished filling his cup, Daemon grabbed it without breaking his attention from Ken. Then he popped his mouthpiece once more. He turned away and drank his second cup and closed the mask again.

"Why don't you kick this guy out of here for me Daemon. I won't charge you for your drinks if you do," James said as he grabbed the bottle once more.

Ken cut a wrathful look at James for his statement.

James returned it to him without hesitation.

"That's not my problem," Daemon replied casually.

"Come on Daemon," James pleaded.

Ken kicked a table that was to his right to get their attention. "I'm not leaving until someone tells me how to get by the Monarchy!" he bellowed.

"You want to keep it down? I'm not in the best mood," Daemon said nonchalantly.

Ken gritted his teeth as he became fed-up with the entire situation. He held his left hand over his chest and activated his Gate. It started to glow from under his glove as he prepared to summon his sword.

Both James and Daemon looked unimpressed, as though the concept of a Soul wielder was nothing new to them. However, James's mouth quickly fell open as he noticed the design of the Gate, "Do you see that!?" he asked Daemon.

Even Daemon's eyes widened noticeably from behind his mask. He instantly grabbed Ken's hand with the speed of a striking snake

Angeon Broken Promises

and pulled Ken in close, interrupting him from summoning his sword.

"Hey!" Ken yelled out as he almost fell over from the force.

Daemon yanked the glove off Ken's hand to get a better look at his Gate. Ken tried to snatch away, but Daemon's grip only tightened. "Calm down kid, I'm not going to hurt you. I just want a better look," Daemon said while scanning over the Gate on Ken's hand. Even James leaned over the counter in awe of it.

"What is it?" Ken said uneasily. He didn't know if he wanted to hit the guy in the head for pulling him around or hear what was so special about his Gate.

"I've never seen one like that before," James said as he stared at it.

"Me neither. It doesn't make sense," Daemon replied while holding Ken's hand up to his face.

"Can someone please tell me what's going on with my own damn hand!?" Ken cried irritably.

Daemon let it go as Ken pulled away, "Does it really work?" he asked.

"You're ignoring me just to piss me off, aren't you?" Ken replied.

"If your Gate works, I'll answer your question about getting by the Monarchy. I'll also tell you what's so special about your Gate," Daemon said, bypassing Ken's statement.

Ken put his hand back over his chest while activating the Gate again. "It's a deal. Although, I was going to use it anyway," he said as he held his arm out to his left side and extended his fingertips. A circle of light with the same design as his Gate hovered in front of his hand, then he reached inside and pulled out his sword.

"It really works!" James expressed.

The Gate faded from the air, and Ken stood with his sword in hand. "Now tell me, what is so special about my Gate!?" Ken demanded.

"It's because of the outside design on it," Daemon answered. "A Gate must be surrounded by a solid outer circle to work. However, yours has a design that breaks the circle. Which means the Gate should not function."

Ken looked over the Gate on his hand, then stared back at Daemon, "Alright, what's so significant about that?"

Daemon shook his head and shrugged his shoulders, "To give you a comparison, it's like starting a fire under water. Something that should be impossible," he answered.

Ken placed the sword on his back and had a seat on one of the stools, "Okay, well the Gate thing makes no difference to me. Now tell me how to bypass the Monarchy to get to Sales," he said impatiently.

Daemon crossed his arms and sat back on the stool for a moment. He seemed like he was trying to decide if he should tell him or not. "Are you prepared to die?" he asked, breaking the silence.

Ken was taken back by his statement. "What do you mean?"

"You've already made yourself an enemy of the Monarchy by attacking one of their soldiers. If you go any further, they won't show any mercy to you next time you run into them," Daemon said in serious tone.

Ken shrugged his shoulders arrogantly. He assumed Daemon read the missing person poster to know that he fought with a soldier. "It's too late for that talk. I beat up three soldiers yesterday. One of them was a captain," Ken said while chuckling.

"You're full of crap!" James said in disbelief.

Ken glared at him from the corner of his eye. "It's true, her name was Ulgenda."

Daemon perked up at the name, "Ulgenda? You don't say!?" he said curiously. "Did you kill her?"

Ken turned his attention back at Daemon and shook his head. "No, of course not," he answered.

"Then you're going to get yourself and that little girl killed if you keep going like this," Daemon replied coldly.

Ken gave another cross glare at him, "Look, you promised to tell me how to get by the Monarchy. So just tell me already," Ken said boldly.

"Big bro, let's just leave," Serena said with a troubled expression as she pulled Ken's arm.

"Not yet, Serena," he replied callously.

"I don't like how you're acting right now. It's scaring me. This isn't you," Serena argued while attempting to get his attention.

Ken broke from his arrogant attitude as he turned to her. He took hold of her hand and stared into her eyes, seeing worry and fear in them. "I'm sorry Serena. You're right, we need to leave," he said as he calmed down.

"Not so fast," Daemon stated as he stood from his chair. "Are you still going to take her home?"

"Yes, I am," Ken replied.

"I can't stand by and do nothing as you walk that girl into danger," Daemon answered.

"It doesn't matter what we do. The Monarchy is after her. She'll be in danger no matter where we go," Ken retorted.

"Then I'll make you a new deal. We'll go out back and have a fight. If you win, I'll tell you the best route to take to get her home," Daemon declared.

Ken stared at him with intrigue, "Yeah well, I'm currently not a fan of your deals. Especially since you don't keep them. Besides, what's in it for you?"

"If I win, I take the girl with me," Daemon replied.

Ken huffed at Daemon's proposal, "I'm not using my sister as a bargaining chip," he answered heatedly.

"Come on Serena," Ken said, pulling her arm as they moved toward the door.

"I can tell you how to use your Gate better, and help you fix your sword," Daemon called out to him.

"What's wrong with my sword?" Ken asked, glancing back over his shoulder.

"I'll tell you when you accept my challenge," Daemon responded.

Ken shook his head and walked toward the door once more.

"I can tell you who put the Gate on your hand!" Daemon said confidently.

Ken stopped progressing and stood still in front of the door, "How do you know?"

"Because, the outer circle may be different, but the main Gate design is the same one somebody I know uses," Daemon answered while folding his arms.

Ken looked back at him once more with a doubtful stare, "How do you know someone didn't copy his design?"

"Sage's Gate designs are unique to each Sage. None of them has the same one. I can't say why it breaks the outer circle the way it does, but there's no mistaking the rest of it," Daemon affirmed.

Ken desperately wanted to know who brought him to this world and gave him the power to Soul wield. Yet, putting a bet on Serena was something he could not accept.

"Do it, big bro," Serena whispered from behind him.

"What!? No way, I can't do that," Ken replied.

"It's our best chance to find a safe way home. Besides, you look like you really want to know," Serena said while placing her fingertips on Ken's Gate.

"I won't use you to bet with, Serena!" Ken stated.

"Well, I believe you can take this guy. After all the fights I've seen you in so far, I know there's no way you can lose," she replied while winking at him.

Ken stayed motionless, contemplating what to do, "Are you sure?"

"I am, I know you'll win," Serena answered confidently.

Ken felt a new strength rise in him from Serena's fidelity. "If you believe in me, then I guess I'll just have to win," he said as he smiled at her.

"Alright, Daemon let's do this," Ken stated with a cocky grin.

"Great, meet me behind the bar then. We will start immediately," Daemon replied.

Ken and Serena made their way out the front and started to walk around the side of the building. "I'm surprised you wanted me to do this Serena. Just a minute ago you wanted to leave. Now you want me to fight. What's up with that?" Ken asked.

"You weren't acting like yourself. You were really mean and demanding," Serena answered. "But when he offered to tell us all that stuff, I thought we needed to at least try. Besides, on the off chance you do lose, we can just run away," Serena said.

Ken chuckled, "Where's all that faith you had in me?" he said jokingly.

"I said the off chance you lose. I still believe you'll win. Although, a backup plan is always a good idea," Serena stated.

"You're incredibly smart, you know that?" Ken responded while rubbing the hair on her head.

"Stop doing that!" Serena cried out through a giggle.

As they rounded the corner behind the bar, they saw Daemon was already standing outside waiting for them.

"You could've just used the back door," he said as they approached.

"You could've told us that earlier," Ken replied mockingly.

James was sitting in a chair just behind the bar. He had an extra one out for Serena. She sat down and gave Ken a thumb up, "You can do this big bro," she shouted.

Ken smirked back at her and gave a thumb up as well, then walked over to where Daemon was. "So, what are the rules? Since you're unarmed, I assume it's no weapons, right?" Ken asked while grabbing his sword from his back.

Daemon tilted his head curiously, "Who said I was unarmed?"

Daemon tightened his right fist, causing a Gate on it to glow through the tights and black metal that covered it. The Gate he projected was the same one that covered his armor and the same as the symbol on Serena's back. He flicked his wrist, and the Gate opened beside him. It moved down his arm on its own and quickly shot away to reveal Daemon's massive sword. He slammed it to the ground and stood firmly beside it.

Ken gawked at its immense size. The blade alone appeared to four feet tall and more than a foot wide. That wasn't including the hilt, which added at least another two feet. The sword's texture was rock-like with a rough exterior. The general color of it was dark grey. What really impressed Ken was that it had cracks that ran all throughout it which glowed a bright red-orange as if the inside of his blade had incandescent lava coursing inside it. It even seemed like the light in the cracks was moving, like blood flowing through veins.

"You're a Soul wielder. And that sword is incredible." Ken muttered. "Wait, how did you make your Gate do that? I thought you had to hold it over your chest and do all that other crap?"

Daemon picked up the sword and laid it across his shoulder, "That's because I control the Gate, it doesn't control me," he replied smugly. "As for the rules, there are none. We just fight, that's it. I like to keep things simple."

Ken bit down on his bottom lip, "We're just going to swing swords at each other? What if one of us gets sliced?"

"What's wrong? You were quick to draw your sword in the bar; now suddenly you're scared to fight?" Daemon said tauntingly.

Ken glared at Daemon as his expression turned heated. His body trembled as he gazed at his opponent. Something about him made Ken feel uneasy. His sword, his armor, and even his stature were intimidating. *Why am I so afraid to fight?* he wondered as he tried to move his legs.

"Any day now!" Daemon called out to him.

Ken tightened his grip on his sword and held it ready. "I have to do this. I have to fight for Serena," he said to himself as he ran forward at Daemon.

Ken reared his sword back as he charged. He then swung his blade with all his might.

Daemon simply caught Ken's sword with the side of his own, then quickly parried it away, causing Ken's blade to fly from his hands.

Ken's sword landed too far away for him to turn around and pick it up. He jumped back to get out of Daemon's range and racked his mind for another plan of attack.

He's way too strong, Ken thought as his body shook even more.

Daemon placed his sword on his back again, then turned his attention to Serena, "Alright then, I guess you're coming with me," he claimed.

"What are you talking about? This fight is just getting started!" Ken yelled.

Daemon eyed him crossly, "No, you're too afraid to fight. You may think you came at me strong, but I could see the fear in your eyes a mile away," he stated.

"I'm not giving up!" Ken cried out to him.

"Then fight me for real! If you come at me half-assed like that one more time, I'm taking the girl and leaving!" Daemon barked.

Ken activated the Gate on his hand to summon his sword once more.

"Don't do it like that!" Daemon yelled out. "You'll just waste energy summoning your sword repeatedly. Call it to you."

Ken gave him a bewildered look. "Call it?"

"Your sword is a part of your soul. You already know you can place it on your back and it will stick to you on its own. The concept is the same, just at a distance. Think about it being a magnet," Daemon replied.

Ken looked to his sword curiously. Then he held out his hand to it, "Come back to me," he whispered as he focused on it.

The blade slid across the ground and flew into the air and landed firmly in his hand, "No way!" Ken shouted after catching it.

"Ken, look out!" Serena yelled.

Daemon rushed at Ken with his sword held over his head, ready to smash it down.

Ken swiftly jumped to the side as Daemon's sword crashed into the ground where he was just standing.

Ken didn't waste any time. He swung his blade back a Daemon who blocked it with his sword once again.

With their blades locked against each other, Daemon tried to fling Ken's sword from his hands as he did before with a parry. However, Ken used the force of Daemon's swing as momentum to spin around and slash at his opponent's torso.

Daemon reacted by using the hilt of his sword to block Ken's attack.

"Dang!" Ken yelled as their weapons rung from the clash.

Ken immediately raised his leg to kick Daemon away, but Daemon used his free hand to snatch Ken by his shirt before he could execute his attack. Then he threw Ken over his shoulder.

Ken rolled on the ground and stood back up instantly while trying to get his footing.

"You did better that time, but you lack direction," Daemon stated.

"I'm just warming up," Ken replied as he readied his sword.

"That's not what I mean. I'm saying your entire life lacks direction," Daemon added as he placed the tip of his sword in the ground.

Ken gazed at him strangely, "What do you mean my entire life? You don't know anything about me!" he bellowed.

Daemon pointed at Ken's sword, "I can tell everything I need to know about you by looking at your soul," he said. "Your sword is mostly black, meaning you are depressed or sad about something. Typically, it's due to a loved one's death. Of course, that's not always the case. However, the two holes above your hilt tell me you morn for two loved ones," Daemon said casually.

Ken gave him a scolding gaze, but Daemon pursued the conservation.

"The silver edge along the blade represents a sense of justice and righteous acts. Although, it can also mean irrational bravery or arrogance, which can be dangerous," he added.

"Does it also predict my future?" Ken replied cynically.

Daemon merely kept talking, ignoring Ken's remark, "The most telling feature of it though is the shape of your sword. It's wavy and unbalanced. This signifies someone who is lost and has no true purpose," he stated in a grim tone.

"Well, that makes no sense. I have a clear goal in mind. To take Serena home and reunite her with her family," Ken answered with fortitude.

"Yes, you have a goal, but you still don't have a purpose," Daemon said. "What happens after that? What will you do if she is reunited with her parents?"

His question rattled Ken. He never took the time to consider what would happen afterward. They played with the idea of him staying with her family, but he honestly didn't know what he would do after everything was said and done.

"I...I don't know," Ken replied reluctantly.

"You act like you're trying to take her home. As if she needs you, but I believe you need her more," Daemon said in a matter of fact like manner.

Ken stood in silence as he contemplated what Daemon was saying. It was all true to him. He really did need Serena. Everything he did was for her. As though he used her as his purpose to keep going.

Ken's appearance went bleak as reality set in. He fell to his knees, wondering what he was really doing all this for. Was it truly for Serena? Or maybe it was for the hooded man. He even came to think that he did it just because he had nothing better to do in this new world.

"Don't listen to him, big bro!" Serena yelled out to Ken as she stood from her chair. "He's just trying to confuse you!"

Ken gazed at her drearily.

"You have a purpose! You saved me! I was lost and alone before you found me! I didn't have a purpose either, but when you showed up and protected me from that soldier – I gained a new hope! It was you! You became my purpose to keep going Ken!" Serena cried out to him.

Ken stared at Serena, "Do you mean that?"

"That's why I call you my big brother, Ken! Because that's what you are! You're my big brother, and I'm your little sister! We're a family now! Nothing can change that!" Serena shouted.

Ken felt a fire overtake his chest. As though something filled a void that he had forgotten about. A burden he carried without knowing. "You're right Serena! We are family now!" he said proudly as he got back on his feet. "You want to know my purpose, Daemon?" Ken said as his sword began to glow in a yellow light. "It's to protect my little sister. Even when I do get her home to her family. It doesn't mean she'll be safe. The Monarchy will still be after her, and she'll still need her big brother to protect her," he shouted as the glowing became more intense. "My purpose is clear! I'll protect Serena with everything I am!" Ken yelled as his sword changed its form in the all-consuming light.

It went from its curvy shape to a straight edge all the way down the hilt. The back of it was still flat and black, but the silver that covered the edge of the blade now took over half of the sword. It was just as long as it was before, standing at four feet tall including the handle. However, it was now a solid five inches thick all the way up to the tip where it curved back to a point. It did still hold the two holes above the hilt in the same manner it did before.

"So, you're staking your entire purpose on the girl?" Daemon said shoddily. "That's a dangerous route to go."

Ken gazed at him for a moment. Only seconds ago, he would've argued that remark, but he had a different approach for Daemon this time. He turned his attention to Daemon's sword which stood in the ground.

"What is your purpose, Daemon? What kind of path made that sword?"

Daemon grabbed the hilt of his weapon and held it up, "I chose the same road you just did. To protect someone precious to me, but then I lost everything. Now my purpose is no longer so noble, but it is simple. This sword reflects a sole intent. Revenge." Daemon held the sword up high. "Protecting someone is all fine and dandy, but what happens if you fail to protect that person? What will you do then?" he said darkly.

Ken didn't hesitate to raise his sword high as well, "That won't happen! I'll become strong enough to keep her safe from anyone!" he replied with great devotion in his voice.

"Prove it then!" Daemon demanded.

Ken gave an intense look, as though prepared to fight to his fullest. He chambered his new sword to his side and then charged at Daemon with a battle cry.

Daemon also dashed at Ken with his sword ready for combat. They met in the middle and clashed swords. The blades rang out as they smashed together in war.

"You can do it, big bro!" Serena yelled as they fought.

Ken grinned confidently as he held his sword against Daemon's, who pushed against it with his, trying to gain the upper hand. Ken pushed back to equal his force as they held a stalemate.

"You can't match my strength," Daemon said as he felt Ken push.

"I'm not trying to!" Ken cried as he rapidly dropped to a low stance.

Daemon staggered forward when Ken's weight vanished. He tried desperately to regain his balance since all his mass was on Ken's sword.

Ken didn't waste this chance as he shot his leg between Daemon's feet and then used his shoulder to push him back. Daemon tripped over Ken's leg as he stepped back and fell to the ground. Then Ken drove his sword down at him, but Daemon blocked the tip of Ken's blade with the flat of his own.

From the ground, Daemon raised his leg and kicked Ken in his hip. Ken jumped away and disengaged from their bout to make a new plan.

Daemon stood back up and dusted himself off, "Looks like you have some skill after all," he said. "Although, I can tell you've never held a sword in combat before."

Ken smirked. He was already prepared for another round, "What gave it away?"

"Your absence of swordplay," Daemon stated. "If you can't wield a sword then you can't take on the Monarchy."

Ken smiled at him with conviction, "I've had enough talk. I'll show you once and for all that I can protect Serena and take on the Monarchy!" he exclaimed.

"I doubt it!" Daemon replied smugly.

Ken stormed at him once more as Daemon readied his blade. Then just as he closed the gap, Ken threw his sword at Daemon's head. He could see Daemon's eyes widened behind his mask as he ducked.

"What the hell!?" Daemon yelled as Ken jumped at him with a

kick to his chest.

Daemon fell back on the ground and then shot up to his feet to prepare for Ken's next attack.

Ken stood before Daemon with his hand held out in front of him. He saw the realization in Daemon's eyes when he instantly learned what Ken was up to.

Daemon hopped to the side as Ken's sword flew by him from behind. The edge of Ken's blade narrowly missed his left arm.

"How was that?" Ken asked with a proud grin as he caught the sword in midair.

Daemon laughed as he regained his footing, "Well, it seems you got some spirit about you. Maybe it's time I stop taking it easy. Let's see how you do when I fight for real," he said excitedly. From his tone, he sounded as though he was enjoying the fight.

"I don't want anything less! I need to know what a General of the Monarchy is capable of!" Ken said tauntingly.

Daemon stampeded toward ken without squandering a second.

Ken held his sword up and braced to block Daemon's attack. Daemon grunted deafeningly as he landed his sword against Ken's. In that instance, Ken's arms collapsed against his torso from the force of Daemon's swing. He even felt his feet leave the ground as Daemon continued to swipe his sword. It was as though he were swinging through Ken and not just hitting his weapon.

Ken skipped across the ground along with his weapon, like a rock thrown across a pond. He finally stopped rolling and felt pain in his left arm from supporting the impact. He laid on the ground while trying desperately to catch his breath. The hit was so strong that it forced his elbow to hit below his chest and knock some of the air from his lungs.

"You see the gap between us now? You understand what you are up against if you continue?" Daemon called out.

Ken struggled to stand and catch his breath, all while clutching his left arm. He didn't carry an expression of pain or worry though. He lifted his head to reveal a look of excitement and resolve. Hastily, he regained a breath of air. Then he slowly held his hand out and called his sword back to him once again. "If that's the best a General can do, then we have nothing to worry about!" Ken said through gasps.

"That's it, big bro, don't give up!" Serena yelled.

"You don't know when to quit, do you? If you don't stop, then I'm going to hurt you for real," Daemon said threateningly.

Ken cracked his neck to the side as he reared his sword back. "Then I better hurry up and win," he replied.

"What a fool," Daemon said under his breath.

Ken dug his feet in the ground and then dashed at Daemon one last time. He threw his sword at him again just like before, but this time Daemon deflected it to the side with his own blade.

"That trick doesn't work twice!" Daemon barked.

Yet, Ken didn't slow down. He raised his left hand and pressed forward. He watched as Daemon's eyes darted to his sword which laid motionless in the dirt. Then at the last second Daemon turned his blade flat to Ken like a shield.

"I got him!" Ken uttered to himself, knowing that Daemon must've thought he was going to call his sword back.

Once Ken got to him, he stopped and placed his hand lightly on the flat of Daemon's sword. Daemon peeked from behind his weapon while supporting it with one hand on the hilt and the other placed firmly against the back of it. His eyes revealed a puzzled gaze that confirmed Ken's assumption.

"Take this!" Ken yelled as he released a pressure blast into the blade.

Daemon's arms collapsed on himself just as Ken's did from his attack. He flew across the ground and landed against a bolder behind him where he sat with his head hanging down.

"You're not the only one who can send people flying!" Ken exclaimed.

As Daemon sat hunched over and motionless, his mask fell from his face. Slowly, he raised his head and laid it back on the bolder behind him. "I didn't expect you to have a Gate power," he said through a grunt.

His face was severely burnt and misshapen. Ken stared for a

moment and then turned his head as Daemon grabbed his mask and placed back over his face.

Ken felt a slight pain in his hand from the Gate. Same as when he used the pressure blast power repeatedly in the storm. He grabbed it and rubbed the Gate.

"You're overusing it aren't you?" Daemon said as he used his sword to stand up.

Ken nodded his head as he continued to massage it.

"I think that's enough, if we keep going like this neither one of us will be able to fight for a while," Daemon said with a chuckle.

Ken fell to his knees with a sigh of relief, *I don't think I could've kept going anyway,* he thought.

Serena ran over to him with an unsettled expression, "Are you okay!?"

"Yeah, I'm fine," Ken replied while he smiled at her.

She grinned back at him and seemed like she got excited, "You won right?" she inquired anxiously.

"I think we can call that one a draw," Daemon answered for him.

"What!? No way! My big bro sent you through the air. He definitely wins!" Serena shouted back with an irritated look on her face.

"He's right, Serena. It's a tie," Ken said as he stood. He wasn't going to argue the point of who won or lost. In that fight, it became clear to Ken who was stronger. He realized Daemon truly was holding back and knew if Daemon fought seriously, he would be no match.

"I guess that means you won't tell me how to get by the Monarchy or who put the Gate on my hand?" Ken asked.

"Since it's a draw, I'll answer just one question for you. I'll even let you pick which one it is," Daemon answered.

His reply surprised Ken. He didn't expect Daemon to tell him anything. "If I can choose only one, then it would be how to get by the Monarchy," Ken stated.

"Are you sure about that?" Daemon asked with intrigue. "This may be your only chance to find out who put that Gate on your hand?"

Ken looked down at his hand and then moved his eyes to Serena, who gazed back at him in suspense of his answer.

"Yeah, I'm sure."

"As you wish then," Daemon said while approaching them. He watched as Ken rubbed his Gate again. "Does it still hurt?"

"Yeah, what did you mean when you said I overused my Gate power earlier?" Ken asked.

"Sages make Gates with a failsafe in them. Just in case you overuse your Gate or Gate power. You see you risk damaging or breaking it when it gets overused. That failsafe lets you know when you've put too much stress on it," Daemon answered.

"So, this pain is telling me that I'm about to break the Gate?" Ken inquired.

"Pretty much," Daemon responded. "If you give it time, it will recover on its own like a wound."

"What happens if it breaks?" Ken asked as placed his sword on his back.

"If you get a crack in it, it will become weak and take a long time to heal. However, if it breaks or shatters off completely – you'll lose it altogether. The only way to get it back is for the Sage who put it on you to replace it," Daemon said as he motioned Ken to follow him to the back of the bar.

"Why can't another Sage replace it?" Ken asked.

"Because once you've been marked by a Sage, you can't be marked by another," Daemon replied. "So, I believe this is probably the only Gate you'll get for a long time."

Ken peered down at his left hand, the pain was gone, but it was replaced with apprehension. He knew his power was the only hope he had to fight with the Monarchy, which made him realize how important it was for him to be careful using it.

"You got a map?" Daemon asked.

Ken broke from his concentration, "Yeah, it's in my bag," he said while grabbing it from Serena. He pulled out the map and passed it to Daemon.

"We're here, and this where you're trying to go," Daemon said while pointing out areas on the map. "One of the roads the Monarchy uses regularly splits between these two places. If you take the main road, you will get caught. So, what you need to do is cut through these woods until you find this path. It's the first one you'll see. Use the woods as cover, and quietly wait for your chance to pass. Be patient and silent," he said as he directed Ken on the map.

"That seems simple enough," Ken said. He believed it would be more complicated than what Daemon showed him though.

"Well, once you get by the first road, you'll have to get by the second one. It has less coverage for a wider distance. That will be the hard one. Once you get past that and find yourself walking on the trail next to the river. You'll be clear," Daemon said as he stood up and popped his back.

"I didn't hurt you too bad, did I?" Ken asked with a slick grin.

"How's that arm of yours feeling?" Daemon questioned casually as he stretched.

Ken smirked at Daemon's response. He seemed to be better than Ken at ribbing people as well as fighting.

"I see you're good with taking a joke," Daemon said as his sword glowed and then turn into yellow sparks.

"And you're quick with comebacks," Ken replied with a light laugh.

"Well, I need to get going. I have someone important to meet with," Daemon said nonchalantly.

"You better pay your tab first!" James demanded as he glared at Daemon.

"He'll take care of it for me," Daemon said while pointing at Ken.

"What do you mean, I'll take care of it for you!?" Ken yelled.

"After all the information I gave you – the least you can do is pay my bill," Daemon stated.

"Why don't you tell me who gave me this Gate and then I'll pay it," Ken retorted.

"Because I don't think you're ready to know. Although, I will make you one more deal," Daemon said in a more serious tone.

"What kind of deal?" Ken asked skeptically.

"Once you finish taking Serena home, go as far west from there as you can. Then go far north from that point. I'll meet you wherever you end up. If I find you, I'll tell you everything. I'll even take you to meet the guy," Daemon said.

"That's not a bad deal," Ken said while stroking his chin. "Alright, sounds like a plan. Of course, I don't think it'll be that easy," he added. "I'm sure Captain Ulgenda figured out that I'm taking Serena back home. She'll probably have reinforcements."

"I doubt it," Daemon replied as he turned away. "I happen to know her and her brother from my time in the Monarchy. She has a chip on her shoulder because her brother is a higher rank. She'll want to catch you herself to try and get a promotion," he said as he started to walk away.

"Are you sure!? You really think it'll be just her and her subordinates?" Ken questioned in an optimistic tone.

"Yeah, I'm certain of it," Daemon called out as he continued to walk away.

"That's good, right?" Serena asked.

"Yeah, it is!" Ken replied with a confident smirk. "Thanks for everything Daemon!" he shouted.

Daemon raised his hand up without looking back as he pressed forward.

James held his hand out to Ken while scowling at him. "Where's the fol for his drinks?" he said as he rubbed his fingers and thumb together.

Ken let out a sigh as he put a few coins in James's hand. Then James walked back into the bar from the back door.

"I should've asked him to come with us," Ken said as he watched Daemon leave.

Serena shook her head at the notion, "I don't like him that much. He's scary to me," she said as she watched too.

Ken shrugged his shoulders and looked at Serena, "Well, what do you say we buy some food and water to take with us," he said as he started to walk towards the front of the bar.

"Okay, then we're leaving right?" Serena asked as she followed.

"Yeah, the next place we stop is Sales," Ken said with a wide grin.

"I can't wait!" Serena exclaimed.

"I do wish I asked him one thing though," Ken said with a puzzled look.

"What's that?" Serena questioned.

"I wonder who he's going to meet with," Ken responded as they approached the door.

"Good question. You'll have to ask next time you see him," Serena replied.

Daemon looked back and watched as Ken and Serena went back into the bar. Then he started walking once more.

"I can't believe we just happened to run into him like that," he chuckled.

"Was that really him? Was that the one *he* told us about?" a young girl's voice asked Daemon as he strolled.

"Yeah, that's him alright," he replied.

"Wow, what are the chances of that happening?" The unseen girl asked as her voice echoed inside of Daemon's head.

"Pretty damn low," Daemon answered indifferently.

"So, are you nervous about seeing your old friend, Colonel Lightsey again?" The girl's voice asked curiously.

"I doubt he's a colonel anymore, but yes. He's probably improved a lot since back then. If I'm not careful, he'll kill me this time." Daemon said in a serious tone.

Chapter 15

Going Home

Ken and Serena went back into the bar to buy a few provisions from James.

James wasn't too thrilled to see them walk back in. However, when they paid for the food and water, he quickly changed his tune. Once they were prepared, Ken looked over the map again to get their bearings. Then they left the bar and went into the woods. The traveling started off slow. The forest was thick and hard to walk through. Ken thought about using his sword to cut a path but remembered what Daemon said about staying quiet. He assumed they had some distance to cover, so making noise at first wouldn't be a big deal. Yet, he didn't want to put Serena at risk. Thus, he decided to travel quietly from the start.

"This is going to take forever," Serena whispered impatiently.

"I know, but it's the safest way," Ken answered while stepping over a large root. "You just have to be patient Serena. It won't be long till you're home."

Serena's face lite up as they continued to push through the vines, trees, and branches. "I'm so excited! I finally get to go home and see my mom and dad," she said while clenching her arms to her chest as if holding back an excited screech.

Ken thought about what she said before about not knowing if her parents were alive. *I think she's trying to stay positive. I know she understands there's a chance her parents died. But I can't blame her for having hope. In fact, her smile is an inspiration. After everything she's been through, it's incredible that she can smile at all,"* Ken thought while glancing back at her.

As they pressed forward, the trees thinned out along with the obstacles like fallen logs and overgrown roots.

"This is much easier now," Serena stated.

"I think we're getting close to the first road. We should be quiet from now on. Stay close to me," Ken said in a low voice.

Serena nodded her head and followed at his heels as they continued through the woods carefully.

While attempting to be stealthy, the sounds of leaves and branches being crushed beneath their feet became more apparent. They tried to watch each step and avoid twigs and other tree byproducts spread across the ground.

As they moved forward, Ken noticed an area ahead that was open and treeless. He looked back at Serena and nodded his head to her. She nodded back to signify that she understood. They were approaching the first road and needed to be inconspicuous.

Ken moved from tree to tree, peeking from behind each one to survey the area. As he moved to the biggest tree, the path came into view. He looked down at it from atop a hill that dropped to the road. The opposite side of the path had a small mount as well.

We have the high ground, Ken thought as he scanned the area. *That makes this easier.*

From his hiding spot, he noticed a few soldiers walk around the corner of the trail. He turned his back the tree and squatted down; Serena sat down next to him. He put his finger to his lip to signify that she needed to be quiet. Then she nodded back as they waited.

They listened as the soldiers moved down the path. Ken could even hear them carrying on a conversation. It was hard to hear the exact words because of how far they were, but they could still hear their mumbled voices.

"Hey!" a soldier yelled out from the road.

Ken felt butterflies rise in his stomach.

"Hey, you! Over there trying to hide!" the soldier shouted once more.

Serena gawked at Ken with a frightened look.

How could they have seen us! Ken thought while quietly maintaining his position.

"Come out already! I know you're there!" the soldier demanded.

Ken peeked around the side of the tree and saw three soldiers standing just below them. *It's just three, I'll bet I can take them*, he contemplated, trying to psyche himself up for a fight.

"Okay, okay, you win!" a voice called out from the corner of the road.

Ken scanned the area, trying to see what was happening.

Another soldier walked out from behind a tree and approached the others, "You guys got me. I was going to scare the crap out of you!" he said through a laugh.

"Yeah, well nothing gets past me," the other one said as he punched him in the shoulder.

"Hey guys, we shouldn't keep Major Ricket waiting. Stop playing around and let's go already!" another soldier ordered.

"Lighten up man. You know Major Zane is a cool guy. He's not uptight like most the other Angeon majors," the one that was hiding stated.

"Major Zane?" another soldier questioned scornfully. "You better watch it! Using his first name like that is unprofessional!"

They began arguing as they walked down the path. Soon their voices were gone after they rounded a corner and disappeared. Ken and Serena both let out a deep breath of tension as they looked the area over.

"That was scary," Serena whispered.

Ken's body still trembled somewhat as he attempted to calm down. "Yeah, I thought we were done." He scanned the area thoroughly and didn't see or hear anything coming. "You ready?" he asked while preparing to run.

"Yeah," Serena replied.

Ken grabbed Serena's hand and dashed down the hill. They shot across the road and then swiftly climbed up the other side while sprinting into the woods again. They ran for a few minutes until the woods got thick once more and stopped to catch their breath.

They both sat to rest as Ken pulled the map out to check on their progress.

"Now we just have to go to the right, and we will see the next road. Just beyond that one is the path by the river that will get you home," he said while rolling the map back up and putting it away.

He noticed Serena was still shaking from almost getting caught. "You, okay?" he asked, placing his hand on her arm.

"Yeah, I'm alright. It's just if we ran when we first got there, the guy hiding would've seen us. We never would've known he was there," she answered.

Ken shrugged his shoulders and stood up, "I could've beat them even if they did see us," he said in a brash tone.

"You think so?" Serena asked with an impressed glint in her eyes.

"Of course, you're looking at the guy who went toe to toe with a former General after all," Ken stated with his chest puffed out, and his nose pointed to the sky.

Serena grinned at him and jumped to her feet, "That's right! My big bro can handle anything," she stated proudly.

"Now, let's get back on track," Ken said as he started walking again.

Serena seemed to get her nerve back from Ken's display of vigor, which is what he was going for. He knew if she were afraid, it would cause them trouble with the next road.

They found themselves walking through a dense woodland again as they made slow progress. Once the afternoon set in, Ken realized they only had a few hours of daylight left.

We have to hurry, he mused as they continued to shove through the forest growth. Soon after that thought, the area around them began to thin out. "Now we're getting somewhere," Ken said to himself as they pushed through the trees.

Serena got closer to him and grabbed his hand tightly while glancing around nervously. He felt her hand quivering from being anxious again. *I guess she's still scared after all,* Ken thought while putting his hand on her head and roughing up her hair. She gave him an unamused look, but Ken held a thumb up with a wink.

Serena smiled back at him, and her face seemed to lose some of its tension. Then they continued their path.

Ken saw the next road come into view as they approached. There was far less foliage to use for cover, and the distance was greater. They also didn't have the high ground to look out from. If anything, this road was elevated higher than the area around it. They stayed behind a tree as Ken planned what to do.

"This looks like it will be harder," Serena whispered.

"It will be," Ken replied. "Just watch me closely and stay as quiet as you can," he said as he made his approach.

Ken inspected the area as much as he could and saw no sign of soldiers anywhere. "We're going to have to make a run for it, Serena," he said as he listened for voices.

"What if someone sees?" she asked apprehensively.

"It's the only way. The road by the river is just across this one. You have to be strong," Ken said, gripping her hand tightly.

Serena took a deep breath and nodded her head, "Alright, I'm ready."

Ken wasted no time. He galloped toward the road while tugging Serena behind him. They ran through the clearing and advanced on the road. As they crossed it, they scanned restlessly to see if they could spot anyone. However, they didn't see even one soul. They made it to the other side and continued their mad dash to the tree line. They blew into trees for cover and then stopped to rest.

"We did it," Serena uttered between breaths.

"Yeah, we did! We didn't see anyone at all. I think we're in the clear," Ken said as he pulled out a bottle of water and took a few gulps. He then passed it to Serena who drank some as well. "You ready to get home?" Ken asked cheerfully.

"Absolutely!" Serena answered.

They didn't squander a moment to get back up and start moving through the trees once more. "It shouldn't take long to find the path now," Ken said.

Just ahead they heard water rushing. Ken pushed back a branch as saw a path below them next to a large running river.

"This is it," he said as Serena peered from under his arm.

The sight of the river racing by the path was gorgeous and picturesque to her.

Ken wrapped his arms around Serena and slid down the small ledge that lead to the path. He let her go and walked out onto the trail and took in the scenery.

"I can't believe it! I'm almost home!" Serena stated as she beamed jubilantly.

"Let's get going," Ken said as he started to tread their path.

He felt a strong sense of accomplishment as the two of them carried on. He was proud to be able to keep his promise and make Serena happy. Seeing her face light up the way that it did made every struggle worth it to him.

As they came around a bend, Serena jumped with her hands in the air. "I'm almost home!" she expressed loudly.

Ken smiled at her and chortled at her enthusiasm.

Suddenly, they heard a twig snap from behind some trees in the woods beside them. Ken's eyes darted to the side as if reacting to something. He dropped the bag from his back, and before it hit the ground, he had his sword held in front of him.

A loud swish cut through the air as Ken blocked a quick strike from a steel whip. The sound of metals clashing echoed in the air as Ken gazed fiercely from behind his sword.

Serena screamed and ran toward Ken.

Two Monarchy soldiers shot behind them from the woods as Captain Ulgenda stepped out to greet them.

Ken held his blade with one arm while throwing the bag back on his back with the other. He looked at the soldiers behind him who had their swords drawn and ready. They seemed to be the same two from the restaurant. One of them even had a scab over his eye from Ken shooting the metal bearings at them.

"You took me by surprise last time!" Ulgenda said casually as she approached. She rubbed her stomach in the area that Ken hit her with his pressure blast. "That attack of yours really hurt. I didn't know you had a Gate power, but this time it'll be different," she said with a malicious grin.

"Take the girl! I'll deal with him," she demanded to her subordinates as she twirled her whip in the air.

"Ken!" Serena cried out as she got behind Ken's leg.

The two soldiers began to move in on them slowly. Ken's eyes scurried back and forth between them and Ulgenda.

They're going to attack from both sides. I can't stop it all. I'll just have to a take a hit, Ken thought as he stood his ground.

The soldiers jumped at him from behind with their swords pointed to his chest.

Ken quickly pushed Serena to the side and ducked beneath their attack. Then he released a pressure blast into the torso of the first one. The soldier was sent flying into a tree which knocked him unconscious.

The second one tried to step back, but Ken quickly unleashed a series of rapid punches to his face while dropping his sword. Then Ken finished with a spinning hook kick to the soldier's head.

Just as Ken finished the assault, Ulgenda's whip struck him on the back of his right shoulder.

Ken heard a deafening crack as he fell to his knees, "AAHHHH!" he yelled. He couldn't raise his right arm through a piercing pain that ran through his shoulder.

She must've broken my shoulder blade, Ken pondered as he dropped the bag on the ground again.

"Big brother!" Serena cried as she ran back to him.

Ulgenda looked at her soldiers who were laying on the ground passed out, "Useless trash!" she spat as she loomed over Ken. "I'll be sure to remove them from my team when this is over. Although, when I come back with you two, I'll probably be promoted anyway," she said insidiously.

"Serena, grab the bag and run," Ken muttered through his teeth.

"I can't!" Serena answered, now tearing up.

"I'll be right behind you I promise. You need to go right now. I'll protect you!" Ken ordered.

"I won't leave you," Serena said as tears rolled down her cheeks.
"I said go!" Ken barked.

Serena jumped back from his reaction. She hesitated for second but then grabbed the bag and proceeded to run by Ulgenda.

Ulgenda smirked as Serena went by her. The captain reached out to grab her but jumped back instantly as Ken flew by with his sword aimed at Ulgenda's arm.

Ulgenda readied her whip and watched as Serena ran while Ken blocked her path. He held his sword with his left hand as his right dangled by his side.

"You won't be able to do much like that," Ulgenda said tauntingly.

"You'd be surprised how far someone can go for the right purpose," Ken replied with a glare.

Ulgenda twisted her whip in the air and flung it at Ken with lightning speed.

Ken raised his sword to block the attack while charging at her. The whip smashed into his blade which deflected it as he closed the gap between them. Ken threw a roundhouse kick that Ulgenda blocked rapidly with her arm. Then he jabbed at her face with his sword.

Ulgenda sidestepped away from Ken's attack and then wrapped her whip around Ken's blade while yanking it out of his hand.

Ken instantly reacted by dropping down to a low stance and performing a sweep kick beneath the captain. He caught one of her legs which forced her to stumble back.

Ken stood up quickly to follow through with another attack, but the pain in his shoulder grew more intense and paralyzed his movements. "Damnit!" he groaned as he staggered.

Ulgenda tossed his sword into the woods. She seemed to make it point to grab it by the back of the blade instead of by the hilt.

"You're pretty good. It's a shame that you're Amony scum. Otherwise, you would've made an excellent soldier for the Monarchy," she said as she raised her whip and struck it at Ken.

Ken jumped to the side of the attack as the tip of the whip smashed into the ground next to him, causing the dirt to puff up from it like dust.

Ken stepped back a few more feet to observe her carefully.

That whip only has a limited range. If I stay this far away from her, she won't reach me, he thought while staring her down.

The Gate on Ulgenda's hand began to glow as a small circle of light appeared in front of her.

"She's opening her Gate?" Ken questioned as he watched in suspense.

Then another circle of light appeared a few feet from Ken's face. He stepped back promptly as Ulgenda flung her whip into the ring in front of her. The other end of the whip shot out at Ken from the second circle of light that was close to him.

At the last second, he moved his head out of the way just enough to miss being decapitated. The lights faded away, and Ken gawked at the captain, "What was that!?" he exclaimed.

Ulgenda merely grinned conceitedly at him as she raised her whip once more.

Ken raised his left hand up and held his palm out to her while maintaining his position.

"Your Gate power won't do you much good at this distance!" Ulgenda jeered as her whip popped and snapped ominously in the air around her.

She heard a rustle in a brush behind her and glanced back as Ken's sword flew from the bushes at her. Her eyes widened before she flung herself to the side to dodge Ken's blade. The edge of his sword caught the armor of her left leg as it shot by and landed in his hand.

Ken took this as an opportunity to catch up to Serena. He turned away and ran the same direction that Serena went while placing his sword on his back.

Ken looked back at Ulgenda and saw she was already on her feet. He noticed Ulgenda check the back of her leg which had some blood coming out over the armor around her calf muscle. He heard the captain yell out savagely just before chasing them in a fit of rage.

Ken sprinted down the path while clutching his right arm tightly. He tried to keep it from moving around, as it caused a great deal of pain when it jostled. As he dashed, he saw Serena running ahead of him. Then she gazed back and noticed him as well.

"Ken, behind you!" Serena cried out.

Ken turned his head and saw a circle of light manifest directly behind him. He skipped to side as Ulgenda's steel whip lashed out from the portal, narrowly missing him.

"You won't get away from me this time!" Ulgenda yelled as she pursued them.

The circle of light appeared once more behind Ken as he ran side to side dodging Ulgenda's attacks. She continued to create the small portals and fling her whip at him as they ran down the trail by the river. All Ken could do was run in zigzag patterns and look back every so often to avoid her attacks as she chased them.

Ken realized she was gaining ground on them. The pain in his shoulder was making it impossible to keep running and dodge her attacks simultaneously. He gazed around desperately trying to get an idea for how to escape, then focused his attention on the river.

That's it! Ken thought while evading another attack. "Serena, jump in the water!" he yelled out.

Serena looked back at him with a fearful mien, "Are you sure?" she asked between breaths.

"Yeah, just do it!" Ken demanded.

Serena did just as instructed and jumped into the river.

"What are you doing you, idiot?!" Ulgenda shouted.

Then Ken jumped in behind her. The current was strong and was pulling them down the river just as fast as they were running.

"Serena! Swim to the other side!" Ken yelled as he struggled to swim with his one functioning arm.

Serena was faring better than he was, yet still was having a hard time with the current.

Another portal appeared before Ken as he fought to stay above the river. Ulgenda's steel whip lashed out and smacked the water beside him.

"You'd rather her die than give her over to the Monarchy?" Ulgenda shouted as she continued to follow by land. She created another portal and tried to hit Ken once more.

Ken dove under water attempting to avoid Ulgenda's relentless attacks on him. Then came back up for air. At this point, Ken realized just how much he underestimated the strength of the current.

"You will never escape me!" Ulgenda bellowed.

Ken gave a livid grunt, becoming fed-up with Ulgenda's onslaught. Another portal appeared in front of him, but instead of avoiding it he reached his left palm inside it. When he did, his hand came out the other portal in front of Ulgenda's face. She gasped when she saw it come toward her. Immediately Ken let out a pressure blast at point-blank range which sent Ulgenda smashing into a tree. He quickly pulled his arm back from the portal as it closed to avoid possibly losing his hand.

"Serena!" Ken called out as he scanned around desperately for her, now that he didn't have anyone attacking him.

"I'm over here!" Serena yelled as the water pushed her around.

Ken swam to her the best that he could with his gimp arm. He powered his way through the pain in his shoulder as he kicked with both legs and paddled with his left arm.

Serena tried to swim against the current toward him, but her attempt was futile.

Ken ducked his head into the water while swimming as hard as he could to get to her, looking up between strokes to keep an eye on his direction. As he closed the gap, Serena reached out for him while fighting rigorously against the raging waters. Finally, Ken grabbed her hand and pulled her to him as the river continued to sweep them away.

"The water is getting rougher!" Serena cried out over the sound of the river crashing against rocks that were on each side of the banks.

"It wasn't this bad earlier!" Ken replied.

He stared ahead and saw more rocks that seemed to be getting closer to the center as they were pushed further down. "Hold on to me!" he shouted while trying to maneuver around the rocks.

The current picked up more speed as they whipped by the boulders. Ken was able to make slight turns to dodge them just in time. Then, they approached one head on. He tried to swim around it but quickly realized he couldn't. He turned his back to it and shielded Serena to keep her from hitting it first. Ken's right shoulder clipped the side of the rock causing the injury to get worse and flare with greater pain.

Ken screamed out in agony as his body went limp. He could no longer hold Serena with his left arm and started to lose consciousness as the river carried them away.

Serena wrapped her arms around Ken and yelled his name frantically trying to keep him awake.

"Ken! Ken!" she cried as he sank.

Suddenly, Ken's eyes went wide. He wrapped his left arm back around Serena. "No, I can't go out just yet!" he exclaimed, furiously kicking his legs to stay above water. With every movement of his body, he could feel a powerful twinge of pain in his back.

"It's going to be okay, big bro. I don't see any more rocks in our way," Serena assured as she gazed out in front of them.

As they floated downstream, they heard the roar of water crashing from a distance. Ken looked ahead and saw where the river seemed to dead end and drop. His heart felt as though it stopped when he grasped what they were approaching. "A waterfall!?" Ken bellowed in disbelief. "Where is that stupid fox!?" he cried.

Serena gripped him tight, gawking at it in terror.

Ken racked his mind desperately trying to devise a plan. Then he noticed Serena still had the bag on her back.

"That's it! Serena, turn around and face the tree line," Ken commanded while trying to push her off.

"I can't," Serena cried while gripping his shirt.

"We don't have time for this! Now let go so I can save you!" Ken ordered.

Serena reluctantly let go of Ken's shirt and turned her back to him.

Ken grabbed her arm, ensuring she wouldn't drift away.

"What about you?" Serena asked as Ken placed his left hand on the bag.

"Don't worry about me, I'll find you in Sales. Now brace yourself, this might hurt," Ken shouted. He dove under the water and got beneath Serena so he could achieve a proper angle. He planned to use his pressure blast power to launch Serena out of the water and onto the ledge by the river before they fell down the waterfall. He knew it could hurt her but hoped the bag on her back would soften the impact.

Ken's Gate began to glow as he proceeded with his plan. Then, just as he fired his pressure blast – Serena rolled away from his hand and dodged the burst of air.

Ken rose back to the surface and grabbed Serena as she drifted, "What are you doing?" he yelled furiously as the waterfall closed in on them.

"I can't! I can't leave you!" Serena wailed while crying heavily against Ken. "I can't do it alone! Not without you!" she exclaimed.

Ken tried to pull her off so he could get her to safety, but she wouldn't let go no matter how much he tried. "You're going to fall down the waterfall with me! Don't do this!" he shouted, still trying to save her.

Ken glanced over his shoulder, realizing it was already too late.

"I won't leave anymore family behind!" Serena cried as she buried her face into Ken's chest.

Ken wrapped his left arm and both his legs around Serena to protect her from the fall.

"Serena!" he cried out as they went over the side and disappeared into a cascading abyss of white mist.

Chapter 16

Family Reunion

Serena tumbled and twisted under the torrential force of the waterfall. She kicked and paddled desperately fighting to find the surface. With every stroke, she couldn't tell if she was going further under or raising to safety. The current dragged and whipped her away like a helpless rag doll. Soon panic set in as her mind went to the worst-case scenario. She feared that this was her end, that she was drowning and that no one would come to save her this time.

Just as she reached her dismal conclusion, she felt something solid push beneath her frame. She found herself washed up on a grassy shore, rejected by the water's grasp. She coughed violently between gasps, frantically trying to catch her breath. She dragged herself out of the water and stood on her hands and knees while trying to calm down and steady her breathing.

After catching her breath, Serena scanned around the scene for Ken. She saw the tall waterfall at the back of the blue lake that endlessly poured into its plunge pool. The lake was surrounded by leafy green trees and grey boulders. The landscape was beautiful, healthy, and alive with fluttering butterflies and birds.

Serena stood up and noticed the bag she wore wash up on the edge of the water. She grabbed it and pulled it onto dry land. Then she continued to gaze around for Ken.

"Big bro!" Serena cried while searching the shore. She walked the edge of the water and saw a figure lying halfway out of the lake. She rushed over to it and found Ken laying on the ground with his legs still in the water.

"Ken!" she shouted while dashing.

When Serena got to him, she saw his left hand shaking and could hear slight groans as he breathed.

"Are you alright?" Serena asked as she pat his back.

"AAAHHHHH!" Ken screamed out from her touch.

Serena gasped and pulled her hand away, "I'm sorry," she said as she placed her hands over her mouth.

"Serena, I can't move," Ken mumbled gruffly. "My back hurts too much to do anything."

"What can I do?" Serena asked as she hovered over him.

"Grab the vile of mystic water, it's around my neck," Ken answered between agonizing inhales.

Serena reached into the back of his shirt and found a string around his neck. She pulled it up slowly from around his head and under his chest.

"I forgot about this. We got it at the Monarchy hospital," Serena said as her eyes lit up. "We can heal you with it!" she shouted cheerfully. She popped off the top of the vile and prepared to give it to Ken.

"Wait, you're not hurt, are you?" Ken asked.

"No, I'm okay. Now drink it," Serena insisted while holding it to his mouth.

Ken opened wide and gulped down the solution in one sip, then he dropped his head onto the grass as he waited for it to take effect.

"I wonder how long it takes to heal," Ken uttered – wincing from that small movement.

"When the doctor used it on you before, it healed your gash instantly. It was like the water washed the cut away." Serena answered.

Gradually, Ken could feel the pain in his back become less intense, "I can feel it working," he said as he started taking deeper breaths. "In a few minutes, I bet I'll be good to go."

Serena smiled while releasing a breath of tension. She gazed out at the water while waiting for Ken to heal.

"That was really scary," Serena said.

"Yeah, it was," Ken responded.

There was a silent pause for a moment before Ken spoke again. "Serena, why didn't you listen to me when I tried to save you? You could've died."

"Because I can't do this alone," Serena replied halfheartedly. "Plus, you're my big brother. I can't abandon you like that."

"No! I won't accept that answer," Ken barked. "If I'm going to be your big brother then you have to listen to me. My job is to protect you, Serena. That's my purpose now. I can't let you throw away your life like that," he stated while starting to move his legs.

"You don't understand, Ken. I don't know what to do. Without you, I'd be lost," Serena retorted grimly.

"So, you would rather die than let me save you?!" Ken shouted.

"No, I just...." Serena tried to answer but couldn't think of what to say.

"You have to live Serena. You must keep fighting even when I can't. If you give up just because of me, then everything we've done will be nothing!" Ken stated as he started to move his right arm.

"I'm just afraid. I'm afraid to face what happens next by myself," Serena said while pulling her knees to her chest and wrapping her arms around them.

"I know it's scary. The idea of being, alone that is; but you're strong Serena. You're stronger than you give yourself credit for. I see it in you every day," Ken said. He was now able to put his weight on his arms while attempting to push himself up.

"You really think so?" Serena asked.

"I know so. Seeing you smile after everything you've been through is inspiring to me. After my parents died, I was bitter and angry at the world. Yet even though you're separated from your family, you still find it in your heart to be happy and caring. That takes someone strong. Stronger than I ever was," Ken answered.

Serena smiled from behind her arms while gazing at the water. "Thank you, big bro," she said lightly.

"Just promise you'll listen to me from now on. I don't know what I'd do if something happened to you," Ken said as his healing progressed. He sat down next to Serena and stretched out his legs.

"Alright, I promise," Serena replied with a grin. "Are you feeling better now?"

"It's still not fully healed, but I am feeling way better. Let's just give it a little more time," Ken said as he took in the scenery. "It's a beautiful place."

"Yeah, I really like it. To be honest, it seems kind of familiar to me," Serena said, turning her face up in thought.

Ken raised his arms and then stood on his feet. He reached down and touched his toes to get a good stretch. His back still felt super tight, but the injuries seemed to be mostly healed. He could tell it would take more time to be one hundred percent.

"Looks familiar to you, eh?" he asked while trying to stretch different areas of his body.

Serena pondered as she continued to take in the area, "Why does this look so familiar?" she whispered.

Without warning, Serena sprang up with a gasp, "I know where we are!" she exclaimed. "This is a spot my family used to come to for picnics and swimming! We're just outside of Sales!" Serena shouted as she ran up to Ken.

"That's great," Ken answered while continuing to stretch.

"Right behind us is a trail that leads to the village. We're almost there!" Serena said ecstatically as she grabbed the soaked leather bag.

Ken smirked and finished his stretching. "Well, in that case, we better get moving," he said while grabbing the bag from her.

"I'll lead the way," Serena shouted while directing Ken. She walked between two trees and then pointed out a thin trail in the woods.

"Oh, I see the way now," Ken said as they walked.

Ken felt the wet clothes start to chafe as they progressed through the trail. He figured she was just as uncomfortable in her clothes as he was.

"Hopefully we'll be able to get some clothes in Sales," he said.

"I can just get clothes from my closet. I'll bet my dad's clothes will fit you. You're about the same size. I'm sure he won't mind," Serena replied, skipping down the path.

Ken started to feel a slight pain in his left hand. He rubbed the back of it and realized it was the gate warning him that it was overused. He assumed that it was hurting the whole time, but he never noticed since the pain in his back was far superior.

"I wonder why that fox never showed up," Ken said curiously.

"I'm not sure. It does seem to come around when there's trouble," Serena replied.

Ken shrugged his shoulders. "Maybe we'll see it again soon," he said casually.

"Aww, you miss it, don't you?" Serena said with a giggle.

"No way, it's just helpful is all," Ken responded as his face turned red.

"By the way, I think we need to name it," Serena added. "Let's call it Meeko."

"Meeko? Why Meeko?" Ken questioned.

"I don't know. It just seems to fit," Serena said innocently.

Ken rolled his eyes and gave a smirk. "If that's what you want," he answered.

Serena laughed as they steadied down the trail. "It's up here, just ahead of us!" she said as she ran ahead of Ken.

"Hey, don't go so far ahead of me. The Monarchy could be here!" Ken shouted as Serena jogged.

She quickly went around the final bend of the trail and disappeared from Ken's sight. "Serena!" he called out as he ran after her.

When Ken made his way around the same corner, he saw Serena standing completely still with a branch clasped in her hand. She had it pulled to the side, so she could see beyond it.

Ken approached her with a glare. "How many times do I have to tell you to listen to me!?"

Serena didn't look back or reply. She stood motionless staring out from behind the branch.

"What is it?" Ken asked as he got beside her.

Serena's mouth was agape, and her eyes were wide.

Ken pulled the branches away from his view to see what frightened her. He gazed out and saw a village that was in ruins. Small houses were destroyed and plundered with broken windows and walls. There were many areas on the ground where chunks of dirt were missing from a wild battle. There was not a square foot of space that was free of debris. The place looked as though a tornado had ransacked it.

Serena stepped out slowly from the tree line as she scanned it over. Ken followed behind her in awe of the destruction.

"This is horrible," he whispered.

Serena took off running and yelled desperately. "MOM! DAD!" she cried out as she rushed toward her house.

Ken followed at her heels, keeping an eye out for any soldiers.

Serena stopped in front of her home which was not spared the same fate of the town. Most of the windows were broken, and there were holes and gashes throughout the house. Serena cried for her parents once more as she hurried into the structure.

"Serena!" Ken shouted as he followed her in.

"MOM! DAD! I'M HOME!" Serena yelled while dashing around the house frantically. She noticed the back door was opened and remembered where they were when she was kidnapped.

Serena slowly made her way out the rear of the house and saw the tree her mother was under when she was protecting Serena.

Serena looked beneath a tall branch that hung over most the yard. Below it was two gravestones laying side by side. One read Jace Kenshi, and the other said Amelia Kenshi.

Serena sluggishly hobbled over to them. She stood before the graves silently.

Ken walked out the back door and saw her standing between the two gravestones. He closed his eyes and turned his head away as a tear fell down his cheek. His worst suspicion was confirmed.

Serena dropped to her knees between the graves, then laid her palms over each one. Her throat became choked up as she struggled to get a breath in. Then she moaned loudly as she sobbed.

"MOM! DAD!" Serena cried out as she gripped the dirt between her fingers. Her moans and gasps made Ken's heartbreak as tears flowed down his face as well. He approached her quietly and got on his knees beside her. Then he rubbed her back, attempting to comfort her.

Serena turned to Ken and thrust her head into his chest as she wept heavily against his torso.

Ken wrapped his arms around her and stroked the hair on her head slowly as she cried. He knew she needed to get it out. Plus, he knew exactly how she felt.

"Oh Ken, a part of me… a part of me knew," Serena said between deep convulsions of snorts.

Ken remained quiet as he continued to ease her.

"But I still had hope!" she bellowed.

"I know you did," Ken said softly.

"I don't know what to do now!" Serena exclaimed as she peered at the graves from under Ken's chest.

Ken let out a deep depressing breath as he observed the graves as well. "Tim said most of the people here died, but I didn't want to believe it," he whispered.

"What?" Serena asked as she leaned back from him.

"Tim said this might happen," Ken said once more as he wiped a tear from his eye.

"You didn't tell me about that," Serena said between sniffles.

"I didn't want to worry you, Serena. I didn't know if it was true. Also, you already had a feeling about it, so I didn't want to push the subject," Ken answered.

Serena stood up and stepped back from Ken while rubbing her eyes. "So, you knew all along then!" she shouted while backing away.

"No, Serena, it's not like that!" Ken replied as he held his hand out to her.

"You knew they were gone and didn't tell me! You brought me all the way here just to see for myself didn't you!?" Serena yelled furiously.

"That's not it, Serena! Please, just give me a second to explain," Ken pleaded as he approached her.

"Stay away from me!" Serena bellowed before running into the woods.

Ken called out to her, but she never looked back.

Ken lowered his head and smack his palm to his face. "I should've seen that coming," he said quietly.

I should just give her some space for now, he thought.

Ken stared at the graves for a moment and remembered what it was like for him when he lost his parents. The unrelenting loneliness and the fear of what would happen to him next came rushing back like an old, unwelcomed friend. All he could think about was how Serena must be feeling the same way right now.

"Serena is suffering. No matter how much she says she wants me to leave her alone, I know I still need to be by her side," Ken mumbled to himself.

He took off in the same direction as Serena. "Serena, where are you? The Monarchy could be around! Please just tell me where you are!" he shouted as he searched.

The sun was starting to go down. The sky became golden just over the tops of the trees as the sun hit the horizon.

It didn't take long for Ken find Serena. She was leaning against a large boulder in a small area cleared of trees. She glared at him and then put her face to the rock as she wept.

"Go away!" Serena demanded in a muffled tone.

Ken was relieved to find her safe. He stepped out from the tree line and got down on his knees. Purposefully leaving some distance between them, so he didn't intrude on her space.

"I'm sorry, I should've told you what Tim said," Ken stated remorsefully. "I know this is the last thing you want to hear, but I understand how you feel."

Serena's eyes shot at Ken from under her shoulder. "You don't know anything!" she wailed.

They sat in silence for a moment, then Ken spoke up again in a soft still voice.

"When my dad died, it tore me apart inside. He was my best friend. The one I would turn to when I was hurt or scared," he said warmly. "Thankfully my mother was there to help me through his passing. But then she died a short time later. My stepdad didn't care enough to try to console me, and I had no friends or other family to get me through it. I felt utterly alone. Like no one cared that I was falling apart. Like it was my responsibility to get over it and move on," he said in a somber tone.

Serena gazed back at him slightly. She still seemed upset, but her expression was softer. Ken kept his distance and maintained his conversation.

"All I wanted back then, was someone to tell me it was okay. Someone to hold me and say that I wasn't alone. That I was still loved and that I had someone to turn to," Ken said as tears welled up in his eyes.

"For me, that person never came. I grew up bitter and mad at the world and all the people around me," he said while wiping drops of grief from his face.

"I don't want you to go through that Serena. Because you're not alone, I'm here for you. I'll be your someone to lean on. I'll be the one to tell you it's okay. I'll be the one to hold you when you're scared. I'll be the big brother you need me to be," he said as his voiced cracked.

Serena's face twisted as she tried to hold back her tears. She got up from the boulder and scurried toward Ken with her arms open. She couldn't hold back any longer and cried profusely as she dashed to him.

Ken ran toward Serena and met her halfway. He wrapped his arms around her frame and clutched her tightly.

"I'm so scared, Ken! I just want my parents back!" Serena bawled.

"I know, little sis," Ken replied as he held her close.

Night fell around them as they stayed in that spot huddled together for what felt like hours. Soon, Serena calmed down enough to separate from him.

"I want to see them again," she said dully.

"Alright, let's go then," Ken replied.

They made their way back to Serena's house and stood in front of the graves together once more. Ken stayed quiet as they stared at them – waiting for Serena to speak.

"Mom, dad, you don't have to worry about me here. I have a big brother now," Serena said while gripping Ken's hand. "I know I'm going to be okay because he's going to protect me from now on. So...so...you can..." she started to choke up while talking.

"So, you can rest easy," Ken said while kneeling before the graves. "I'm going to take care of her for you. I'll be her big brother from now on, and keep her safe," he added as he placed his hand over the graves.

"Thank you, big bro," Serena said while wiping her eyes.

Ken stood up and looked back at Serena. "You need to get some rest," he said.

"Can I sleep here, one last time?" Serena asked while gazing back at her house.

Ken hesitated to answer. He thought about Ulgenda and how she may be coming for them right now. Then he considered that maybe someone else would find them. He peered into Serena's sad green eyes and knew there was no way he could refuse her.

"Alright, Serena, we'll stay here tonight," Ken replied reluctantly.

Serena walked into the house and showed Ken her room. It too was damaged. Many of her things were destroyed or broken, but her bed was still intact. She also still had some clothes that were in good condition inside what was left of her closet.

Ken turned away as she changed into a different set of clothes. Then he tucked her into bed.

"You feeling, okay?" Ken asked.

"Yeah, I'm okay. Thanks to you, big bro," Serena answered with a melancholy smile.

"Just call for me if you need something," Ken said before walking out. As he approached the doorway, he looked back and saw she was already asleep.

"She must've really worn herself out," Ken said as he walked out to the front porch. "I can't blame her though. She's been through more than any ten-year-old girl should ever have to deal with. Especially in the last two days. Between Ulgenda attacking us at the restaurant and the trail – then falling over a waterfall – and then finding out her parents are gone. She deserves a good night's sleep."

Ken surveyed the wreckage of the village once more as he imagined what the battle was like. Seeing all the gashes in the ground along with all the other weird damage done to the buildings made him wonder if Angeon powers were involved in the fight.

"So much destruction," Ken whispered.

I wonder if I really am strong enough to protect her from powers that can do things like this," he pondered as he rubbed his hand across a large scare that ran up the side of Serena's home.

"It's too late for doubts now. She's counting on me to be strong," Ken said as he tightened his fist.

He walked around the house a few times to make sure no one was around, then stopped by Serena's parent's graves.

"You can count on me," he said in a whisper just before going back into the house.

Chapter 17

Broken Promises

Throughout the night, Ken guarded the house as Serena slept. He went in and out of her room repeatedly to make sure she was safe and sound. As the evening carried on, Ken decided to explore the other houses for valuable resources, such as food, water, and anything else that may come in handy. One thing he kept an eye out for was a new map since the previous one was destroyed by water. While he searched, he made sure not to go too far from where Serena rested and checked on her between houses.

Most of the buildings he examined were cleaned out of food and valuables. He assumed scavengers, soldiers, and random people in general, were to blame. However, he did manage to find some bread and fresh water along with a new map and a better bag. He felt a little guilty about taking things from the houses, but he knew it was necessary to get the proper provisions.

As Ken went from house to house, he noticed gravestones behind each one. It seemed what Tim told him was true. Only a handful of people survived. Although, Ken saw no evidence of any survivors at all. He went as far as to think the entire town was slaughtered in the battle. He wondered who buried all the townspeople, and then assumed the Monarchy did it after everything was over.

Once he gathered enough items, Ken went back to the house and rechecked on Serena. She was still asleep, wrapped up comfortably in her blankets.

Ken placed the bread, water, and map down on a small table in what he guessed was the living room. Then he sat on the porch outside and let out a long, exhausted yawn as he stretched his arms above his head.

He stared as the sky and the clouds turned from dark night to cotton candy blue and pink. The sun was beginning to rise much to his disbelief.

"Wow, morning already?" he uttered while watching the sun make its way over the horizon.

The heavens turned from their pink and blue amalgam to a golden amber as the sun peered over the tops of the trees. The dew on the ground glistened like diamonds when the light's touch reached it.

"Even this disaster-stricken town looks beautiful in the sunrise," Ken mumbled to himself.

From behind, he heard a thud come from in the house. He quickly went into it and ran straight to Serena's room. Upon opening the door, he saw she wasn't there.

"Serena!" Ken called out as he searched the house. He walked outside the back door and saw her sitting in front of her parent's graves. She didn't appear to be crying or upset. She was only sitting with them silently.

Ken let out a sigh of relief. He wanted to ask her how she was feeling but decided he would leave her be for now. He walked back into the house and grabbed the map then unraveled it and looked it over on the couch, which was missing most of its cushions and was cut and damaged.

"Better make use of this time and find a new place for us to go," Ken said as he scanned over it.

While searching the map, Ken's eyes became droopy and his head slowly tilted down. He popped back up to stay awake, yet his eyelids got progressively heavier as he fought with them. Soon, the map fell to the floor as he drifted into a slumber.

Ken woke up to find Serena sitting next to him on the couch. She was dressed in dark blue pants, a pair of brown work boots, and a white shirt that had stains from grass and dirt. It clearly was used for outside work. She was stuffing some more clothes into the bag when Ken noticed her.

"Was I asleep?" Ken asked muzzily as he sat up.

"Yeah, I thought you could use the rest, so I left you alone," Serena replied. "I got you some clothes. They're on the table," she said, pointing to a small pile of garments across from them.

As Ken approached the pile, he felt how stiff and uncomfortable his clothes were. "I didn't even think to look for clothes while I was out last night," he said in a groggy tone. "Where did you find these?"

"Those were my dad's," Serena answered softly.

"Oh, Serena I couldn't," Ken said.

"It's okay, most of his clothes are gone anyway. Someone must've stolen them. I'd rather you have what's left instead of someone else taking them," Serena said dully.

Ken picked the clothes up and looked them over. The pants were a navy blue with various stains and marks on them. They were made of a thick material that would be perfect for rigorous outside work. The shirt was plain white with a few marks on it as well.

"Alright then, thanks, Serena," Ken replied with a tone of guilt in his voice.

Serena turned her head so that he could put the clothes on. Ken took off his brown leather vest and placed it to the side so he could wear it again later. The pants were slightly big on him, but Serena had a belt laid out with the clothes that made it fit.

"The clothes we're wearing are what my dad and I wore when we did work in the village," Serena said as she finished putting clothes in the bag.

"You both worked?" Ken asked.

"I just helped sometimes. I didn't do much, but he got me these clothes for when I wanted to go do jobs with him," Serena answered.

"Well, these are really nice pants. The material is excellent for hiking through the woods. Also, they are broken in and super comfy," Ken claimed.

He started stretching and throwing a few kicks while admiring the quality of the pants. They may have been stained and well used, but he liked them all the same. Serena was happy to see that he was pleased with them.

After throwing a few more kicks, Ken grabbed the bread and water he found and gave some to Serena.

"Here, I found this last night. We should eat to get our strength up," Ken said while passing some to her.

The bread was stale but still good to eat. It wasn't much, but it was enough to get them moving.

As she ate, Serena's eyes became gloomy, "So, where are we going from here?" she asked in a somber tone.

Ken could tell she was sad about leaving. However, he was relieved to hear her ask at the same time. He knew they couldn't stay any longer. They already pushed their luck as far as he thought it would go.

Ken reached down to the floor and grabbed the map, "Well, I believe we need to do what Daemon said. We should head west until we hit the coast. Then go north until we run into him again," he said while looking the map over.

"There is a small town not far from here according to this. We should make that our next stop," Ken said while rolling the map up.

"Okay then," Serena mumbled.

"By the way, I think you should bring this with you," Ken said as he passed Serena a picture. It was a small photograph of her and her parents. She was in the middle, her father was to the left, and her mother was on the right. They all seemed happy together in the image.

Serena's eyes lit up as she grabbed it from him. "Where did you find this?" she shouted happily.

"It was in a small broken frame on the floor," Ken replied with a grin.

Serena wrapped her arms around Ken for a hug as her eyes went misty. Ken patted her head and then grabbed the bag. "Did you put everything from the other bag in this one?" he asked.

"Yeah, I threw the soaked clothes and map away, but I left the money and metal bearings in there," Serena answered while wiping her face.

"Oh yeah, I might want those," Ken said. He reached in the bag and grabbed the small brown pouch with the metal bearings in it. He tied them to the side of his pants for easy access. "Alright Serena, you ready to go?" he asked while putting the vest back on.

"Yeah, just let me see them one more time," Serena said while walking to the back door.

Ken gave a half smile and followed behind her.

Serena stood before the graves of her parents, staring at them in silence. Her eyes dampened as she let out a shaky sigh.

Ken placed his hand on her shoulder to let her know he was there. Serena made a faint smile and then leaned her head against his side.

"Promise we'll come back to visit them," Serena said in a drab tone.

"Of course we will, little sis. That goes without saying," Ken replied.

They stood in place for a few more minutes and then Serena turned to Ken after rubbering her eyes dry. "Alright, I'm ready to go," she said.

As Ken and Serena headed toward the tree line of the village, they stopped and looked back at it one more time before going into the woods.

"I wonder how long it will be before we can visit them again," Serena queried.

"It won't be long. We'll be here again before you know it," Ken replied as he ruffled Serena's hair.

"Stop doing that!" Serena giggled.

Ken turned to the woods and started to walk away. "Let's go, come on," he said while laughing with her.

After walking for a few minutes, Serena pulled on the side of Ken's shirt. "Can we take a trail this time? Walking through the woods is getting to be a pain," she said while stepping over a log.

"We need to be extra careful right now. It's better that we play it safe," Ken replied.

"Shouldn't we avoid going to a town then?" Serena asked.

"Yeah, but we need more food and water. I'm hoping we can sneak our way through and get what we need. Maybe we can even find an inn to hide at for most of the day," he answered while rubbing his chin.

"I don't think we should try for another inn," Serena said reluctantly.

"Why not?"

"Because every time we pay for a room something bad happens before we can even use it," Serena answered in a frank tone.

Ken put his hands behind his head and looked up at the blue sky through the branches and leaves. "I guess we really do have bad luck with inns," he said while reminiscing about the last two times they got a room. The first time, Serena got kidnapped, and the second time Ulgenda found them at the restaurant.

"You make a good point Serena. No more hotels then."

Serena seemed lost in thought for a moment like she was reconsidering her statement. "I wouldn't mind sleeping in a nice comfy bed though. Maybe the third times the charm," she added in hopes that Ken would change his mind.

"You just said we shouldn't get one," Ken replied in an irritated tone.

"Yeah, but I don't want to sleep on the ground anymore either," Serena retorted while folding her arms.

Ken let out a sigh while rolling his eyes. "We'll think of something when we get there. Maybe someone will offer us a place to stay like Tim's family did," he stated.

"I doubt it," Serena replied skeptically.

"I guess we'll just have to see."

Ken stopped abruptly and grabbed Serena's arm. He pulled her close and scanned the area with an intensity in his eyes. His face also became rigid as though ready for a fight.

"What!? What is it?" Serena asked as she gazed around for soldiers.

"You didn't hear that?" Ken said, his eyes still darting around.

"Hear what?" Serena questioned.

"I heard movement somewhere around us," Ken replied. "Show yourselves! I know you're here," he shouted, but no one came out.

The air became silent as they stood in place, listening for more signs of life around them.

"I said come out!" Ken demanded once more.

A daunting figure moved out from behind a wide tree that was in front of them. A man standing at least seven feet tall appeared. He was incredibly stocky and unnerving in size and presence.

"Alright, guys no need to hide anymore," the man called out in a deep, voice.

Five men came out from behind trees that encircled them. Each one was holding knives and grinning maliciously.

"Damn, they have us surrounded," Ken thought as he gazed at them.

The large man laughed darkly and then crossed his arms. "I'm the guy they call Bandit Bull, leader of this team of scoundrels. We were just on our way to pick over whatever is left of Sales when we heard you two coming a mile away," he said in an eerily cheerful tone.

"What do you want?" Ken asked crossly.

"Can't you guess by my name kid? Give me all your money and everything in that bag," Bull demanded.

"Hey boss, I heard him call that girl Serena earlier," one of Bull's henchmen said. "You think she's the one from the missing person poster? You know, the new one we saw yesterday?"

Bull stared at Serena curiously, then made a snaggle toothed grin. "I think you're right! The hair is different, but she looks similar. If it is her, she's worth one hundred thousand fol!" he exclaimed.

Ken grit his teeth and glared at them, trying to think of a way to handle all six at once.

"It all fits. She's supposed to be with a guy who's wanted for assaulting a Monarchy Soldier too. He's worth another twenty-five thousand!" Bull said eagerly. "We hit the jackpot fellas!"

"Serena, I'm going to fire these ball bearings at the boss. When I do, I want you to run. I'll take care of these guys while you get out of here," Ken whispered.

Serena looked at him to protest, but Ken shook his head. "Remember what I told you before. You have to listen to me," he said as he grabbed the pouch with the metal bearings in it. "Don't worry, I'll find you," he added as he raised his left hand with the pouch gripped in his palm.

"What are you two whispering about?" Bull barked.

"Now!" Ken yelled as he fired the metal bearings at the boss with his pressure blast.

The bearings flew straight into Bull's face and upper torso without fail. Bull screamed out in pain as he covered his mug from the attack.

Ken quickly summoned his sword through his Gate as Serena started to run. He then realized Bull's henchmen were staring at him while chuckling. They didn't seem the least bit concerned about the volley of metal imbedded in their boss's face.

"Ken look!" Serena cried while pointing at Bull.

Ken focused his attention on the boss who was smiling at him. Bull was missing an eye and had a bloody face with gashes in it from the attack.

A light blue transparent orb that hung around Bull's neck started to glow. The cuts on his face disappeared in the bright blue radiance and his eye grew back in his socket.

"What!?" Ken exclaimed as he watched.

Bull laughed obnoxiously as his face healed. He placed his finger and thumb on the light blue orb and rolled it between his digits. "You can't hurt me as long as I have this!" he said arrogantly.

Ken scoffed and stared Bull down. "Thanks for telling me! I'll just have to cut it off with your head!" he retorted.

Bull snapped his fingers and all five of his men charged at Ken with their knives.

"Serena, keep running!" Ken yelled as he fought against them.

Bull reached out swiftly and grabbed Serena before she could go. He picked her up by her shirt while clutching her with only one arm.

"KEN!" Serena screamed out in fear.

"NO! SERENA!" Ken bellowed as he battled with the henchmen.

"You guys handle him while I deal with the girl," Bull ordered as he walked away with Serena.

"LET HER GO!" Ken demanded as he kicked one the men back.

Ken raised his gate to his mouth and then yelled at it desperately. "Hooded man, I know you can hear me! PLEASE! SAVE HER!" he screamed as he struggled to fight back against the five henchmen.

Instantly, a red portal opened in the air between Ken and Bull. The flying fox dropped out the bottom of it and soared at the boss. Its claws began to glow and extend as it jammed them into Bull's head.

"AAAHHHH!" Bull yelled as he dropped Serena and grabbed the fox.

He threw the fox off himself as the orb shined once more and healed the damage the fox did to him.

"Run Serena! Get out of here now!" Ken shouted again.

Serena staggered as she stood. She gazed back at Ken with terror in her eyes then turned away and ran.

"You won't get away from me!" Bull claimed as he chased after her.

"Stay away from her, or I'll kill you!" Ken yelled at the top of his lungs as he tried to run after Bull. However, one of the henchmen jumped in front of Ken and slashed at his right shoulder. The vest took the hit and saved him from a bad gash. Then the others attacked him from behind.

"PROTECT HER!" Ken ordered the fox as he fought them off.

The fox got back up after being thrown and glanced over to Ken – then scurried after Serena and Bull.

"Get out of my way!" Ken commanded as he slashed and kicked at the henchmen who attacked him relentlessly.

"We almost got him. Go for the throat!" one of them yelled. The thug jumped at Ken who rapidly spun around and drove his heel into the bandit's face.

"I said get out of my way!" Ken howled furiously.

His fear for Serena became intense as the fight dragged on. All he could think about was something horrible happening to her. Then he heard her scream out from somewhere deep in the woods.

"SERENA!" Ken cried as his body began to shake.

"Get him now!" one of the men yelled as he charged.

Ken's eyes went wide with furry as his blood boiled. He ducked under the bandit's guard and ran his sword into the thief's stomach and out his back. Then he coldly flung the body off his blade.

The bandits all gasped at the sight of their dead colleague.

"Let me go, or I'll kill you all!" Ken threatened in a dark growl.

One of the bandits began to wobble as he gripped his knife harder. "You killed my brother!" he shouted as he jabbed his blade at Ken

Ken merely stepped to the side of the attack and slashed across the bandit's waist.

The thug fell to the ground as he bled out and gurgled.

Afterward, Ken stared the rest of them down menacingly from under his eyes.

The other three stepped back in fear as Ken approached them.

He started to run after Serena and went passed the rest of the henchmen. Then one of them threw a rope tethered by two metal balls at his legs – which wrapped around Ken and made him fall to the ground.

All the henchmen charged at him as he struggled to cut the rope off his legs.

"Kill him!" one of the men shouted as he pounced for Ken.

Just before suffering the attack, Ken cut the rope and rolled away as the bandit drove a knife into the ground where his head was.

Ken heard Serena scream out his name desperately from the forest again.

"SERENA!" Ken cried out, gripping his sword furiously.

Another bandit came at him while thrusting a knife at Ken's face – but Ken smacked his arm out of the way with a block, then smashed his left palm into the bandit's stomach. He roared and released a pressure blast into the thug which made blood spew from the bandit's mouth as he flew into a tree.

Ken charged at another one without hesitation and mercilessly slashed at his torso as the bandit tried to escape. The thief fell to the ground as he bled out from his chest and burbled agonizingly.

Ken turned his attention to the last one who picked up a second knife. The bandit looked scared and riled up as he shook fearfully. Ken rushed at the thief with great hast and a murderous glint in his eyes.

The bandit shrieked as he charged back at Ken with both knives up and ready. Rapidly, Ken dropped his body below the bandit's knives and sliced through the center of the thug's waist as he ran past him. Ken continued to dart forward without even looking back at the bandit.

The thief stood perfectly still as Ken disappeared into the woods. Blood suddenly gushed out from the center of the henchman's body. Then he collapsed lifeless on the ground.

Ken dashed through the woods yelling Serena's name frantically as he went. He cut and slashed through branches like they were butter, trying desperately to find her. His heart raced faster and harder as panic set in while he searched. His breaths became heavy and sporadic while screaming out her name repeatedly with no reply.

"Where are you!? Answer me! SERENA!"

Soon he became dizzy from hyperventilation. He leaned against a tree to tame himself. "I have to calm down. I can't help her or think clearly like this," Ken said as he took long deep breaths. After a moment, he noticed a few broken branches in front of him. They looked like someone busted them as they ran by.

Ken followed the trail of snapped twigs while his eyes darted around for any sign of her. "Serena! Serena!" he called out as he pressed on, but still heard no reply.

His mind started to go through different scenarios of what could've happened to her. How she could've been captured, passed out, or even—

No, she's okay! I know she's okay. She just won't answer me because she's scared, Ken thought as he continued his search.

"Fox! Where is she!" Ken hollered in hopes that the fox would appear with her.

Suddenly, Ken heard a light squeak to his left. He glanced over and saw the fox limping between trees. He rushed to it and saw it had taken a hard hit.

"Where is she!?" Ken asked fussily.

The fox gazed at Ken with despairing eyes and then pointed his nose to an open spot beneath a tree.

Ken looked where the fox directed, his eyes grew wide as his mouth gaped open.

Serena was laying on the ground motionless under the shade of the branches.

Ken stared at her in disbelief. His breaths became shaky as his throat choked. His body began to tremble while he stared at her in silence hoping that any minute she would pop up and tell him she was alright.

Slowly, Ken started to approach her. It took everything he had to pick up one foot and then place it down. As he gradually made his way to her, his eyes focused intently on her still frame.

"S…Se…Serena," he whispered through the pain in his gullet.

Finally, he got a grasp of himself and ran toward her.

"Serena!" Ken cried out sorrowfully.

He dropped to his knees where she laid and extended his reach toward her. His hands shook even more violently as they hovered above her body. Sluggishly, he lowered them on top of her figure which was unmoving and without presence.

With his fingertips, Ken traced Serena's arm up to her face where a trickle of blood ran from her mouth and down her cheek. Ken brushed her hair from her brow to reveal her closed eyelids and angelic face. Her skin was still warm, but without the lively glow he came to expect from her.

Ken shuttered as he looked her over. His eyes weld up with tears which fell from the tip of his nose to the side of her face.

"No…no…this can't be real," he whispered mournfully.

Ken leaned down low and put his hands under her body while wrapping his arms tightly around her frame. He clutched her against his chest and sobbed. He touched his forehead to hers, supporting the back of her head with his palm.

Ken gazed up at the sky as his faced twisted in anguish. "No…no…no…NO…NO…NO…SERENAAAAAA!" he screamed while holding her closely in his arms.

Chapter 18

Angeon

After grieving over Serena, Ken carried her back to Sales. He found a shovel by one of the houses and started to dig her a grave between her parents. He didn't have a gravestone to place at the top of it. Instead, he took the picture of her with her parents and placed it at the head of the grave.

He sat on his knees in silence at the foot of her resting place and stared at the photograph with a despairing grimace. The flying fox followed him back to Sales and was curled up next to where she was buried. It too seemed to be grief-stricken by her death.

"Some big brother I turned out to be," Ken whispered as his eyes got misty.

"After all that talk about how I would protect you. I promised I would keep you safe. I promised I would be there for you!" he stated while placing his hands on top of the soil that covered her body. He hunched over her grave and gripped the dirt between his fingers.

"I should've been stronger. I should've fought harder!" Ken exclaimed.

Tears fell from his eyes onto the ground that sheltered her body. He began to quiver as he sobbed. Then he heard the fox make a noise as it adjusted its body. Ken looked to it for a moment and suddenly felt a powerful rage build in his chest.

"This is your fault," he said while glaring at the fox whose ears popped up at his statement.

Ken stood up slowly and clenched his fist. "You were with her. You were supposed to be protecting her," he said darkly.

Ken approached the fox in a disgruntled manner which frightened it. It ran from him and scurried up the tree that hung over the graves.

Ken chased after it but was too slow. It sat atop a branch and stared down at him as he kicked the base of the tree.

"This is all your fault!" Ken screamed while repeatedly striking the trunk.

"Why didn't the hooded man come instead of you!?"

Ken placed his left hand on the tree and released a pressure blast which caused the leaves and branches to shake.

"Where is he!? Why haven't I seen him!?" he barked while blasting the tree a few more times.

The pain from overusing his gate power became worse with every burst, yet he ignored it as he rampaged.

"Why did he send me to protect her!? Why didn't he do it himself!?" Ken questioned irately while blasting the tree even more.

Bark began flying off in splinters while he continued his onslaught. The pain grew exponentially worse from the Gate straining.

"Is he happy? Is he satisfied? Is this what he wanted?" Ken bellowed.

After firing another blast, Ken's Gate cracked down the center of his hand. He looked it over and then scowled at fox. "I'll bet if I break the Gate, he'll come to fix it!" he shouted.

Ken placed his hand on the tree once more and discharged another blast. Fragments of wood violently expelled from the tree and into the air.

The crack on his Gate grew and spread across his hand as the pain became crippling. His body trembled as he attempted to keep his hand on the tree for another blast.

The fox jumped from the limb and flew into the woods. Ken saw a faint red-light shine for a moment and assumed it used its portal to go away.

Ken held his hand on the bare wood of the tree where his attacks stripped off layers of bark and timber. He focused intensely and prepare for another blast. Just as his Gate glimmered for another shot, he dropped his hand and fell to his knees.

"Why am I here? What is my purpose?" Ken mumbled as he

wept.

Afterward, he heard a voice calling out from the center of the village. "Where are you!? I know you're here punk!" it said in a burly man's tone.

Ken thought that it sounded familiar. He stood up using the tree to support himself and listened as the voice called out.

"You killed all my men! I heard you yelling a moment ago! Where are you!?" the voice yelled out heatedly once more.

Ken's expression became intense when he realized it was the man who went after Serena in the woods. He dashed out from behind the house and saw Bandit Bull standing in the center of the village. Just the sight of him made Ken's heart race with fury.

Bull saw Ken and gave him a cross stare. "You killed all my men you bastard! Now I'm going to pay you back!" he hollered.

Ken exposed his teeth as his breathes became staggered. "You killed my sister," he uttered quietly from under a shaky whisper.

"What? I couldn't hear you! You must be too scared to talk!" Bull taunted.

Ken activated his Gate and then flicked his wrist like Daemon did – causing it to open in front of him instead of by his side. The cracks that were on his hand were also visible in the Gate that hovered before him. He reached his left hand inside as it shined brightly.

"I said, you killed my little sister!" Ken screamed as he pulled his blade out from the circle.

His sword changed from its black and silver color scheme to a more sinister appearance. The entire weapon was now black from hilt to tip. Except for the edge of the blade which was now blood red and serrated as though it had teeth instead of a sharp trim. The center of the sword had three diagonal hollow gaps that were rectangular.

Ken pointed his blade at Bull while he glared at him with homicidal intent. "You'll be the one to die here!" he barked in a threatening voice.

Bull reared his head back and laughed profoundly at Ken's display. "You're right about one thing, I did kill the girl. When I finally caught her that damn fox jumped on me and blew fire in my face. So, I dropped her and grabbed it from my shoulder and threw it off to the side. Then I had to chase her down again," Bull said. His tone was irritable as though reliving the experience.

"The whole time I chased her, she cried and whined for help. Then I finally grab the little pipsqueak, and she screamed: 'Ken, Ken, save me Ken!' It was pathetic." Bull mocked.

"THAT'S ENOUGH!" Ken yelled out crossly.

"That's not the best part," Bull added with a devilish grin. "After crying for you to save her, she bit my arm. She bit it good too. Broke right through the skin. So, I grabbed her by the neck and threw into the closest tree," he said as he snickered.

Ken's chest pounded as his expression went from being angry to uncontrollably livid. "SHUT UP!" he screamed while clenching his sword with both hands.

Bull reached behind his back while cutting a sneer. He pulled out a long sword that resembled a katana in shape and form.

"I was a little pissed with myself though. I couldn't turn her in for money since I killed her and all," he said casually while shrugging his shoulders.

Ken raised his sword and charged at Bull with full speed. "I'LL KILL YOU!" he shrieked.

Bull smiled haughtily as Ken approached.

Ken threw his sword at Bull ferociously while closing in. It spun and whipped through the air while tumbling toward its target.

Bull was taken off guard by the attack and tried to dodge the sword but was too slow to escape it. The tip of the blade pierced his stomach and drove into him until it stuck halfway into his gullet.

Ken leaped into the air and performed a flying side kick into the hilt of his sword and pushed it all the way through Bull's body.

Bull gurgled and choked as blood spilled from his back and abdomen. The light blue orb began to glow and heal Bull – but Ken reached for it with his left hand and grabbed it.

"I WON'T LET YOU LIVE THROUGH THIS ONE!" he bellowed while trying to snatch it off.

However, the pain from overusing his Gate power prevented Ken from thoroughly gripping the orb. He tried desperately to clutch his fingers but couldn't get a firm hold on the orb which rolled around the palm of his hand as it shined intensely.

Seeing his chance – Bull quickly raised the sword in his right hand and ran it through Ken's solar plexus.

Ken's eyes widened as he felt the tip of cold steel penetrate his skin and cut through to his back. He coughed as blood spewed from his mouth, and his hand dropped from the orb.

Bull pulled his sword out of Ken and picked him up and threw him across the ground where he rolled onto his back and laid there while bleeding out. Bull reached into his stomach and slowly pulled Ken's sword out from his belly and then tossed it aside.

The orb's light blue glow began to shine over the gaping hole in Bull's gullet and healed it as he breathed in deeply. "I didn't think you could get one in on me," Bull said as he recovered. "Oh well, at least I killed you."

Unexpectedly, the hole in Ken's stomach glimmered the same color as the light blue orb. His wound healed and closed as he started to take deep breaths.

"What!?" Bull yelled in disbelief. "It must be from when you grabbed the orb," he stated. "Yeah, you were holding it when I stabbed you. How lucky, now I get to kill you again!" he said with a sinister grin.

Ken coughed and wheezed as the light faded away. He stayed on the ground while staring at the blue sky. His vision went back and forth from being blurry to clear as he recovered. Then he heard a faint voice speak to him.

"Ken...Ken...I'm here Ken. I'm with you," it said as he noticed a transparent white form floating above him. The voice was soft and innocent, like the tone of a child. "Ken, you have to get up. He's going to kill you," it said as Ken's vision became clear.

He saw Serena hovering above him. Her face and body were clear and white like a ghost. He reached out slowly to touch her, but her body was intangible.

"S...Serena?" Ken questioned in a dazed tone.

"It's me, big bro, you have to hurry or he's going to kill you!" Serena stated in an urgent tone.

Suddenly Ken's eyes widened as he became alert. He saw Bull running at him with his sword raised to slice him in two.

Ken held his arms over his face out of reaction while Bull swung his sword to cut him in half. As the blade bore down on Ken, he closed his eyes and braced for impact. Ken heard a loud clanking noise, like the metal of a sword hitting something hard. Then he heard Bull cry out.

"What the hell!?"

Ken opened his eyes and saw a bright silvery white wing shielding his body from above. It extended from Serena's back and appeared to be made from solid light.

Serena used the wing to smack Bull back and send him rolling on the ground.

Ken placed his hands down and pushed himself back up to his feet. He gazed at Serena incredulously.

"Serena – is that really you?" he questioned with a blank stare.

"There's no time, big bro. He's getting up. We need to stop him once and for all. Grab your sword, and I'll give you my power," Serena answered.

Ken was confused by the whole situation, but when he looked over at Bull and saw him getting up, he knew she was right and decided to figure things out after Bull was dealt with.

Ken raised his hand and called his sword which flew from the ground to his palm.

"Now what do we do?" Ken asked as his expression change from confusion to resolve.

"Raise your sword above your head with both hands," Serena commanded while floating behind Ken's head.

Ken followed her orders and raised his sword steadily above himself. Serena held her hands out to Ken, and his body started to glow as a white fuming arura of light encased him and rose to his sword. As the energy became more intense, it twisted and wrapped around his blade. Rapidly the power started to solidify from a fuming smoke like form to a thick white fire like energy that surged up the sword from hilt to the tip.

Ken felt the power grow and become more concentrated as it left his body and condensed around his weapon. He felt the blade quiver and shake as the aura encased his sword and raged loudly above him. The noise coming from it was like rushing water falling into a pond.

Bull stood up slowly and shuddered. From his eyes, he saw Ken standing with his sword held high and a white fire like light that raged and whipped around his blade. A pair of angelic white-silvery wings were spread wide behind the sword. Bull noticed Ken was staring him down unforgivingly from under the display.

"Hey, let's talk this out for a minute," Bull begged as he fell to his knees. "With my healing stone and your power, we could join forces. No one could stop us! What do you think!?" he yelled out as he tremored from intimidation.

Ken didn't answer. He merely continued to glare at Bull with complete distain.

"Ken, do it now!" Serena cried from behind him.

Ken tightened his grip on the handle as his expression became even more severe. "This is for… MY SISTER!" he yelled as he swung the point of the sword down to the ground.

When the tip touched the dirt – the white aura left the blade and expanded hastily as it raced across the terrain. It grew and thundered as it tore a scare into the ground beneath it.

All Bandit Bull could do was scream as it made its way to him. When the energy reached his body, it instantly shined a bright blue that matched the orb and expanded five times larger than it already was.

The air filled with the over whelming sound of the energy as it pulverized the land and forest behind the village. Wind roared and the ground around them shook like an earthquake as the attack surged.

Slowly the energy quelled and faded away until it was gone, leaving behind a large gash in the ground where it stormed. When the dust settled a gaping hole was exposed in the tree line. All the vegetation in the path of Ken's blast were utterly obliterated. The destruction seemed to go about a quarter mile into the woods and left nothing but a deep empty scare in the forest.

Ken stood frozen in place. He was still holding his sword with tip to the ground, gawking at the destruction from the attack.

"Are you okay, big bro?" Serena asked as her wings dissipated.

Ken straightened up while taking in the view from their attack. He turned to Serena to respond. However, when he saw her ghost-like form, all the guilt and anguish from her death came back to him. He reached out to touch her cheek, but his fingers passed through her as though she weren't there at all. He fell to his knees and stared at her fleshless, pale, ghostly form.

"I'm sorry Serena, I let you down," Ken whispered despairingly as tears rolled down his cheeks.

Serena opened her mouth to respond, but before she could say anything, they heard a voice call out behind them.

"Whoa! Did you see that, Aisha?! That was some serious power!" a man expressed as he stepped out from behind a building.

"Raiga stop!" a woman shouted as she followed him. "We have to wait for back up Raiga! He's too powerful without an Angeon on our team," she added.

"Are you kidding me!? With power like that, he must be an S class Angeon!" Raiga replied eagerly.

"Ken, we need to leave," Serena said as Ken stood back up and glared at the two newcomers.

The guy called Raiga was a cocky looking man with spiked black hair that had a slight green hue to it. He was about the same height as Ken but was more muscular and seemed to be in his late twenties. He wore a tight tank top that was dark forest green with black fingerless gloves. His pants had a few pockets that went down the side of his legs and were also black like his gloves.

The girl he called Aisha had a more modest look about her. Her hair was light brown with a pink hue and was pulled back in a low braided ponytail. She wore a tight pink and brown tank top that covered her midriff. She had a matching pink and brown skirt which reached the top of her knees and had light pink fabric running down the center and brown leather like material down the sides of her waist. Under that were brown tights that also went down to the tops of her knees.

"From the way they talk, it sounds like they're with the Monarchy," Serena said in a concerned tone. "We have to get out here."

Ken gazed at them crossly. "No, we need to take them out, Serena," he replied. "It's their fault you're like this. It's because of them that all this happened to you in the first place. They deserve to suffer the same way you did," he muttered darkly.

Serena was shocked by his response. It was something she didn't expect to hear from her big brother. "Ken, you have to go," she pleaded.

Ken ignored her request and readied his sword. "I'll get revenge for you. I'll make them realize exactly how bad they screwed up," he stated.

Raiga reached into his pocket and raised a sliver badge into the air. "I'm Major Raiga Fearbuster of the Omni Enforcement Regiment of The Monarchy. You're under arrest for assaulting Monarchy soldiers, kidnapping, using unregistered Angeon powers, and murder," he said while cutting an arrogant grin.

"Raiga! As your commanding officer, I order you to back down!" Aisha demanded.

Raiga's eyes darted back to her. "If he's an S class Angeon then he falls under the K.O.S. ruling, Aisha. Kill…On…Sight! He's too dangerous to let walk around freely. You saw that power. We're obligated to keep all of Etheria safe," he argued.

Aisha looked at Ken and the destruction of his attack. "We can't handle that much power, we need to regroup," she answered.

"He used a lot of energy with that attack, Aisha. I'll bet he's running on fumes right now. This is the best chance we got to take him down," Raiga claimed.

Aisha looked like she wanted to dispute the point further, but she seemed to give in to Raiga's influence. She let out a sigh and then grabbed her badge and raised it as well.

"I am Major Aisha Sono of the Omni Enforcement Regiment of the Monarchy. I am the commander of this team. With the power given to me by the Monarch, I order you return your sword to your gate and lay on the ground with your hands behind your back!" she commanded.

"What if I don't!" Ken replied.

Raiga gave a smug grin at Ken's comment. "Then we'll make you!" he shouted as the back of his right hand began to glow from under his glove.

Raiga's Gate opened before him and revealed its form. It had a diamond shape in the center which had eight other diamond structures pointing out from its corners and sides. A circle connected the protruding diamonds at their center corners. And an outer circle encompassed the entire design.

His Gate flew over his arm and then quickly pulled itself away revealing a large dark forest green kite shaped shield on his right forearm that matched his tank top. The edges of it were silver and bladed. It had black trim around the outer ends just behind the blade that went around the entirety of the weapon. It also had two one-inch holes in the top left and right corners.

"We'll go with formation B Raiga." Aisha said as the Gate on her right hand shined.

It opened and revealed the same pattern as Raiga's. It moved in the same manner as his did as well. Then it disappeared while leaving behind her weapon.

She gripped a small sword that she held upside down. The blade was about a foot and a half long with a subtle curve that followed her forearm and passed the point of her elbow. In it was a thin black line that traced from the hilt and up the center of the sword to the tip. It also had a small triangular shaped hole near the base of it. The sword had a blunt guard that covered the fingers and could be used as brass knuckles. The top of the handle had another six-inch blade which displayed its versatility in battle.

"Formation B sounds perfect to me," Raiga said as he took a

fighting stance.

"Ken, let's go! Please!" Serena begged while floating beside him.

Ken ignored her pleas and focused intently on Raiga who seemed happy to be getting into a fight.

Aisha's expression still showed her reluctance to jump into battle with an Angeon.

Ken gripped his sword and started to walk toward Raiga who moved in on him as well. As they approached each other their walking became faster and faster until they started to run at one another with weapons held ready to strike.

They both yelled out as their weapons crashed together. Raiga smiled conceitedly at Ken from behind his shield which pressed against Ken's blade in a pushing stalemate. They broke apart, and each took a fighting stance to continue the battle.

Ken lunged forward while jabbing his sword at Raiga who used his shield to parry the attack. Raiga then used the opening this gave him to punch at Ken with the tip of his shield.

However, Ken ducked below the swing and rose back up with an upper slash using his sword. Raiga responded by stepping back and to the side quickly to narrowly miss being hit by Ken's blade.

The fight continued in this manner with them slashing, blocking, and dodging each other's attacks repetitively until Ken made a fake swipe with his sword to Raiga's legs which forced Raiga to drop his guard.

When Ken noticed his chance, he swiftly delivered a powerful spinning hook kick to the right side of Raiga's face.

Raiga fell over to his knees and immediately stumbled back to his feet.

Ken smirked as he moved in to make the final strike. He readied his sword by rearing it back to finish Raiga, then he heard Serena call out to him.

"STOP!" Serena bellowed from behind his head.

Just before landing his attack, Ken pulled back his sword and jumped away from Raiga. As Ken looked Raiga over, he noticed Aisha's sword come up from behind Raiga's back. If he hadn't stopped when he did, Aisha would have run her sword through him without even noticing she was there.

"I told you we need to leave, Ken. They're too dangerous," Serena nagged as Ken raised his sword to continue.

"I can take them, Serena," Ken replied with an ominous growl in his voice.

"Ken, I can feel something from you when you're attacking him. You're trying to kill him, aren't you?" Serena asked.

"He deserves it! It's his fault you were taken from your home," Ken stated.

"He didn't do it, big bro. Remember? It was Ulgenda," Serena answered.

Ken huffed at her response, "He works for The Monarchy Serena. He's just as guilty, they're all guilty!" he exclaimed.

Raiga grabbed the bottom of his chin and rubbed it for a moment. "He got me pretty good," he said.

Then he spat out some blood and moved his jaw around until he felt it pop. "Oh yeah, that's better."

"You want me to tag in?" Aisha asked from his side.

"No way, it's just getting interesting," Raiga stated. He held his shield out in front and then smirked at Ken. "Now that I'm done gauging his fighting skill, I can get serious."

Raiga pulled a small handle that was under his shield, causing his weapon to transform. The entire shield slid forward on top of a small platform that was hidden beneath it. The platform stayed laying across his forearm, but the shield moved all the way up until most of it hung over his fist. Then the tip of the shield slid forward as the sides filled in the gap the tip left. It lost its shield shape and now had the form of a sword which was wielded from the forearm instead of the hand.

"Now let's try that again," Raiga said as he took a fighting stance. Aisha stepped back to let the fight continue.

Ken stared at the new weapon while wondering how he should go about fighting against it. "Hey Serena, can we do that blast again?"

Ken asked.

"No, I used too much power with that last attack. I have some energy, but not much," Serena replied.

"Dang," Ken blew while staring Raiga down. "Can you give me a little power to use then?"

"I don't want to kill any more people, Ken. Please, I just want to go," Serena pleaded.

Just as Serena finished, Raiga rushed in on Ken with his newly formed weapon. He slashed, jabbed, and lashed out at Ken.

Ken blocked and dodged Raiga's onslaught but found it more difficult to avoid the slashes than before. Raiga was faster and more precise with his swings. It was like he started taking the fight seriously.

Ken jammed, evaded, and parried every attack that he could from Raiga's blade. However, behind each slash he stopped or avoided was followed by a punch or strike of some kind that he couldn't maneuver while being distracted by the weapon.

Raiga didn't let up an inch as he flailed his sword and shield hybrid at Ken.

Finally, Ken made the split-second decision to use his Gate power and raised his left hand as it started to glow.

Raiga instantly realized what he was doing and jumped back to create space.

Ken stopped the energy from firing at the last moment.

"Was that a bluff? I noticed your Gate is cracked. If you use your power one more time, you'll shatter it for sure," Raiga taunted.

Ken pondered the best way to go about fighting. He couldn't keep up in a sword fight, yet he felt like he could still win. There was just something he didn't see that he knew he could do.

Raiga cut a smirk at him while he readied for another go. "I'll say this much about you. I can see how you beat some of our soldiers. It's obvious you've been in a fight or two, but clearly, you're not particularly good with a sword," he said while holding his left arm out with his thumb pointing down.

Just when Raiga finished his remark, Ken realized what he was doing wrong.

Of course, it's like when I fought Daemon. I'm fighting him on his level. I need to fight him with my skills, not his, Ken thought. He dug his feet into the ground and gripped his sword with both hands.

"Looks like you're ready for me wrap this up," Raiga stated.

Ken just smiled at the comment and sprinted toward Raiga at full speed. Then he threw his sword at Raiga with all his strength.

Raiga's eyes widened as Ken's sword spun at him in the air. He ducked below the blade which flipped and sliced above him.

Ken closed the gap as Raiga tried to stand back up to fight.

Ken shot his foot between Raiga's ankles and used his back and shoulders to push Raiga over his leg and onto the dirt. Immediately, Ken raised his hand and called his sword back to him – which was still whipping in the air as it flew toward the woods. It stopped midflight and jetted back to the palm of his hand. Ken didn't waste a minute raising it above his head to strike down Raiga who laid on his back beneath him.

"Ken, no!" Serena cried out as Ken drove his sword down at Raiga.

Raiga squeezed his eyes together as he braced for death.

Just before the tip of Ken's blade touched his chest, Aisha knocked Ken's sword away and drove her shoulder into Ken's stomach, causing him to stagger back.

Ken raised his sword to fight Aisha, but she rapidly closed the distance between them and unleashed a punishing salvo of slashes at him.

Aisha struck the flat of Ken's sword repeatedly with immense force and speed. Sparks burst in the air with each swing of her blade as it battered Ken's.

All Ken could do was back up as she continued to push him away with her attacks.

Aisha moved his sword away with the guard that covered her fingers and drove her elbow into Ken's side. She followed up with multiple strikes to the inside of his thighs, ribs, and even hit him in the right arm where his bicep muscle meet his triceps. Each attack was performed with a punch or elbow strike and done so swiftly that Ken couldn't react or do anything to stop it. The hits crippled the muscles they smashed, causing him to fall to his knees.

Ken was in complete shock from her moves and technique. Never in his time practicing martial arts had he come by someone so fast and skilled. He gawked at Aisha from his helpless position, waiting for her to make the final strike.

Aisha raised her sword and punched the finger guard at Ken's face. Instantly, Serena's wings appeared in front of Ken and blocked the attack. Serena opened them quickly and pushed Aisha away from Ken.

Aisha slid back and took a stance while staring Ken down with a serious expression. However, the look of intense focus on her face quickly changed to shock as she took in the view of a pair of empty wings floating above Ken's head.

"Raiga, do you see that!?" Aisha called out in bewilderment.

"Yeah! What the hell is going on? Is that coming from his guardian!?" Raiga replied with the same expression.

"That's impossible! Guardians can't manifest their own power!" Aisha answered, still gazing in awe.

"Ken, we need to go while we can," Serena expressed as she hovered over Ken with her wings spread wide.

"I can't. That girl hit me in all the right muscle groups. I can't move my legs or my right arm," Ken replied. He gripped his sword weakly in his left hand and tried to contemplate all his options.

"What do we do, big bro?" Serena asked in a concerned tone.

"If you could give me enough energy to fire another attack, I may be able to buy enough time to escape while the muscles she hit recover," Ken replied.

"It won't be like the last energy I gave you, it'll be smaller," Serena retorted.

"That's fine, just give me something to work with," Ken stated.

"Okay big bro, but please don't kill them," Serena pleaded as her wings faded away. She held out her hands, and Ken once again felt her power start to surge around him.

"He's getting ready for another attack!" Raiga shouted as he rushed toward Aisha.

Ken moved the energy from his body to his sword. The power twisted and wisped around his blade like steam made of white light. He held his sword at the side of his body while winding up to make the attack. The energy became more intense as it ran from the base of the sword to the tip.

Ken yelled out as he swung the blade and fired the energy off at Aisha. Unlike the last blast, this attack came out in the shape of a crescent moon as it shot toward her.

Raiga got between Aisha and the beam as his weapon changed back from its sword mode to its shield form. When the energy reached them, Raiga yelled out and smashed the blast with his shield. It deflected off to the side where it cut down a tree as it as crashed into the woods.

"No way!" Ken shouted.

Raiga then ran at Ken with Aisha following at his heels.

"Serena, I need another one!" Ken exclaimed as they moved in.

"I can't, I'm completely out of energy!" Serena replied in a panic.

Ken gritted his teeth while raising his sword to fight against them. He tried to stand, but his legs refused to move. He jabbed his sword at Raiga who smacked it out of the way. Then Raiga used the broad side of his shield to slam the side of Ken's head which caused everything around him to go black.

Chapter 19

The Deal

"Ken…Ken, wake up."

Ken heard Serena's voice call out to him. It sounded distant and echoed with every word. His head felt like it was spinning and jarring back and forth as though the area around him was moving on its own.

As he struggled to awaken, he thought that he was laying down on something. A thin pad or mattress of sorts. Ken placed his left hand on his forehead but felt something hard and cold like metal hit him in the face. He opened his eyes slowly while holding his hand above his head. As his vision became clear, he saw a metal glove that was fastened down on around his wrist and slipped over his hand. His fingers were stuck pointing straight out in it. It had different marks and seals written on it that were like the Gate on his hand. It wasn't heavy, but it was annoying since he could not bend his fingers.

Ken sat up slowly and looked around his environment. He was in a jail cell with pale white walls and stone-grey floor. There was a metal toilet in the corner. He glanced down and realized he was sitting on a stiff metal frame which protruded from the wall with a hard pad made of chopped up fabric beneath him. The fixtures on the ceiling poured out bright light which made his head hurt. He raised his left hand to cover his eyes but smacked himself with the metal glove once more only adding to the throbbing pain in his temple.

Ken heard a voice say something and laugh just outside of the cell. As his eyes adjusted to the light, he saw black metal bars covering the front of his room. Raiga and Aisha were sitting on a bench in front of his chamber, watching over him.

"How many times you going to hit yourself with that glove idiot!?" Raiga called out in an amused tone.

Ken placed his feet on the floor and made his way toward the bars. He noticed he was wearing the same clothes that he had before they captured him. Once he reached the bars, he scanned around the outside of the cell. He saw a hallway with a shined floor that led up to other lock down units. With his limited space, he couldn't see how far the hall went or wherever it led to.

"So, how's that egg on the side of your head feel?" Raiga asked in a condescending manner.

Ken peered up at him and saw he had a brown bandage on his cheek from where he kicked Raiga.

"About the same as your face I suppose," Ken retorted.

Raiga's expression changed from obnoxious grinning to an irritable scowl. "Want to see if you can do it again, buddy!?" Raiga stated heatedly as he stood from the bench.

"Get in here and I will!" Ken answered.

"That's enough, Raiga!" Aisha ordered.

Raiga turned to her and threw his arms up in the air. "Whose side are you on?" he asked.

"You know exactly where I stand, but you don't have to kick him while he's down," Aisha said while glaring at him.

Raiga sucked his teeth and turned away from her. "Fine, watch him yourself!" he huffed before starting up the hallway.

Ken heard a door pop and slam, after which everything became quiet.

After sitting in awkward silence for a moment, Ken realized he didn't see Serena floating around him.

"Serena! Where are you?" he shouted.

"I'm here, big bro," Serena's voice echoed in his head.

"Where?" Ken asked while looking back and forth for her.

"I'm inside you. When they put that glove on your hand, it forced me to faze into your body," Serena answered.

"Are you okay?"

"Yeah, I'm fine. It didn't hurt me at all. What about you, big bro?

You're the one who got hurt," Serena inquired.

"Well, my head is killing me, and my body is sore in the places that *she* hit me," Ken said with emphases on the word 'she' as he looked over at Aisha. "Other than that, I think I'm ok."

Ken continued to glare at Aisha who glanced off to the side with a guilty expression.

"Where am I?" Ken asked, his tone was harsh and sounded more like a command than a question.

"You're at the Monarchy jail in Ribriann," Aisha answered softly. She seemed distant and wouldn't make eye contact.

Ken couldn't help but notice her mood. He pondered why she was acting so remorseful.

"Ribriann!?" Serena shouted in Ken's mind. "That's the capital of Estaira!"

"What's Estaira?" Ken asked out loud.

Aisha gave him a confused glance. "It's the name of the continent we're on?" she said in a question like tone. "How do you not know that?"

Ken stayed quiet for a moment, thinking about how to respond. Then he concluded that he didn't owe her any explanation at all. Especially since it was her fault they were there to begin with.

"It's none of your business. Shouldn't you be off with your boyfriend or something?" Ken retorted in a snippy manner.

"He's not my boyfriend. He's my team member and subordinate," Aisha replied.

Ken huffed and rolled his eyes at her.

Aisha turned her head away and looked down at the floor with a grimace once more.

What's her deal? Ken thought while staring at Aisha.

"She does seem sad about something doesn't she," Serena said.

You can hear my thoughts? Ken asked Serena in his mind.

"Yeah, when I'm infused with you like this, I can hear what you're thinking," Serena answered.

Huh, I guess I'll have to watch where my mind wonders then, Ken replied while looking back at Aisha who let out a deep depressing sigh.

Her eyes slowly made their way back up to Ken. She opened her mouth to talk but stumbled over her words.

"I...I just...I wanted..." Aisha stuttered.

"Spit it out already!" Ken barked irritably.

"I'm sorry!" Aisha shouted back.

Everything went quiet again. Ken was shocked to hear her apologize and was trying to process a response.

"You're sorry?" he mumbled.

"Yeah, I saw you when you were burying her. I could tell how much she means to you so, I'm sorry," Aisha answered as her gaze slowly drifted away from him again.

Ken tightened his right hand into a fist while gritting his teeth. He then jumped up from his bunk furiously.

"You're damn right you're sorry!" he exclaimed. "Aren't you a Major or some crap?! Why are you here watching me? Shouldn't you be crawling up some supervisor's ass for a promotion since you caught me!?"

Aisha didn't respond, instead she lowered her head even more, as if the weight of her remorse was pushing her down.

"What's wrong with you!? You can't lock me up and then act like you feel bad about it! What's your deal?" Ken bellowed.

As he stepped forward toward the bars, he felt something under his foot. It was a small plastic spoon that was laying on the floor at the edge of his bunk. He picked it up and then threw it at Aisha.

"Answer me!" he shouted as it flew to her.

Just as Aisha raised her right hand to catch the spoon, it stopped in midair and floated in front of her palm.

"Is she doing that?" Ken uttered quietly as he stared at Aisha who sat perfectly still like a statue.

"No, that would be my doing," a voice said from the back of the cell.

Ken jumped forward and spun around. A man with long raven black hair tucked behind his ears stood behind him. He wore a white robe which had gold trimming around the edges. The trim crossed over the front of his chest making a Y shape just under his neck. His skin was pale white, and he wore a smile that creeped Ken out.

"Who are you?" Ken asked.

The man glanced down at Ken's left hand and then walked toward him slowly. As he did, Ken started to back away.

"I go by many names. Father of The Monarchy, Master of Time and Space, The Great Elder Sage. Any of those will do," he answered pompously.

Ken continued to back away from him but bumped into his bunk. "How are you doing this?" he asked as he glanced back to Aisha who was still frozen in the same position with the spoon floating in front of her hand.

"I already told you. I'm the master of time and space," the strange man replied. He stopped approaching after he got a couple of feet from Ken.

"Well, what do you want?" Ken asked while taking a fighting stance.

The man's creepy smile grew wider as he stared at Ken's left hand. Then he pointed to it with his long pale finger.

"I want to see that," he answered.

Ken looked down at his hand and noticed the glove was gone. It vanished without him even realizing.

Serena phased out of his body since the glove was no longer forcing her to stay inside.

Ken looked over his hand curiously and then cut a cocky smile. "That was a mistake," he said while activating his Gate and pulling his sword from it. "Serena, give me some power! We're getting out of here!" he shouted.

"Got it Ken!" Serena answered.

The white aura started to surround Ken as he built up energy.

The man laughed while shrugging his shoulders. "If you want to escape, I won't stop you. I have people to do that for me. But if you leave now, then I can't put Serena back in her body," he said haughtily.

The energy they were building immediately faded away from Ken as he and Serena both gawked at the man in disbelief.

"What did you just say!?" Ken asked.

"I said I can give the girl back her body," the man replied conceitedly.

"Are you serious? Can you really do it?" Ken asked with a desperately hopeful expression.

"Of course, I can! You doubt the power of The Great Elder Sage?" the Sage stated with self-importance.

"How, how can we do it?" Ken asked as he closed the gap between him and the man.

"Let me get a good look at that first," the Sage said while pointing at Ken's Gate.

Ken held up his left hand to the man, who quickly snatched it with his right and then held the back of it up to his eyes. He started to caress the scaring of Ken's Gate with his cold fingertips, tracing out the lines engraved in Ken's skin.

"Yes, this is where I sensed it after all," the Sage said in a hiss like whisper. "This is *his* energy. This is *his* mark," he muttered while turning his head from side to side while rubbing the Gate. "Why, why did *he* put so much into it? Why did *he* invest this much into the boy? What does *he* see? What does *he* know?" he murmured quietly to himself.

Ken started to feel uneasy as the Sage continued to stare and touch the Gate on the back of his hand. The Sage then looked at Ken from above his Gate.

"Do you see this?" the Sage questioned while circling the outside of the Gate with his finger. "Do you understand the significance of this?"

Ken shook his head while giving a freaked-out stare.

"*He's* taunting me," the Sage said with a slight chuckle as he started to quiver. "This Gate shouldn't work since the sword design breaks the outer circle. Yet, here it is. In perfect working order. *He's* showing me how far *he's* come. How advanced *he* is now," he said as his shaking became more intense.

Ken snatched his hand away and backed up a little. He finally had enough of the man acting weird.

"Alright, you had your look. Now, how do we bring back Serena?" Ken demanded.

The man turned away from Ken and paced back and forth in the room. Then he turned back to Ken with a serious look.

"I have a deal for you. A proposition if you will," the Sage said while approaching Ken once more. "The man who put this Gate on you wants to get you back. He won't give up on it. So, I'm going to put a mark on your Gate that will summon me when he contacts you. Then, I will kill him. After he is dead – and only after he is dead, I will give your sister back her body," he said while taping his fingertips together.

"All I have to do is just… be bait? That sounds too easy. What's the catch?" Ken asked skeptically.

The man rolled his eyes and sighed. "There are a lot of politics that are involved in something like this. You see, I can't just free you," he said while rubbing his forehead.

"What do I have to do then? Ken asked.

"You're going to have to join the Monarchy and serve a one-year probation period," the Sage replied.

"Are you serious!?" Ken yelled.

"During that year you'll receive training on how to use your newfound Angeon powers and how to fight better. When your year is up, you'll join the Omni Enforcement Unit," the Sage said, ignoring Ken's outburst.

"What if the hooded man comes to me before the year is up?" Ken asked.

"He won't do that. He's not stupid enough to come here to try and take you. That's why I'm putting you on the Omni Enforcement team. They go out on regular missions far away from the castle. That's when he will contact you," the Sage answered.

"That's not good enough. I can't make Serena wait a whole year," Ken said crossly.

"It's either that or the death penalty!" the Sage replied. His tone suggested that he was getting impatient.

Ken grumbled and threw his arms in the air. "I don't need training or any of that crap! Just send me out there, I'll find him. The sooner, the better!" he exclaimed.

"You're not getting this. The charges against you are severe. I can't just let you leave without consequences. I already gave you the options. I may control space and time, but I am not a patient man, now choose!" the Sage demanded.

"Ken, I'm not so sure about helping him kill someone. I know we killed that bandit, but that was a different situation," Serena contested.

"What choice do we have Serena? It's either this or the death penalty. Besides, the hooded man hasn't done us any favors. If he was a good guy, he would've saved you. If you ask me, he deserves what he gets."

Serena was taking back by Ken's statement. The look in his eye was dark and revealed a side of him she never seen before. "I guess you're right. We really don't have a choice," she answered grimly.

Ken gazed at the Gate on the back of his hand apprehensively. He didn't trust this guy at all. At the same time, he thought it could be the only chance to give Serena another opportunity at living her own life.

"Do we have a deal?" the Sage asked while holding his left hand out to Ken.

Ken stared at it for a moment and then grabbed it with his left as well. "It's a deal!"

Immediately the Sage turned Ken's hand over and placed his right palm over Ken's Gate.

Ken felt the same searing sensation that he experienced when the hooded man put the Gate on him. His face twisted from the pain, but he glanced over to Serena who floated beside him. She watched with a concerned look on her pale, ghost-like face. Instead of crying out, Ken forced a smile at her. He wanted her to see him standing steadfast in the face of this new journey they were taking on together.

When the Sage finished branding his mark, Ken looked over the back of his hand which had steam coming off it. He didn't see any new seals on it but did notice the cracks were gone.

"You fixed it? I thought only the Sage who put it on could do that?" Ken queried.

"Only the Sage who gave you the Gate can replace it. However, a powerful Sage can fix any gate. Although, a Great Elder Sage such as I, *could* put a new Gate on you. If I wanted to," the Sage answered snobbishly.

"Where is the mark you put on me? I don't see it anywhere," Ken asked while scanning his hand over.

"I hid it within your Gate, so no one will see it," the Sage replied. "Now listen up. In about an hour or so the Monarchy will come for you. They will take you to see the Commander General. Just behave yourself, and you'll be fine. Oh, and they will scan your memory to see if you have any affiliation with the Amony. The mark I put on you will make it look like you have no memory from before you found Serena. So, roll with that and pretend you lost it. Don't slip up, though. You won't get any redoes from me," he said hastily.

"One more thing. Before I leave, I'm going to put you in the same position you were in when I got here. It would look weird to her if you instantly appeared to move from where you were," the Sage said while looking at Aisha who was still frozen in time.

"When will I see you again?" Ken asked while rubbing the back of his hand.

"When I'm turning *him* into dust," the Sage replied with a wicked grin. "See you in a year."

The Sage snapped his fingers together loudly which caused Ken's view to completely change. He went from looking at the Sage to throwing the spoon at Aisha in a split second.

Aisha swiftly caught the spoon in midair and then gazed at Ken from behind her hand.

Ken looked around the cell for the Sage, but he was gone. He started to wonder if all that really happened or if it was just a dream. Then he felt a tingling sensation on the back of his hand which had the metal glove back on it. *Did that really just happen?* he thought with a muddled expression.

"Yeah, it did. I remember it," Serena answered inside his mind.

Aisha gave him a puzzled look. To her, he went from raving mad to jumbled and dumbfounded.

"Are you okay?" she asked while throwing the spoon to the side.

Ken glanced up at her and saw her bewildered expression. Then he sat down on the bunk and put his right hand on his forehead. "Yeah, I'm fine. I just got dizzy for a minute there. I guess I was to upset," he replied.

Aisha didn't seem sold on his response, but she didn't pursue it either.

"The creepy man said they would come to get us in about an hour, right?" Serena asked.

"Yeah, we just have to wait until then," Ken replied.

They all sat in silence for the remainder of their time. Then they heard the door pop down the hallway. Raiga, along with three soldiers dressed in white armor with silver trim came down the foyer. Aisha jumped up from the bench to meet them.

"What's going on?" she asked Raiga.

"The Commander wants to see him," Raiga said while pointing to Ken.

"What?" Aisha responded.

Raiga shrugged his shoulders as the soldiers moved toward the cell. "I don't know what's going on, but he wants both of us there too."

"You there! Come to the cell door at once," a soldier ordered Ken.

Ken got up and walked over to the bars as told.

"Now turn around and put your hands behind your back. Then get on your knees and place your forehead on the ground," the soldier ordered.

Ken followed all the instructions given to him and waited. The soldiers opened the cell and then rushed in. They put a pair of handcuffs on Ken that were hinged together and then locked them around his wrist. Two of the three soldiers reached under his arms and pulled him to his feet. Then they walked him out the cell.

Raiga scowled at Ken who glared back at him. "Bag him!" Raiga ordered.

One of the soldiers put a cloth bag over Ken's head so that he couldn't see.

"Hey!" Ken cried out. He felt them pull him by his arms as they moved him up the hallway.

Why put a bag over my head? Ken thought as he felt them tug him along.

"That is a little uncalled for," Serena replied.

Ken heard the door pop, and they started to walk some more. Then another door popped open, and he was yanked into what Ken assumed to be another hallway. He could hear the echoes of their footsteps which reminded him of walking down the hall at school when everyone else was in class. As they pressed on, he could hear the soldiers whispering to each other.

"Why would the Commander want to see him?"

"I heard the king himself ordered the Commander to talk with him personally."

"Well, I'll bet the Commander will make an example out of him and carry out the execution himself," they all uttered amongst themselves.

They're in for a surprise, Ken thought as they rounded a corner.

Suddenly, they came to an abrupt stop. Ken heard a door open and was then led forward again. The sound in the area around him changed from echoing footsteps in a hallway, to a quiet and still atmosphere. As he stepped, he felt that there was a rug beneath his feet instead of hard tile.

The soldiers stopped him from moving and made him stand in place. Then something hard hit the back of Ken's knees causing him to fall into a chair that was thrust behind him. One of the soldiers pulled the bag off his head.

Ken found himself sitting in a large room with a giant brown desk in front of him. Draped over the front of it was a white cloth with an insignia sewn in gold on the front of it. The symbol was a shield with a crown that hovered above it. The shield had two swords that crossed each other in front of it. It also had a symbol of some sort engraved into it where the swords met in the middle. Ken assumed it was a Gate like what he had on the back of his hand. From each side of the shield rose two wings that spread out and upward to complete the symbol.

Behind the desk sat a man with long silky black hair that was tied into a ponytail in the back. He stared at Ken with his burnished yellow eyes and a curious expression. He wore white armor with gold trimming that outlined the edges of his breastplate and shoulder guards. The stomach plate of his armor was the only piece that was solid gold.

To his right was a younger looking man who appeared to be in his mid-twenties. He had platinum white hair and azure eyes that focused on Ken. His armor was also white with gold trim. However, his stomach plate was silver instead of gold. The most interesting thing about this guy to Ken was that his left arm was in a sling. As if he had been injured recently.

Behind those two men were two other people standing perfectly still in each corner. They wore dark brown robes with hoods that covered their faces.

As Ken gazed around the room, he saw five soldiers to his left and five more on his right. Each wearing white armor with silver trim. They stood in front of books shelves that lined the entire wall on both sides. Aisha and Raiga stood behind him along with the soldiers that walked him in.

He looked down and noticed the rug beneath his feet was blood red throughout the room except for the dark blue circular mat under the desk. Behind the desk was a large window with extravagant curtains that matched the rug and had gold-colored ropes that tied them back to wooden rails that protruded from the wall. The entire room was regal and the perfect fit for a king or someone of great rank. Everyone in the room was silent and stared at Ken with stern expressions.

"I am Commander General Eugene Crow. I am in charge of the main headquarters and castle of the Monarchy," the man behind the desk said.

"I reviewed the report on your capture and saw where your guardian can manifest her own power. Is that true?" he asked while putting his hands together and resting his chin on them.

"Her *name* is Serena," Ken retorted.

"Such insolence! You will not address the Commander in that manner!" one of the soldiers cried out behind Ken.

Commander Crow casually raised his hand to the soldier. "Now, now, we don't need any of that," he said with a calm demeanor.

The soldier was taken back by the Commander's response but stood back at attention by the bookcase.

"Yes, Commander!" he replied.

"Let me try this again. Is it true that, *Serena*, can manifest her own power?" the Commander asked, maintaining his cool, level-headed tone.

Ken nodded his head without saying anything. The same soldier that scolded him cut a loathing look in his direction. Ken could tell he wanted to yell at him some more.

"Remove the suppression glove," the Commander ordered.

Everyone in the room glanced around at each other nervously. They all seemed surprised by the Commander's order.

"Did I not just say to remove the suppression glove?" the Commander inquired in an irritated tone.

"Yes, Commander!" one of the soldiers behind Ken shouted nervously as he pulled out a key and used it to take the glove off Ken's left hand.

The Commander noticed the unrest amongst the soldiers in the room and chuckled. "Are you all afraid of him? You're in a room full of Generals, Majors, and Soul Wielding soldiers. I believe we can handle any problem he may try to cause," he said in an amused tone.

After the soldier removed the glove, Serena phased out from Ken's back and floated just over his head. Ken noticed The Commander and the man next to him look up at Serena along with the two people in brown cloaks behind them. However, no one else in the room seemed able to see her.

"Hello there, Serena. Would you mind showing me this power you have?" the Commander requested in a light tone as though talking to a child.

Serena looked down at Ken with an uneasy expression.

"It's okay, Serena. Show them," Ken said.

Serena nodded her head at him and then created her wings. They fired out from her back and hovered above Ken while shining their pure white glow. Many of the soldiers gasped or jumped back from Ken, but all of them gazed on with wonder. The Commander stood from his chair as he took in the sight of beaming angelic wings hovering in his office.

"Magnificent!" the Commander shouted.

The younger man next to him even looked shocked at the spectacle.

Serena drew her wings back and made them fade away. Afterward, she lowered herself to float next to Ken.

The Commander clapped his hands and laughed, "Our great King is truly brilliant!" he exclaimed. "I told him about the report. You want to know what he said?" The Commander asked jubilantly. No one answered, though. They all just waited for him to finish.

"He said that we must have you in our ranks! Someone with such a unique power could be a great asset to the cause of protecting Estaira!" the Commander cried out while raising his hands in the air.

Everyone in the room was astonished by the Commander's words. It was apparent some of them wanted to protest, yet none of them were foolish enough to say anything against the King.

"What is your name young man?" the Commander asked.

"Ken…Ken Malachite."

"Splendid! What do you say, Ken? Want to serve a higher purpose for the King? Or would you rather take whatever penalties await you after the trial?" the Commander questioned with a confident grin, revealing he already knew Ken's answer.

Ken hesitated for a moment. Part him felt like he was going to throw up over what he was about to say, but he knew to give Serena her life back he had no choice.

"I'll serve the King," he answered reluctantly.

"Perfect!" the Commander shouted while snapping his fingers. One of the cloaked men left the wall from behind the desk and approached Ken.

"It is my understanding that you lost your memory, is this correct?" the Commander asked.

Aisha gave Raiga a look from the corner of her eyes.

"Don't look at me. I didn't put that in the report. I have no way of knowing if he lost his memory or not," Raiga whispered.

"Since we don't know anything about you or if you're secretly part of the Amony, my Sage will check your memories to see if you have a connection to them or not," the Commander said.

The Sage stood directly in front of Ken. From his position, Ken was able to see under the hood. The Sage wore a faceless, skin-colored mask that creeped Ken out. The Sage raised its arms and extended its long bony fingers to the side of Ken's temple. Then the Sage put its fingertips on Ken's head.

Ken saw flashes of his memories pop before his eyes as if he were dreaming. He saw when he first found Serena, when he cut down the burning tree at Hanks, when he fought the Puppet King, and even his fight with Ulgenda. All his recent memories from the last week poured from his mind like pictures from an album spread out on the floor. Suddenly, the Sage removed its hands, and all the images disappeared from Ken's eyes.

"He has no memory before finding the girl," the Sage said.

The tones and pitch of the Sage's voice changed back and forth between sounding like a man and woman as it talked. Some of the tones were burly and then boyish while the others were womanly and then childlike.

"Even the memories he does have are hard to see. He won't be getting any of his old memories back," the Sage added.

"Excellent! He's a clean slate!" the Commander expressed. "It's just as our great King Volgia said. I wish I had his wisdom and insight," he added as his voice went giddy with admiration. "The King even planned for what to do with you if you said yes and cleared the memory check. You will be on a one-year probation period starting tomorrow. During that year, you will receive training from Brigadier General Lightsey since he's currently out of commission anyway and has powers similar yours," the Commander said while glancing over to the young man with white hair beside him.

"It would be an honor to fulfill the King's wishes, Commander," Brigadier General Lightsey said while bowing.

"I'm going to place you under Major Sono and Major Fearbuster's watch during this year. You will live in their assigned apartment, and they will guide you back and forth to the castle," the Commander said.

Ken heard Raiga grunt behind him as if fighting to keep from yelling out.

"Do you have a problem with that Major Fearbuster?" the Commander asked.

Raiga bit down on the inside of his lip before answering. "No…Commander," he replied.

"Good! Since you two are short one member anyway, this will make use of your extra time flawlessly. You both will oversee his transportation to and from the castle and keep track of him at night," the Commander said.

"Commander, permission to speak, sir?" Raiga requested.

"What is it?" the Commander answered impatiently.

"What if he tries to escape, sir?" Raiga questioned.

The Commander snapped his fingers, and both the brown cloaked Sages approached him.

"Put a shock barrier around their apartment with the corresponding seal on the suppression glove," he ordered.

"Yes, Commander," both the Sages said in unison.

One of them grabbed the glove from the soldier holding it and seared a new symbol into it. Then the Sage gave it back to the soldier. Afterward, both Sages went out the door to accomplish their task.

"Put the glove back on him," the Commander ordered. "He will wear the suppression glove at all times, unless he is training with

Brigadier General Lightsey. Is that understood?"

"Yes, Commander!" Aisha and Raiga said together.

After the soldier finished putting the glove on Ken's hand, Serena faded back into his body.

"Your one-year probation starts tomorrow with training first thing in the morning. Now, take him to the apartment," the Commander ordered.

"Does he need to be bagged, sir?" a soldier asked.

The commander put his hand on his chin in thought for a moment. "Yes. He's still technically our prisoner until tomorrow, so we will follow proper protocol," he answered.

"Yes, Commander!" the soldier responded.

He put the bag over Ken's head and then two of the soldiers reached under his arms and lifted him up to his feet.

Do I really have to wear this freakin bag again? Ken thought.

"It does seem kind of dumb for you to wear it since you're about to be working here," Serena replied.

Ken felt the soldiers tug him as they moved toward the door. Once they went out the doorway, he heard the loud echoing footsteps down an empty hallway. He also heard Raiga irritably muttering something to Aisha behind him.

"This is insane! We are one of the Omni Enforcement Units – not a daycare for criminals!" Raiga said in a not-so-quiet whisper.

"Don't be so loud, Raiga. You'll get in trouble if the wrong person hears you complaining about the Commander's orders," Aisha replied.

Raiga grumbled petulantly in response.

Ken heard another door open and felt warm air hit him. He heard birds chirping and the sound of wind rushing by. He assumed that meant they were outside.

"Load him into that van," Aisha order.

Ken felt them pull him down a ramp and then walk him across grass. Then he heard the squeak of doors open as he walked up a small flight of stairs.

"Sit here!" Raiga ordered

Ken felt a hand push him in the chest which caused him to fall onto a bench behind him. The squeaky doors closed, and the bag was yanked off his head.

He was in the back of a grey van sitting with Aisha and Raiga as it transported them to their apartment. Raiga had an outraged expression on his face as he stared toward the front of the van. Aisha, however, maintained her melancholy look from before.

"What have we gotten into?" Ken asked Serena.

"They may turn out to be nice people," she replied optimistically.

Ken cut a look at Raiga, "I doubt that."

After a few minutes of driving the van stopped, and the back doors opened again.

"We're here," a soldier called out.

Aisha and Raiga exited the van, and then a soldier helped Ken since his hands were still cuffed together.

"Is the seal set?" Aisha asked a soldier standing by her.

"Yes Major! The shock seal is laid down and is active," he replied.

Raiga glared at Ken with malice in his eyes. "You hear that? If you try to escape or leave without Aisha or me, you'll be shocked until someone comes to get you. Do me a favor and test it. I want to see if it works," he leered.

Ken wanted to tell him to get lost but thought better about it.

"Keep still," one of the soldiers commanded as he tried to unlock Ken's handcuffs.

Once they were off, a Sage approached Ken and grabbed his left hand. It put its palm over a symbol on the metal glove which began to glow. When the Sage removed its hand, the mark was gone without a trace. Afterward, Serena floated out from inside Ken's body.

"I'm free!" Serena stated happily.

"The Commander ordered that your guardian be freed," the Sage said in its weird multi-toned voice.

"Come on, we'll show you your room," Aisha said as she and Raiga walked inside.

"Wow, this town is beautiful!" Serena claimed.

The road they stood on was made of cobblestone. Brick buildings lined the street which made a crescent shape in front of a large cobblestone stairway. The stairway led down to a dark-green, grassy patio with walkways that stretched out toward the castle that towered in the background of the city. The castle was gigantic in stature and was made from white brick. Towers that touched the sky extended from all areas around it with windows that speckled the outside. In front of it was fields of bright pink petaled trees that painted the ground beneath it.

"Hurry up!" Raiga yelled out to Ken from the door.

Ken quickly made his way up the steps and into the house. The layout was relatively simple inside. The kitchen table sat in the middle of the room with a small kitchen area to the left of it. To the right of that was sitting area with two small bookshelves lined with a few books. In the back of the room was a set of stairs that lead to a hallway.

Raiga pointed at Ken with his finger and then motioned for him to follow. Ken shadowed him up the stairs and saw five doors down the hall. Two on the left, two on the right and one in the back.

"This first door is my room," Raiga said while pointing at the first door on the right. "The one across from it is the bathroom. The next one up from the bathroom is Aisha's room. Stay away from it!" he declared while scowling at Ken. "The second one on the right is your room, and the one in the back leads to the balcony."

Ken opened the door to his room and gazed around inside it. It was cozy and rather small with a hardwood floor and plain white walls. It had a small bed and dresser with a window that had curtains over it to block out the light.

"Stay in here. We'll bring you food and water. Don't come out until we get you in the morning for training," Raiga demanded.

Ken opened his mouth to respond, but Raiga slammed the door before he could say anything. Ken stood in place for a moment and let out a long sigh.

"This room seems pretty nice," Serena said as she floated in circles around Ken.

Ken opened the curtains of the window which revealed the castle and all its glory in the background. The fields of pink-petaled trees that led to the castle were more visible from the window than the ground. They were in four rows, each separated by pathways leading to the castle.

Before that was a large park with a few green trees spread here and there throughout it. There were multiple paths that fanned out in different directions against the lush green grass of the park. One path ran from a set of cobblestone steps to a walkway which was in front of the apartment.

"It really is beautiful, isn't it?" Serena said softly to make conversation.

Ken didn't reply, he only stared out the window quietly. He placed his palms down on the window-rest and tightly gripped it with his right hand.

"You okay, big bro?" Serena asked.

"How…how can you still call me that?" Ken whispered back to her. "After I… I let you die," he muttered as his eyes turned red and puffy.

"That's not true. You didn't let me die. I know you tried everything you could," Serena replied.

"You died because of me. You called for me, and I didn't come! You needed me, and I wasn't there!" Ken declared as tears rolled down his cheeks.

"Big bro, it's not your fault," Serena said once more.

"It is my fault! You should have never had to go through something like that! You should be standing next to me right now in your own body. If anyone should be in the ground, it's me!" Ken cried out.

"Big Bro," Serena said softly, unsure of how to respond.

"But I promise you this. I will push through this year with everything in me. I will fight hard and become stronger. I will train harder than I ever have before. That way, when you do get your body back. I'll have the strength to protect you. No one will ever hurt you again!" Ken stated as he wiped the tears from his face.

"I know you will, big bro, and who knows? Maybe you'll make some friends during your training," Serena replied in a lighter tone.

"I'm not here for friends. Other people will only be a distraction from our goal. Besides, I doubt those two want to try and be buddy-buddy with me. I personally want to knock Raiga's block off, and I don't even know how to read Aisha," Ken said while continuing to stare out the window.

"You never know, a lot can happen in a year," Serena replied.

Ken stayed quiet for a moment and looked to Serena who hovered to his left. He raised his hand to touch the side of her cheek, but it phased through her face. He bit down wrathfully, upset with his own shortcomings. In contrast, Serena gazed at him tenderly.

"Serena, I swear to you—" Ken said as his voice shuttered and shook. "I will keep my promise and bring you back."

Chapter 20

Enock and Eliezer

The Great Elder of Time and Space was staring out the window of a castle stationed in a drab, lifeless wasteland. The ground around it was vast and empty without vegetation or life. The only thing that decorated the landscape was the grey castle and a giant set of bones just outside that appeared to belong to a dragon.

As the Sage gazed blankly at the bones on the ground, a bright green light erupted in the room behind him. A circle appeared in the air and moved its way down, revealing a large muscular man.

The newcomer was completely bald and stood at least seven feet tall. He was shirtless and wore a skirt that was made from navy-blue leather that hung below his knees. He had tattoos that covered his grey skin with red designs from the top of his head to the bottom his feet. He also had a necklace that hung down below his chest that was decorated with bones and teeth along with a bright green orb that hung from the center. The man's eyes were white and had no pupils or retinas.

"You call for me, brother?" the man said in a deep burly voice.

"Yes, Eliezer. Come here," the other man answered without looking back.

"How many times do I have to remind you to call me Eli," Eliezer said. As he approached, he looked down at the stone floor of the castle and saw a dead man sprawled out on the ground, lying at his feet.

"Ignore that for now. Have a look at this," the man with black hair said while pointing to a design engraved in the stone wall beside him. He still did not break from the window.

Eli stepped over the dead man and looked at the etching in the wall. It was a copy of the Gate Ken has on his left hand.

"What do you think of it?" the man asked Eli.

"It's nothing, the design breaks the outer circle. It's certainly not a Gate or a Seal. Are you trying to make new Seals or symbols Enock?" Eli asked while looking it over. "Wait, some of it looks like *his* work."

"It is *his* work!" Enock answered, now breaking his attention from the window and approaching Eli.

"Well, what does *he* expect to accomplish with this? It won't work after all," Eli stated.

"Actually, it does work. I've seen it for myself," Enock retorted.

"Preposterous!" Eli spat.

"It's true. It's a Gate, and it really works," Enock said while putting his hand over the design and rubbing it with his fingers.

"How!? How did *he* make something like this work?" Eli shouted.

"I don't know. I tried to see if I could do it too, but you see how that turned out," Enock answered nonchalantly while looking at the corpse. He had the same Gate as Ken etched onto his right hand.

"Zeek was always the most talented when it came to Gates and Seals, so it doesn't surprise me that he found something new to tease me with," Enock said with an unenthusiastic air.

"If you're going to call *him* by his name then at least use his full name, Ezekiel. He was only Zeek to me back then, but not now," Eli stated scornfully.

"Someone's still butt hurt," Enock mumbled.

Eli merely rolled his eyes, although since he had no pupils, it looked like his head only tilled up slightly.

"Let me get to the point," Enock said as he walked back over to the window. "Have you been sensing Zeek pop up here and there lately?"

"Now that you mention it, I have briefly sensed his energy a few times this week," Eli answered.

"Well, that's because Zeek poured some of his power into a Gate that now belongs to a boy I have in the Monarchy," Enock said.

"He did what!?" Eli Exclaimed.

"I don't know why he would put his own power into it, but that's why we were sensing him. It seems every time the boy uses his Gate power, Zeek's energy becomes visible to us for a split second," Enock said, ignoring Eli's outburst.

"Why would *he* do that!? Can the boy use *his* powers?" Eli asked in a seemingly frightened tone.

"I just said I don't know, and no, the boy can't use Zeek's powers at all. He's not a Sage. He's an Angeon and a Soul wielder," Enock answered.

"That doesn't make any sense at all. Why would *he* give this boy a special Gate with *his* power in it if the boy can't use it?" Eli asked.

"That's why I brought you here, to see if you had any ideas. If not, then I thought I would at least let you know what I've found," Enock said.

"I never could figure out what Ezekiel was thinking," Eli stated. "But if he put some of his power into the boy's Gate, then all we have to do is kill the boy, and Ezekiel will be that much weaker."

Enock shook his head and smiled. "I thought that too, when I first met the boy. Then I put some thought into it. If Zeek put that much into the kid, then he's not just going to just give him up. I'm going to use the boy as bait to draw out Zeek. Then after I kill Zeek, I'll kill the boy as well. You know, tie up any loose ends. I don't want even a sliver of his power left behind," Enock said with a wicked grin.

Eli smirked when he heard the plan. "That's a good idea. How long do you think it'll take Ezekiel to show up for the boy?" Eli asked.

"He won't show up at the Monarchy castle, so he'll probably wait till the boy joins the Omni Enforcement Unit with the Monarchy," Enoch replied.

"How long will that take?" Eli grumbled.

"A little over a year," Enock said. He sighed slightly after answering. He knew Eli wouldn't like that response.

"Just send him out now! The sooner we kill Ezekiel, the better!" Eli burst out.

"You know I can't just send him out. The boy has attacked soldiers, kidnapped a young girl from us, and has even killed peolple. The subjects would be in an uproar if the King just forgave him and sent him out to do missions for the Monarchy," Enock retorted.

"Then just replace the King after it's over. Volgia is just another one of our pawns anyway," Eli said.

"Volgia does good work. He hasn't let the mantle of King go to his head. I'd like to keep him around," Enock said while making air quotes around the word King.

"Wait, kidnapped a girl? You mean the same one Ezekiel freed from the Monarchy? The one they were looking for?" Eli asked, referring to Enock's previous statement.

"The very same," Enock answered.

"So, he planned for the boy to become an Angeon then? He purposefully made the boy kidnap the girl so he would get her power when she died?" Eli inquired.

"It's all just speculation right now, but yes, I think that's why he did it. Of course, I won't know for sure until I'm scanning through Zeek's memories before turning him into dust," Enock said casually.

"Anyway, I was just letting you know what my plan was. By the way, any luck on the blue stone?" Enock asked as he turned his attention back to Eli.

"No, I'm still searching," Eli answered.

"Well, search harder. With Zeek making moves like this, there's no telling what he might have planned. If he finds it first, then he will become a real threat," Enock said while pulling a blood red orb from inside his white robe and rolling it around his fingertips.

"I know, I was searching for it when you called me here," Eli replied while rolling the green orb on his necklace around his digits.

"Oh, that reminds me. Your pet died again," Enock said while walking back to the window.

Eli followed him and looked down at the dragon bones that laid at the foot of the castle. He held out his hand, and the green orb started to glow brightly along with the tattoos that covered his body.

The dragon bones began floating in the air and assembling themselves to form a full, living, dragon skeleton. It opened its mouth as if it were roaring but made no sound.

"Why won't you let me get rid of that thing?" Enock asked. "It's an eyesore."

"Because when I get the blue stone, I'll restore it to its proper body," Eli answered. "Is that all you have for me?"

"Yes, you are dismissed, Eli. Continue your search for the stone," Enoch answered.

"As you wish, brother," Eli retorted.

He created another green circle of light and stepped into it and disappeared.

Enock went back to the window and watched as the dragon skeleton fell apart into a pile of bones once more. He then turned his attention to the grey sky and smiled darkly. "It won't be long now, Zeek."

Thank you for reading Angeon Broken Promises. If you enjoyed the story, please rate and leave a review online. Thank you again for your support and be on the lookout for Angeon Fading Bonds.

Made in the USA
Columbia, SC
11 February 2023

960be480-b17d-4e18-8e8e-51d1cdf0ede2R01